PERFECT

Book 1 of the Genesis Trilogy

L.A. KESSLER

Visit L.A. Kessler at: Lisa-Kessler.com
Sign up for Lisa's newsletter: goo.gl/56lDla

Edited by Double Vision Editorial, Danielle Poiesz
Cover design by Lisa's Lair
Interior Design by BB eBooks
DNA Icon made by Freepik from www.flaticon.com is licensed under CC BY 3.0

Manufactured in the United States of America

First Edition May 2022

Also by L.A. Kessler

The Genesis Trilogy

PERFECT

FLAWED

TAINTED

As Lisa Kessler

The Muse Chronicles

LURE OF OBSESSION

LEGEND OF LOVE

BREATH OF PASSION

LIGHT OF THE SPIRIT

DEVOTED TO DESTINY

DANCE OF THE HEART

SONG OF THE SOUL

The Night Series

NIGHT WALKER

NIGHT THIEF

NIGHT DEMON

NIGHT ANGEL

NIGHT CHILD

The Moon Series

MOONLIGHT

HUNTER'S MOON

BLOOD MOON

HARVEST MOON

ICE MOON

BLUE MOON

WOLF MOON

NEW MOON

The Sedona Pack

THE LONE WOLF'S WISH

SEDONA SIN

SEDONA SEDUCTION

SEDONA SCANDAL

SEDONA SURRENDER

SEDONA SERENITY

SEDONA SACRIFICE

SEDONA SUSPECT

SEDONA SANCTUARY

SEDONA SALVATION

The Salem Pack

WOLF'S WITCH

The Sentinels of Savannah

MAGNOLIA MYSTIC

PIRATE'S PASSION

PIRATE'S PLEASURE

PIRATE'S PERSUASION

PIRATE'S PROMISE

PIRATE'S PARADOX

Summerland Stories

ACROSS THE VEIL

FORBIDDEN HEARTS

A WINTER'S WISH

Standalone Works

BEG ME TO SLAY

FORGOTTEN TREASURES

Dedication

This one is for my amazing daughter, Panda.

I love you!

PERFECT

by L.A. Kessler

"Perfection is attained by slow degrees; it requires the hand of time."

—Voltaire

1990

PROLOGUE

DR. JAMES TURNER'S size-twelve loafers clicked against the worn linoleum floor, echoing down the cold, white hallway like a clock and marking the seconds as they ticked away. It was a constant reminder of the time slipping away.

How long would this baby live?

Dread sapped the energy from his body as he stared down at the small bundle he was holding in his arms. The newborn was healthy, and her parents were demanding to see her. He had no right to keep her from them, but he wished he had another option.

Shaking his head, he kept walking, forcing himself closer to their room. This was the fourth daughter he'd delivered for Dr. and Mrs. Huff.

None of the others had lived to see their first birthday. Crib death had claimed them all.

CPS had inspected their home. There had been no signs of abuse or neglect, so police and child services had deemed the deaths tragic but not criminal.

Dr. Turner hoped this baby would be safe. He had run every test at his disposal, and to the best of his knowledge, this little girl was a perfectly healthy newborn.

But the other infants had seemed every bit as healthy…

Something knotted in his gut as he weighed her chances of survival. He was beginning to wish he had asked the nurse to bring the couple their baby. Looking the other way would have been so much easier.

But he couldn't. Something was happening to these infants. It couldn't be coincidence that they had all died. Crib deaths happened, it was true, but it was extremely unlikely to happen three times in the same family, especially to otherwise healthy babies.

But if they weren't dying in their sleep, then how?

Deep down, he was afraid he already knew the answer. That was why he had insisted on bringing this child to them himself. He hoped that by talking to the Huffs, seeing them hold their little girl, that he might be able to make a difference in her future. That maybe this infant would survive.

He had to try.

With each echo of his footsteps, Dr. Turner's trepidation multiplied. He stopped when he reached the door and looked down one last time at the baby in his arms. For a split second, he yearned to keep on walking. Just wander out of the hospital and give this infant to a couple who couldn't have children of their own, people that would love her and keep her safe.

But he couldn't do that, no matter how much it

seemed like the right thing to do. Kidnapping was a crime, and he drew the line at breaking the law. He was probably overreacting. He had to be. Surely, if there was any chance of foul play, Child Protective Services would have taken action against the Huffs. But just in case, he'd documented every aspect of Mrs. Huff's delivery, as well as the infant's initial test results and prognosis. This time, if she fell to the same fate as the other babies, maybe his documentation might lead to an investigation.

Shifting the tiny bundle into one arm, he carefully opened the door and entered the room. The baby's father spun around with cold, emotionless eyes. He was tall and slender with a pronounced pointed nose and short brown hair.

Dr. Huff uncrossed his arms. "We were beginning to wonder about you, Dr. Turner."

"I apologize for the delay," he replied. "I was running some tests to be sure your precious little girl here stays nice and healthy. Given the previous family history, I thought it pertinent to be extra cautious in this case."

A silent glance passed between the new parents, sending a chill down Dr. Turner's spine. While most couples who had previously lost babies were anxious, almost desperate, to hold their new infant, to touch it and love it, Dr. and Mrs. Huff made no such effort. In fact, they hadn't even moved close enough to see her yet. It was awkward, almost ominous to witness. The cool detachment in their eyes made Dr. Turner wonder if they even wanted this child.

Maybe they were simply afraid to love the infant for fear she might die like the others had. He didn't know, but something about the way they were staring at each other concerned him. Almost like two wolves circling their prey and giving each other silent signals before attacking.

Dr. Turner cleared his throat, pushing the disturbing image from his mind as he turned toward the biochemical research physician—although no one in the local medical community knew exactly what kind of research he did—and made a gesture to offer him his baby. "Would you like to hold her, Dr. Huff?"

The infant's father didn't move. Dr. Turner's smile faded when neither Dr. Huff nor his wife made the slightest effort to see their child.

They both just stared at him.

Making a final attempt, Dr. Turner took another step closer. "Don't worry, she's healthy as an ox and beautiful as a butterfly. Come take a peek."

Again, neither parent moved. Mrs. Huff looked over at her husband and gave him an encouraging nod, but he remained stiff.

"Does she have ten fingers and toes?" he asked cautiously.

Dr. Turner started to frown. "Yes, ten of each."

"And she doesn't have a coned head, does she?" Mrs. Huff interrupted.

He froze for a moment, caught off guard by their questions. "No."

"And no nasty birthmarks?" Mrs. Huff's nose crinkled in disgust.

Dr. Turner shook his head, hoping his uneasiness wasn't showing on his face as he approached Mrs. Huff's bedside. "None."

Cautiously, he handed the infant to her mother. If he didn't do it now, he might find an excuse not to give her to them at all.

She took her new baby girl and held her in the crook of her arm, her free hand gently caressing the infant's soft brown hair.

Dr. Turner relaxed. Maybe he had been overreacting. "She's just perfect."

Mrs. Huff looked up at her husband. Her lips curved into a thin smile and her eyes gleamed—but not with the joy Dr. Turner was accustomed to seeing in a new mother's eyes. There was a ferocity there he didn't understand.

She focused on the tiny bundle. "Did you hear that, Ed?"

Dr. Huff nodded and came closer to her bedside. They stared at their daughter for a moment, and whispered together, "She's perfect."

"Be ye therefore perfect, even as your Father which is in heaven is perfect."

—Matthew 5:48

1999

CHAPTER 1

BILLY PEDALED HIS bike faster as he past the large Victorian house. Something about the people who lived there bothered him. He couldn't put his finger on it, but a ten-year-old imagination could dream up all sorts of hideous reasons…

Which made him even more anxious to get past their property.

He stayed focused straight ahead. No way was he going to look up at those windows again. What if that ghost stared back at him? Okay, so she might be a really pale girl, but she never played on their street and no one knew her name.

Obviously, she must have been the spirit of a girl who died in the house, or maybe it had been built on an old burial ground like in that *Poltergeist* movie. His mom said he had an overactive imagination, but he didn't want to find out if any of his guesses about the creepy things in that house were true anyway. He just wanted to get to school.

John Harding Elementary was small, but Billy liked it. He attended a larger school in downtown Los

Angeles for kindergarten and first grade, but after his big brother passed away, his parents moved to the suburbs for a fresh start. Moonlight Cove was just southwest of Los Angeles, north of Malibu.

LA seemed like a lifetime ago. He entered Harding in second grade and never looked back. He was starting fifth grade today.

The suburbs hadn't been bad. It was a nice change to have the whole school know your name. It made him feel like a big fish. So what if the pond was little?

Billy pressed the pedals backward to slow his bike. This was the only intersection between his house and the school, and he swore to his mom on his comic book collection that he would always stop and look both ways for cars, even when no one was coming. Cars had a way of not seeing little boys on bikes, his mother would say.

Arguing with her when it came to things like that was pointless.

But he wasn't *little* anymore. Thankfully, he'd grown over the summer and was proud to say he now stood nearly five feet tall. Fifty-eight inches to be exact. It didn't make him the tallest fifth-grader in his class, but he towered over the kindergartners.

Most everything about him was pretty average, only his bright-green eyes set him apart. His mom was Latina, and he had her brown skin color and black hair, but he got his dad's green eyes. A few girls in school were starting to comment on them, but he wasn't exactly sure how he felt about that yet.

Girls were a mystery to Billy. Annoying gigglers one minute, and then the next he'd catch himself doing some idiotic stunt just to make one of them smile at him. Girls had developed some sort of power over the boys this summer, and none of them could resist. Interactions were more confusing with each passing day.

He didn't understand them, and according to his dad, he probably never would.

Billy parked his bike at the school and locked the chain around the rack with nervous anticipation. He hated the beginning of the school year with a passion. Not only did it mean the start of homework and tests but it also included a new teacher with a whole new set of rules and new expectations that bothered him.

He'd finally gotten the hang of doing all his homework in cursive with his last name first, just the way Mrs. Allen liked it, and now he had to start all over again.

And to make things even worse, this year he had Mr. Hart. Everyone said he was hard, and all the kids knew his secret nickname: "Mr. Hart the Old Fart." And when a teacher had a secret name like that, you knew he was bad.

In fact, he might not even be human. It was possible…

Billy's mom would disagree. She'd say his imagination was running away with him again.

He glanced down at his feet. At least he had cool new shoes this year. Money had been tight since his brother had gotten sick. He'd overheard hushed, late-night conversations between his parents about medical bills, so Billy knew better than to complain about his clothes, but this summer things had changed. His dad had gotten a new job, and his mom had taken Billy back-to-school shopping.

She'd surprised him when he'd floated the idea of a bright-white pair of Nikes with a blue swoosh on the sides and she'd actually said yes. Not only did these shoes make him run faster but he'd be a king among the other fifth-graders at school.

Billy adjusted his backpack and headed for class. He entered his classroom quietly and found his name card sitting at a desk near the back of the room. Relief washed through him as he smiled and took his new seat. There was nothing worse than finding yourself in the front row. Not that it would matter much in this class since it was well-known that Mr. Hart had super-human hearing and could catch a kid whispering from across the room.

Even so, being near the back was always safer.

Todd waved from the other side of the room. Billy grinned. He hadn't expected to get to sit near one of his best friends, but at least they got to be in the same class. Ever since third grade, none of his teachers had allowed their desks to be anywhere near each other.

He was beginning to smell a conspiracy.

Billy and Todd had become best friends as soon as he'd started at their school. Todd had been assigned to be Billy's buddy on his first day, and they quickly discovered they both loved comic books. Todd was a little taller than Billy and wore his black hair shaved close to his head. He was also good at every sport he tried, a natural athlete. Billy wasn't terrible at baseball and soccer. He'd even made it to the All-Stars in Little League last year, but Todd had a gift. He could hit, catch, throw, and run with any kind of ball you tossed him.

Sometimes Billy caught himself envying Todd.

Zack was the third man in their group. He was a little pudgy and pale with freckles, but no one could make them all laugh harder than Zack. Unlike Billy and Todd, he didn't play any sports. He had a mild case of asthma and his mom worried even more than Billy's about him getting hurt.

This year Zack ended up in Mrs. Price's class. Although he seemed a little disappointed to be separated from Billy and Todd, he got the better end of the deal. Mrs. Price was one of the easiest teachers in school.

The bell rang, and silence fell over the class when Mr. Hart stood up from his desk. He was tall. Basketball player tall. His light-brown hair and brown eyes made him look pretty normal at first, but Billy had heard the stories about him. Mr. Hart was tough as nails and, more than likely, an alien from outer space, sent down to torture fifth-grade humans with too much homework and science tests that even Einstein couldn't pass.

Billy sighed. If only he could blame this on his overactive imagination.

THE FIRST WEEK of school flew by, with notes home to parents for curriculum night, homework agreements, and placement testing for the new school year. With a few days under his belt, Billy suspected the rumors about Mr. Hart might be wrong. So far, he'd been strict, but from everything Billy had witnessed, he was also fair. He didn't tolerate gum-chewing or note-passing, or talking out of turn or pranks, but other than that, Mr. Hart was kind of okay, in a teacher sort of way.

Billy would never admit it to his friends, but he was almost starting to like Mr. Hart. Although he did go a little heavy on the homework.

When the final bell rang on Friday afternoon, Billy struggled to contain his excitement. His mom had agreed to let Todd and Zack spend the night.

They met at the bike rack, putting on their back-packs as they plotted the evening's activities.

"So do you think your dad will let us use his tent to camp in your backyard?" Zack asked, then grunted as he fumbled to get his arm through the second strap of his backpack.

Billy shrugged. "I dunno. It's up in the rafters in the garage. I can ask my mom if we can use it."

"Cool!" Todd exclaimed, tossing his books over his shoulder as he unlocked his bike. "I'll bring my flashlight, and we can tell ghost stories."

Billy smiled. Of the three, he was the best storyteller.

"Yeah," Zack agreed, finally getting his backpack on. "And whoever gets scared first has to do whatever we say."

Billy laughed and nodded. "Okay… Won't be me, though!"

"Yeah, sure…" Todd grinned, holding on to the handlebars of his bike. "I'll have you both crying for your mommas."

"Shut up, Todd!" Zack said.

"Aw, make me, Z-Man," Todd replied, and they all burst into laughter.

Memories of their summer superhero game always guaranteed bouts of uncontrollable laughter. Billy had dressed up as Sunspot from the *X-Men* comics, while Todd went for the Falcon, but when Zack showed up with a big beach towel tied around his neck and a huge *Z* painted on his T-shirt declaring he was Z-Man, Billy and Todd cracked up so bad they almost wet their pants. Zack's angry whining about how he thought they were supposed to make up new superheroes only made it worse, but eventually, he was laughing right along with them.

A happy memory.

Billy clung to those since he'd lost his older brother.

He said goodbye to Zack and Todd, and pedaled home from school. Going home took a little longer than getting to school because it was mostly uphill. He usually made it without having to get off and walk his bike, but if it was really hot, walking was unavoidable. He hated those days. Passing the Huffs' dark, Victorian house when the heat was rising from the pavement made everything move like a wiggly mirage. It almost felt like the house was watching him.

But today, he pedaled right by. He didn't stop until he coasted down the slight incline of his driveway and dropped his bike in front of the garage. Sure, his mom would yell at him to move it later, but for now, he had more important things to do.

FROM HER UPSTAIRS window seat, Juliet peeked through her black-out curtains, staring down at the outside world below. The boy from across the street pedaled his bike past, just as he did every day during the school year. She wished she could be normal like him.

She was nine years old today. Almost double digits. Juliet sighed. None of her siblings had ever lived this long. Her momma told her that made her special, but she didn't think that was such a great thing anymore.

Being special was lonely. The only thing she wanted for her ninth birthday was to go outside like the other kids, just like the boy riding by with his backpack hooked on his shoulders.

School would be fun, too. She often imagined being in a classroom, but she knew that wish would never come true. She couldn't even open the drapes anymore. Her momma put a stop to that right quick. Now if she wanted to see the kids, she had to be careful not to let anyone catch her peeking.

"Juliet?"

She flinched at the sound of mother's stern voice and jumped back from the window. "Yes, Momma?"

Her mother went straight to the window, jerking the drapes closed all the way. She spun around, pointing at Juliet. "The sunlight has ultraviolet rays. Remember what they can do?"

"Damage my skin," Juliet recited, wishing she had heard her mother's footsteps on the stairs so she could have avoided this confrontation.

"And?" Momma put her hands on her hips.

"I could get freckles." Juliet had only seen them on the cover of a book once.

"We can't have that, now can we, perfect girl?"

They never openly discussed what would happen if Juliet ever did get a freckle, or a cut, or any other imperfection, but she suspected she knew. Her parents had already buried seven of Juliet's baby sisters, and she wasn't sure how many had died before she came into the world. Perfection wasn't easy. None of her younger sisters had lived to see their third birthday, and most of them never made it to their first.

She'd asked once where the babies came from. Her momma patted her head and told her papa made them and then something called a surrogate held them in their bellies. Juliet wasn't exactly sure what that meant, but she didn't ask again. It didn't matter where her sisters came from.

All that mattered was staying perfect.

The thought of being "flawed," as her parents called it, sent chills down her spine, making her fingers and toes tingle. Terrible nightmares haunted her at night. And they had a way of coming true in her house.

But even so, it was so hard not to dream about going outside. She could almost imagine how the sun would warm her face and the dirt would crunch under her bare feet and between her toes. Sometimes, she dreamed she was walking barefoot around the neighborhood with the boy with the bike from across the street. In her dreams, he would invite her to play with his other friends. They would laugh and run, and she would be one of them. Normal.

She loved those dreams.

"I'll keep the drapes closed." She laid her hands in her lap. "I'm sorry."

"Good girl." Her mother went to the door. "I need to feed the baby, and then I'll be back to braid your hair." Her mother's tone darkened. "Watching the outside world leads to dangerous thoughts. I'm trying to protect you. All your sisters would have given anything to be perfect like you are." She pointed toward the window. "It's filthy and full of disease out there. It's no place for a perfect girl like you."

"Yes, Momma." But Juliet couldn't help but wish it were.

"Brush out your hair and put your pajamas on." Her mother left the room, and Juliet sat down at her vanity to being her afternoon ritual, combing out her long, dark curls. At least fifty strokes—that was Momma's requirement. Brushing her hair when her mother would just come and braid it anyway seemed silly to her. Almost as silly as getting dressed in day clothes and then changing back into pajamas before it was even dark out. It wasn't like she was going to go outside anyway, and no one would ever see her, but she also knew better than to question her parents. It usually made them angry. Especially her mother.

Martha Huff was nothing like the smiling moms in the cereal ads in the magazines. Her momma had deep frown lines around her mouth, and her dark-brown eyes were small and close together—nothing like Juliet's. Every once in a while, Juliet would catch a glimpse of her mother looking out the window lost in thought, and in those moments, her brows would soften, the wrinkles in her forehead smoothing out, and Juliet could imagine what her mother might have looked like when she was a girl. She might have been pretty...

Momma always had her brown hair up in tight a bun and wore rubber gloves on her hands, and her apron was always filled with cleaners and disinfectants. She never wore makeup like the ladies in the magazines. Momma said she was a "no-nonsense gal." Juliet wasn't sure what that meant, but she supposed it didn't really matter.

A sigh escaped her as she stared at her face in the mirror. It was her birthday, but she looked exactly the same. She didn't look a year older. Her skin was the same color with just a hint of rose in her cheeks and lips. Nothing had changed.

Juliet steeled herself and began a slow, meticulous review of her reflection for any sign of a blemish or flaw. Her mother would make her own evening inspection soon, but Juliet couldn't help it. She needed to know in advance that she would pass her mother's visual audit. Deep down, she realized that if she found a pimple or a scratch, there was no way to escape.

She had to be perfect.

Not finding any new flaws, she pulled on her latex surgical gloves and got up to change into her night clothes. It was a very careful, specific process. First, she removed her turtleneck, cautiously lifting it over her head so she didn't catch her ears, and then replaced it with a clean, long flannel nightgown. Next, she slid the sweatpants and panties off, and carefully stepped into a fresh pair.

She picked up the day clothes and dropped them into the hamper with the others. Every day it was the same. The only thing that changed were the colors. She used to dream about owning a pair of jeans like the boys on her street, but her mother thought they were too dangerous.

What if she caught her skin in the zipper?

At least her mother allowed her to dress herself now. Until she was eight, that had been her mother's job, too.

"We can't have you trying to step into your pants and fall over. You might get a bruise, perfect girl," her Momma would always say.

Juliet shuddered at the thought. A bruise would be impossible to hide from them. The year before, she had accidentally scratched the back of her neck right at the hairline with a sharp fingernail and hiding it had been the hardest thing she had ever done. That was why she was always careful to wear her latex gloves now. She couldn't chance that happening again. And if she ever bruised herself… She didn't dare think about it. She couldn't.

"Ready for cake, birthday girl?" Her momma walked into her bedroom again, and without missing a beat, her fingers went to work, braiding Juliet's long hair while her eyes slowly moved over Juliet's face, silently inspecting her for any blemishes.

Juliet's mouth curved into a hopeful smile in the

mirror. "Can I have a birthday party this time? Please?"

Her mother's stern frown made Juliet instantly wish she could take back the words.

"You know we can't, Julie." Her mother shook the brush at her reflection in the mirror. "Why do you always want things you *know* you can't have? Do you enjoy seeing your papa and me feel like ogres? We're only protecting you. All it would take is one dirty little child to come in here and sneeze." She sighed. "And you know what would happen?"

Juliet cringed in her seat. She kept quiet. Her mother wasn't really asking for an answer anyway. Momma was funny like that.

"You could get sick! That's what could happen," Momma ranted. Juliet didn't say a word. No sense making it worse by interrupting. "You've been perfect for nine years! And what about poor Julie-Eight?"

Her newest baby sister. Her parents always named the new babies Julie after Juliet because she was their first perfect girl. Her father mentioned there had been babies before Juliet, but they were all flawed. He called them failed experiments. But the babies born after Juliet each had a number after their name. She figured it was like those rulers from the history books her Momma homeschooled her from—King Louis the Fourteenth and Prince John the Third.

Julie-Eight was Juliet's eighth sister. The other seven didn't stay perfect.

Juliet never allowed herself to get too fond of her

siblings even though Julie-Eight was so cute. It hurt too much when they got a sniffle or a diaper rash. Her momma would carry the baby out of the nursery, which was really the other side of Juliet's room, and the next time she would see her infant sister, she'd be lying too silent in the crib. Then another mound of earth would pop up in their backyard. Juliet could see them from the back window of the house, like an unspoken reminder that anything less than perfection meant…death.

"Julie-Eight is barely a month old and you're wanting to expose her to germs? Are you really that selfish?"

This was a question her mother *did* expect her to answer. "No, Momma. I'm sorry."

Her mother shook her head, her frown slowly fading as she stroked Juliet's hair. "I know you are, perfect girl. We'd let you have the biggest party in the world if we could, but those people in the outside world don't deserve to sit at the same table with you… You're perfect, and you'll always stay that way because we keep you here where we can protect you."

"Yes, Momma," she replied.

But deep down in the secret places inside her heart, she didn't care if those outside people were flawed. She wanted to meet them and talk with them anyway. And if birthday wishes really came true, she would, because that was all that she was going to wish for. Just for one night, to be normal—that would be the best gift she could ever receive.

CHAPTER 2

When his dad finally pulled in the driveway, Billy ran out to greet him. Before his dad could get inside the house and take off his lab coat, Billy asked if he and his friends could use the tent.

Once his father agreed, Billy helped him bring it down from the rafters, while his dad went through the usual lecture about remembering to put the storage bag inside after they set it up so he wouldn't lose it. Billy nodded. He'd agree to almost anything to guarantee use of the green, five-man tent complete with zippered windows and door. It was one of the few things Billy had that none of his friends had. Backyard camping with the guys always made for hours of fun. Billy could hardly wait.

At five o'clock, Todd's bike tires screeched to a stop in Billy's driveway.

"Hey, man!" Billy called as he headed out to help Todd carry in his stuff. "My dad said we could use his tent! He even got it down for us."

"Cool," Todd replied, taking off his backpack and carefully stuffing bungee cords into the front pocket as he looked around the garage. "So where's Zack?"

"I dunno. He should be here soon, though." Billy pointed at the backyard. "Wanna start setting up the tent?"

Todd nodded, stashing his duffel bag in the corner of the garage. He helped Billy carry the tent into the back, and they started setting it up.

As they hammered the last stake into the ground, Zack finally showed up. He parked his bike and immediately pointed out other spots around the yard that would have been better for the tent.

"Get lost, Zack," Todd grumbled. "No way we're pulling out these stakes now. They're too damn hard to get in."

Billy glanced around with a grin. Todd had been the first of them to start peppering their conversations with curse words. Billy's mom would kill him if she ever heard them coming out of his mouth, so the added danger made it even more thrilling, but his timing for using then wasn't very smooth yet. For now, he just admired Todd's clever use of them.

"Fine." Zack mustered an unimpressed shrug. "But don't expect me to help when you put it in such a dumb-ass spot."

"You just don't want us to put you to work." Todd said as he and Billy struggled to slide the tent poles into the impossibly small straps of the tent.

Todd was right. All three of them knew Zack was a master at finding excuses to get out of any kind of manual labor. Billy's mom said Zack was a thinker, not a doer.

Whatever he was, he sure wasn't helping pitch the damn tent.

Billy and Todd finally finished and went back to the garage to get their gear. Billy's mom had left them some flashlights, as well as a bag of chips, sodas, and peanut butter and jelly sandwiches. They figured they'd sneak back later for cookies.

Any excuse for an undercover mission.

After eating, some light baseball card trading, and what felt like an endless discussion about who was going to win the World Series and why, it was finally scary story time.

Billy loved this part. Usually, it ended with him and Todd laughing while Zack ran to the mailbox and back in his underwear. With any luck, it might be covered with Scooby Doo or some other humiliating cartoon character. Billy was grateful his mom had stopped buying those for him. Having Spider-Man on your butt was cool when you were six or seven years old, but they were in fifth grade now… Nope, plain white Fruit of the Looms were just fine.

Todd started the game with a spine-tingling rendition of *The Golden Arm*, which had them all jittery but no one begged for the safety of the house just yet, so the game continued. Zack's story was next.

Watching Zack tell a scary story was fun. His blue eyes would get so big inside his round face, he looked like he might explode if he got any more excited. And the further he got into a story, the faster he'd tell it.

"Okay, guys, you know the house across the street over there? The one with the pointed roof?"

Billy nodded, his stomach tightening into a knot. That was the house he sped by on his bike every day on the way to and from school. He'd never seen anyone go in or come out, and the stories about why were impossible to count. And none of them were good—not one.

"Yeah, well, I heard my mom talking to Mrs. Briggs about it," Zack said. "There's a girl up there in the top room, and they never let her out."

"No way…" Todd rolled his eyes. "This is supposed to be scary, Z-Man, not stupid."

"Oh shut up, dumb-ass, and listen," Zack said. "My mom says the girl's parents homeschool her 'cause she's got some kind of disease or somethin'. And if she comes out of her house and touches somebody, she could kill our whole neighborhood!"

Todd laughed and Billy tried to do the same, but it was forced. He had seen something—or someone—staring out of that high upper window before.

"It's true, you guys!" Zack insisted. "If she ever got out, there would be an outbreak and we'd catch her disease and die. My mom says that keeping her here, so close to normal people, should be illegal. She needs to be locked up or something."

The girl in the upper window flashed in his head again. It sounded like she was already locked up.

Todd shook his head. "Your mom's full of shit, Zack."

Zack tried to punch Todd in the shoulder, but Todd blocked the weak attempt. "She is not. Take it back!"

"Does your mom know her name?" Billy asked.

Todd and Zack stopped fighting for a moment and turned to stare at Billy, making his cheeks heat at the sudden attention.

"I just wondered…" Billy shrugged. "Just makes it more believable if she has a name, you know?"

"No way!" Todd teased. "You have the hots for Disease Girl!"

"Shut up, Todd, I do not." Billy glared at Todd and then looked over at Zack. "Never mind. It's all a lie anyway."

"I know the family's last name is Huff," Zack answered. "And my mom said the mailman told her the inside of their house is covered with pictures of their daughter. He told my mom it was like a shrine or somethin'."

That was it. The story was getting a little too real and too creepy. Billy tightened his arms around his knees, pulling his legs in tight to keep the fear from showing. The last thing he wanted was to end up walking down the street in his underwear.

"If she's so contagious, how come her parents are still alive?" Todd asked.

Billy shifted, waiting for Zack to answer. It was a

good question.

"I don't know." Zack shrugged. "Maybe they wear those special suits. You know the ones they gotta wear to work with radiation? Or maybe they're aliens, or—"

"Let's go find out!" Todd interrupted.

The excited look of determination on Todd's face made Billy's heart sink into his shoes. There was no stopping him now. They would be going, even if Todd had to drag them after him.

Zack gasped and shook his head rapidly. "Oh no. No way. We could die, man." He crossed his arms and shook his head. "I'm not going."

"Yeah." Billy nodded, relieved to see he wasn't the only one who didn't want any part of spying on the Huffs. "Besides, my mom would ground me for the rest of the year if we snuck out in the middle of the night."

"She won't catch us." Todd stared them down. "I can't believe this. My best friends are scared wusses!"

"Are not!" Zack dropped his hands to his sides, balling them into fists. "We're just smart, that's all."

"No way. You're both scared." Todd glanced between them. "So I win…"

Billy cringed inwardly. He and Zack would have to do whatever Todd wanted. That was the rule; it had always been the rule. Billy wasn't going to try to weasel out of it now, but he caught himself *hoping* Todd would tell them to walk down the street in their underwear. In fact, Billy might be willing to run down the street buck naked if it meant he wouldn't have to go sneaking around that creepy house with Disease Girl and whatever else might be hidden inside.

"You don't win," Zack argued. "I told the story, so if anyone wins, it's me!"

"Not my fault you creeped yourself out with your own story." Todd shrugged. "I still win, and I say we're going to go see if this Disease Girl exists."

Billy sighed. His fate was sealed, and after a few minutes of serious peer pressure from Todd, so was Zack's. Whether they liked it or not, they were going to spy on the Huffs.

The first step of their undercover operation was to prepare their vehicles. They needed their bikes to be stealth and silent, so the cards they'd wired into the spokes of their back tires, the ones that clicked and hummed like motorcycle engines as they pedaled, had to go.

He led his friends into the garage to gather supplies—wire cutters, a pair of work gloves, and a screwdriver—from his dad's toolbox. Billy twisted his sweaty hands in his pockets, nervous, his pulse pounding in his ears. His dad's number one rule was to stay out of his garage. His number two rule? Never, *ever* touch his tools without asking.

They'd managed to break both rules at once. Great.

Using his dad's wire cutters, Billy carefully snipped the piece of wire that held his old baseball card against the spokes and yanked it free. Over his shoulder, Zack tucked his flashlight into the waistband of his pants.

"Hope you're not planning on bringing that, Z-Man," Todd whispered.

"Hey, there's no way I'm going to Disease Girl's house without a light to signal for help."

"You're gonna get us caught is what you're gonna do," Todd said.

"Am not," Zack grumbled. "I'm taking it just in case. Besides, we can use it for self-defense, too."

"Self-defense?" Billy whispered.

"Sure." Zack shifted the light from hand to hand. "If anyone tries to bother us, we can knock him out with the flashlight. Just whack 'em on the back of the head."

Billy nodded, but he did *not* like where this was going. They weren't just sneaking cookies from his mother's kitchen cabinets. This was… This was real.

Real scary.

"Whatever, Z-Man. Just don't turn it on, okay?" Todd got on his bike. "You guys ready?"

Billy wanted to say no, but what was the point? He didn't want to be a chicken. Besides, the sooner they left, the sooner they could get back to the safety of the tent. He swung his leg over his bike. "Ready."

Zack finally got the flashlight adjusted to his liking and grabbed his bike, too. Silent as three highly trained international spies, they rode out of Billy's driveway and down the street toward the Victorian house.

CHAPTER 3

JULIET MADE HER silent birthday wish, blew out the candles on her cake, and secretly prayed it might come true this time. Let this be the year she could go outside, even if it was just for a minute.

"Can I cut it, Momma?" Juliet watched her mother's eyes shift to her father's.

"What do you think, Ed?"

"Please, Papa?" She pleaded. "I'm wearing my gloves, and I'll be real careful."

He finally nodded his consent, and she grinned. She'd never been allowed to hold a knife, let alone use one. Her fingers trembled as she took the knife from her mother. Momma cast one more questioning look at her father, and Juliet quickly plunged the blade through the cake, making the first cut before they had second thoughts.

After Juliet had carved out three pieces, her mother collected the knife and took it to the sink, reminding Juliet to eat slowly. No stomach aches. She savored the frosting, closing her eyes as she tried to memorize the sweet flavor. Sugar caused cavities and pimples, so it was usually forbidden to her, but on her birthday, her parents made an exception.

Her father placed a square box in front of her. Her eyes widened. "A present?"

She'd read about them in books, but she'd never received one before.

"It's from my vitamin company, not us."

Of course. Her father wouldn't even remember her birthday if it weren't for all the detailed daily physical records of her progress he had to keep for his company. He was nothing like the dads in her books. Nothing about her family or her house was like the books.

She carefully lifted the lid of the box and found another smaller pink box inside. Curiosity took over as she reached in and pulled it out. There was a small gold latch on the front. She glanced at her parents for approval before she dared to lift the lid. A wobbly tune chimed as a ballerina snapped upright, circling in front of a tiny mirror.

Juliet gasped, watching her turn in circles. "She's so pretty."

At the bottom of the box was a small green pin. She picked it up, studying the symbol. It looked like a figure eight on its side and it covered the planet.

Her father swooped in and took it from her. "That shouldn't have been in there."

"What is it, Papa?"

A muscle tensed in his cheek as his eyes shifted over to her mother. "I need to get back to work."

He left the room without looking back, and Juliet closed the box. The music stopped, and silence descended again, suffocating her.

"Better get to bed." Her mother picked up the cake box and dropped the mostly untouched sheet cake into the garbage.

Juliet looked in the trash can. The lid had popped up, exposing the cracked letters of her name on the discarded birthday cake. Broken and no longer welcome in this house.

"'Night, Momma." Juliet climbed the stairs with her present, careful to take them one at a time in the slow, cautious way she'd been trained. Missing a stair could leave an imperfection behind.

When she got to her room, she set the jewelry box on the small dresser next to her pillow and went into the bathroom to brush her teeth. Then pulled the covers back and slid into her bed. She lifted the lid, staring at the ballerina spinning inside. Even that tiny dancer had more freedom than she did. She'd asked if she could learn to dance like that after she found a story about *The Nutcracker* in one of her mother's magazines.

Momma had said it was too risky. Life itself seemed too risky. Maybe it was.

But she still ached to be a part of it. She yearned to experience it.

She pulled off her latex gloves and reached out to touch the tiny dancer in the jewelry box. Every ridge in her little plastic body seemed intricate, perfect. Juliet stiffened at the thought and closed the box. The ballerina would never see center stage. She'd never jump or even dance. She was a prisoner inside that box, doomed to spin whenever the music played, whenever someone opened it.

Just like me.

Juliet blinked back tears and went into the bathroom to brush her teeth again. All it would take was one canker sore in her mouth, one cavity, and she wouldn't be perfect anymore. The problem was, half of her longed for a flaw, anything to release the pressure of perfection. But her sensible side won out.

She had to be perfect. Her life depended on it.

WITHOUT A WATCH, Billy couldn't be sure of the time, but the street was quiet and dark. Hardly any lights were on inside the homes as they rode along. The Huffs' place was only three houses down on the other side of the street, but it seemed a lot farther away now—and colder, too, if that was possible. A chill shot down his back. Much colder.

Todd led the way, parking his bike at the edge of the street, one house away from the Huffs'. Billy stopped close behind, with Zack screeching his tires so he didn't run right into them.

"Damn you, Zack!" Todd spat, managing to make a

whisper seem like a scream. "You're gonna wake everyone up!"

"Shut up, Todd! I had to stop…" Zack put his kickstand down.

Billy struggled for words that wouldn't come. All he could do was stare up at that big Victorian house and wish he were back home. Everything about the house spooked him, from the squeaky weathervane perched on the tip of the sharp, pointed roof to the empty swing on the dark porch that never got used.

Sometimes he wondered if the Huffs were really just ghosts, haunting the big, ugly house. No one ever saw them outside. They didn't even have a mailbox. The mailman had to drop their mail through a slot in their front door. No matter how you sliced it, the Huff house was creepy.

Todd led their top-secret mission, quietly moving deeper into the shadows, away from the street. Billy and Zack followed close behind, neither boy eager to get separated. Every shadow lurking in the glow of the streetlamps seemed cold and unfriendly. The farther they walked, the more Billy felt like they were being watched.

After finding a dark spot to climb the fence into the backyard, Todd stopped and whispered to the others. "No sign of dogs. Let's go."

"Go?" Zack asked. "You mean, over that? No way…"

"Fine, then. You stay here all by yourself. Come on,

Billy."

Billy's stomach tightened into a hard knot. He shifted his gaze to Zack and then looked back over at Todd. Billy was the swing vote. If he chickened out and went home with Zack, Todd would razz him about it forever, but at least they'd get to go home, back to the tent. No way Todd would do this alone. But if Billy decided to go with Todd, Zack would be forced to come along. He wouldn't wait in the dark by himself.

It all rested on Billy's shoulders. And as he stared up at the Huffs' house in the moonlight, he'd never wanted to chicken out more in his entire life.

Todd was already surveying the fence, probably hoping someone would be following him soon. Billy sighed. Todd really didn't want to go nosing around the Huffs' place alone, and the way Billy saw it, no one would.

Maybe he'd play along for now. Once Todd realized there was no way over the fence, they could all leave and Billy wouldn't have to admit he was afraid. Everyone could win.

"Come on, Zack." Billy waved him over. Zack grumbled behind him, but he followed anyway. Billy stopped beside Todd and sized up the tall fence. "It's pretty high. Maybe we should just go back, huh?"

"No way." Todd grinned. "We've come this far."

He hopped up and grabbed on to the top of the wood fence, then slowly walked his feet up the fence. Billy and Zack stood together as Todd climbed over the top and dropped to his feet on the other side.

"He made it," Billy whispered.

Todd was over the fence and inside the Huffs' yard; this was really happening. And before Billy realized it, he'd pulled himself up and over, too.

He and Todd waited impatiently for Zack to arrive and jumped back, barely stifling their giggles when he landed face-first in the dirt. Billy and Todd helped him to his feet.

"Nice landing, Z-Man," Todd whispered.

"Screw you," Zack said, dusting himself off.

They peered around the dark backyard. Creepy shadows haunted Billy everywhere he looked, following him with their invisible eyes. Where was the light coming from?

He glanced up, and the hair on the back of his neck stood on end. The lamp in the top-floor window was still on. It was the only window lit in the entire house, and he couldn't help but wonder who—or what—was up there.

And he prayed whoever it was couldn't see them.

"Okay, we saw it. Let's get out of here," Billy whispered.

Todd gave him a disgusted frown. "We came to find out if Disease Girl exists, not hop the fence and leave. Come on. Let's split up and see what we can find."

"Splitting up is a bad idea." Zack scanned the shadows. "We should stick together and go back to Billy's before we get caught."

"We'll be fine. Besides, if we split up, we'll find proof faster, and then we can get out of here sooner." Todd flashed them a smile. "We'll be quick."

Billy was ready to agree to anything if it meant they could go home, and within a couple of minutes, he was heading around the side of the house. He stopped when he came to the trash cans. He'd watched enough episodes of that new show *NCIS* with his mom to know it was a gold mine for evidence. You could always find clues in other people's garbage.

He didn't have a flashlight, but he could see well enough in the pale light from the moon. Donning his dad's work gloves—a good investigator never left behind fingerprints—Billy quietly picked through the Huffs' trash. It was hard to concentrate on his task with his heart racing. His eyes kept shifting from the trash up to the side door.

What would he do if it opened? He tried to push the thought from his mind and ignore the door, focusing on his task, but what *would* he do?

Run. That was exactly what he would do.

He didn't find anything interesting in the first can, but when he lifted the lid of the second can, he found something. Something special.

It was a cake box with a bakery sales slip taped to the lid. Billy carefully removed the slip and held it up, trying to read it in the moonlight.

Happy 9th Birthday, Juliet!

Disease Girl was a year younger than Billy was. He folded the slip and stuffed it into the front pocket of his jeans before quietly replacing the lid. This would be enough evidence to get Todd to leave. He turned to go find his friends, but behind him, the doorknob squeaked, turning. Billy froze.

Run, bastard! Run like the wind!

But his body didn't respond. Billy looked over his shoulder as the door swung open. Whatever horror was about to come through that door, he wasn't going to be able to get away.

He held his breath as he saw that one thing he'd never expected to see.

Juliet. It had to be. She was shorter than him by a couple of inches and stood just inside the threshold of the door in a blue flannel nightgown. Her long brown hair fell past her shoulders, and she had these big brown eyes… Suddenly, he remembered he had no business being in her yard and spun around to leave when a soft voice stopped him in his tracks.

"Please don't go."

Billy turned back, surprised to see her smiling.

She lifted her hand in a small wave. "Hi."

"H-hi… I'm Billy." He pointed toward his house. "I live down the street."

"I know. I mean, I know you live nearby. I see you riding your bike to and from school." Her smile widened into a grin that he found more contagious than he would ever admit.

He started to speak but stopped when he noticed her hand on the doorknob. She was wearing one of those plastic gloves that doctors sometimes wore.

"Why do you have on doctor gloves? Are you sick?" He waited, proud of himself for not blurting out that he knew she had a rare disease that could wipe out their entire neighborhood.

He kept his distance, but she didn't seem sick or diseased or anything. Maybe that was how those contagious diseases worked. You couldn't see them, but they were there, just waiting to infect you.

"I always wear them." She held her hands up, turning them over in the dim porchlight. "I'm perfect, and my momma says I have to stay that way."

Billy frowned. Normally, he'd think anybody who told you they were perfect needed to be taken down a peg or two, but something about the way she said it…bothered him.

"No one's perfect, even with doctor gloves on." He met her eyes again. "If you're not sick, then how come I've never seen you outside before?"

"Oh, I'm not allowed to go out. Not ever."

Billy pinched his eyebrows together in confusion. "Everybody goes outside."

"Not me."

"Are you Juliet?"

Her eyes sparkled, and Billy had to admit, she

looked kind of pretty when that happened, not diseased at all.

"Yes." She nodded. "Juliet Huff. And you're Billy…?"

"Manning. Billy Manning." He checked over his shoulder, getting antsy to leave. "You won't tell on me for coming here, will you?"

He held his breath, praying she wasn't a tattletale wrapped in flannel.

She shook her head. "No, course not. I'd be in so much trouble if my parents knew I talked to anyone. I could never tell."

"You've really never been outside?" Billy couldn't imagine being cooped up in his house for a week. Was it really possible she'd been trapped inside for her entire life?

"Never." Her long lashes shielded her downcast eyes.

Butterflies went berserk in Billy's belly, that weird sensation in his gut that only a few girls produced. Without meaning to, he climbed the stairs to her porch until he stood face-to-face with Juliet Huff. She didn't look anything like the Disease Girl he had pictured.

She was actually kind of…normal. And in a girl sort of way, pretty.

Her gaze rose to his face, and his ten-year-old heart pounded. Was she waiting for him to say something? He wasn't even sure why he had come up there.

"H-Happy birthday, Juliet."

For a second, her mouth formed a surprised circle, and he cringed, sure he'd made a mistake. For all he knew, maybe her birthday was last week. He'd picked through her trash, but he was no detective. He was about to apologize and run away when she lifted her gloved hand up toward his face.

He almost ran away. Almost.

But something made him stay. This girl wasn't sick. She just seemed...sad. He flinched when the cold rubber glove came in contact with his cheek. He hadn't expected her to touch him, but he couldn't bring himself to pull away. She stared at her finger on his skin, as if she needed to make sure he was real or something. Finally, her hand dropped to her side.

She started leaning closer to him, and time slowed. His pulse pounded in his ears as her lips lightly brushed his cheek, lingering against his skin. She smelled so clean—too clean, almost as if she'd never been dirty in her entire life.

Her face lit up with a smile as she drew back. "Thank you for making my birthday wish come true. Even if it was just for a minute."

Heat rose in Billy's cheeks as he struggled to find something to say. He'd never been kissed by a girl, not even on the cheek. And what if she *was* diseased? Did he have it now?

Before he could come up with anything to say, the sound of a woman's voice shocked him back to reality. The woman sounded angry.

"Who's out there? I hear you!"

The color drained from Juliet's face. When she spun around toward Billy again, fear burned in her eyes as she whispered, "She's coming. Run, Billy."

He gave her one last look and tore down the steps and into the darkness of the backyard, his new Nikes digging into the dirt with every step.

He couldn't see, but he could hear Todd's soft call. "Psst, Billy. Over here..."

He turned toward his friend's voice, still running at full speed, but just as quickly, he lost his footing. He couldn't keep his balance, and suddenly, he fell. The air shot out of his lungs as he hit the ground, his hands barely managing to shield his face from the cold, hard earth. He lay in the dirt, gasping and unable to move. While he wondered if he was about to pass out, the yard around him was bathed in an eerie light. Billy managed to turn his face away from the house and prayed no one could see him.

Todd and Zack shrunk back into the thick bushes by the fence. Billy could barely make them out in the dim shadows cast by the porch light. His eyes slowly adjusted to the night, and he finally realized what had tripped him. He bit his lip to keep from screaming.

There were three straight rows of small sunken squares of dirt in the Huffs' backyard. He had fallen while trying to run through the first row of them. But nothing grew. It didn't look like rows of a flower bed. They almost looked like...graves.

A flashlight beam swept the yard, and he hoped his black clothes would shield him. Billy didn't risk turning his head. He'd rather not know how close he was to being caught. He held his breath, lying as still as possible. After what felt like years, the door opened and closed, and the porch light finally went out.

Billy got up and ran for the cover of the bushes, trying very hard not to think about what those rows of sunken dirt squares he'd lain on top of might have been.

"Jesus, that was close!" Todd pulled Billy against the fence with them.

"You were lying on the graveyard," Zack said.

"The what?" Billy gasped, his chest heaving as he gasped for air.

"The graveyard." Zack pointed toward the spot where Billy had tripped. "It looks like a bunch of graves, doesn't it? Just needs a few headstones."

"Does not," Todd said, giving Zack a nudge. "It's probably some kind of vegetable garden or something that hasn't started growing yet. Nobody buries bodies in their backyard. It's illegal."

Billy was already on his way up and over the fence. Todd was right. They couldn't really be graves, but either way, Billy didn't want to find out. He wanted to go home.

One by one, they jumped to the ground and pedaled in silence back to the safety of Billy's backyard.

"Did you guys find anything?" Todd asked as they

dropped their bikes in Billy's driveway.

"Nope," Zack said.

Billy realized they were both staring at him, and for a second, he almost said something about meeting Juliet. He shoved his hand in his pocket, his fingertips toying with the tag from the thrown-away cake box, but he didn't pull it out.

He wasn't sure why, but he shook his head. "Nope, I didn't get anything, either."

They went back to the tent and slid into their sleeping bags. Todd and Zack rambled on about the adventure and what might really be inside the Huffs' house, but Billy wasn't listening.

He couldn't stop thinking about the girl who had never been outside. The one who wore rubber gloves and acted as if she'd never seen a boy up close before. He wasn't sure why he hadn't told Zack and Todd about her. Normally, he told them everything.

But something about her made him want to protect her.

CHAPTER 4

JULIET CLOSED THE door and tried to back away, but it was too late. Her mother pressed her lips together in a scowl that made her whole face tip down into a frown of disapproval. She clenched her hands into tight fists as she came toward Juliet.

"What do you think you're doing?" her mother shouted.

Juliet pressed her back against the wall, trying to make herself even smaller. "Nothing, Momma. I…I just came down for a drink of water."

"Liar!" she bellowed, throwing a kitchen chair out of her way.

It slid across the linoleum floor and slammed into the cabinets. Juliet flinched and covered her ears as she slid down the wall. Neither of her parents had ever touched her without rubber gloves, and never out of anger, but she'd never seen her mother in such a rage, either.

"When did you become a liar, Juliet? I haven't slaved away for years to keep you perfect for you to start lying to my face! I saw you closing that door, and

God help you if you set foot outside–"

"I didn't, Momma," she cried, scooting backward, away from the raw anger burning in her mother's eyes. "I just wanted to look, that's all."

Juliet's heart pounded in her ears. She screamed in terror when her mother lunged forward and grabbed her upper arm, yanking her to her feet.

"*That's all?* Do you understand what you've done?"

She winced as her mother drew her hand back to strike.

"Stop!" her father yelled. "Don't touch her!" His chest heaved as he stumbled into the kitchen. His eyes widened as he stared at her mother's hand on her arm. His voice dropped to a menacing snarl. "Let her go, Martha."

Her mother released her, and Juliet staggered backward, struggling to keep her balance. She couldn't risk a bruise. She'd never heard her father shout before, and the sound startled her almost as much as the rage on her mother's face. Cowering in the corner of the kitchen, Juliet wished she were invisible.

"She was going outside, Ed!"

He grabbed her mother's wide shoulders. "Get a grip on yourself! Dammit, Martha." He shook his head. "What if you had hit her? One welt and I'd have to start all over again. Nine years of research down the drain."

All the anger seemed to fade from her mother's face. "I know." She stepped back, straightening her apron. "I know. I saw her there with the door open and I...I was just so angry."

Her father's ice-blue eyes fell to Juliet's face, and she cringed.

"That's understandable. But we can't use physical discipline." He walked over to the corner and knelt down in front of her. "Get up."

Juliet swallowed the lump in her throat and stood. "Papa, I didn't mean—"

"I don't want to hear it, Juliet," he interrupted. "Opening that door was inexcusable and completely forbidden. You have no idea how important my research is, and what you did tonight was dangerous and ignorant." He led her down the hall and opened the closet door. "I won't hit you, but I *will* teach you to obey the rules of this house."

Juliet stared into the dark closet and slowly began to realize he was going to lock her in it. Her heart raced as she looked up into her father's unfeeling eyes. "I won't ever do it again, Papa. I promise."

"You'd better not. Now get inside."

Her mother stopped behind him. "We're trying to protect you."

Juliet looked from one face to the other, searching for any spark of kindness. Her heart sank. There would be no mercy. Without a word, Juliet went into the closet.

The lock clicked into place behind her, suffocating her in darkness. Beyond the door, her parents' voices were muffled. She couldn't make out their words over the loud pounding of her pulse in her ears. She reached out with her gloved hands for any source of comfort from the blackness. A long coat hung on a hanger. She pulled it free and wrapped it around herself. Closing her eyes, she sat down with her back to the wall and imagined she was outside again.

She could still see Billy's smile in her mind, and his green eyes would probably be etched in her memory forever. He'd wished her a happy birthday. He didn't look dangerous and dirty, as her parents had always said the people from the outside world were. He seemed kind and friendly.

A dangerous thought crept into her mind. What if her parents weren't protecting her at all?

"The safest road to hell is the gradual one—the gentle slope, soft underfoot, without sudden turnings, without milestones, without signposts."

—C. S. Lewis

2008

CHAPTER 5

BILL'S NEW SILVER pickup was everything he hoped it would be. This year he would drive himself back to UCLA at the end of summer. No more depending on the parentals for a ride. Freedom.

He was nineteen now, and for the first time in his life, he had the entire house to himself while his parents were on a three-week tour of Europe. No curfews or required phone calls home to "check in." So far adulthood didn't suck. He was keeping his grades up in college and already registered to vote and had bought his first losing lottery tickets. His future was right in front of him for the taking.

But he wasn't in a hurry to let the summer pass by. His friends, who were more like family, were home, too, and part of him was already dreading leaving them behind again. None of them talked about what life after college might look like. Frat parties, coeds they dated, and the joys of living away from home were their usual conversation topics. But once they graduated, this town might not be home anymore, and they all knew it.

Zack was attending MIT and majoring in software engineering like his father, and Todd had gotten a full scholarship to USC for football. No one had been surprised. Todd had led their mediocre high school team to the CIF state championships two years in a row. The college scouts had pursued him all through their senior year.

Bill had managed to get a partial academic scholarship to UCLA. With dreams of being the next great American novelist, Bill majored in English Literature while working part-time as a barista. It was the perfect job for people watching.

He pulled into his driveway and turned off the headlights. He left the stereo on and opened the back window of the cab. It was too nice a night to go inside already.

Bill got out and untied the sleeping bag he stashed in the back. Laying it out, he got into the bed of the pickup and lay down to stare up at the stars. He had planned on cruising into the city with Todd and Zack tonight, but Todd's girlfriend had thrown a fit, and they'd ended up canceling. She wanted to spend every minute with him before they went back to school on opposite coasts. Bill couldn't really blame her.

After high school graduation, Todd and his girlfriend, Cindy, had decided to stay together. And so far, they'd managed their very long-distance relationship. But this summer Bill had seen the first signs of jealousy and cracks in their bond. They loved each other, but

Bill had a sinking feeling that might not be enough. Could they last another school year?

Even though Todd and Cindy had good intentions, she was attracting attention from New York while singing at the New England Conservatory of Music and Todd was often interviewed on television as one of the star football players for USC. They were both outgoing and good-looking. It didn't take a brain surgeon to see that it would be an uphill battle for them to keep the miles—and other people—from coming between them. But Bill hoped they would beat the odds.

He was glad he didn't have a girlfriend right now. His last one had scooped his heart out with a spoon. He rubbed his chest absently. She'd been in the drama department. He should've taken that as a sign. But he'd been dazzled by her laughter, her lips. Shit, everything about her had left him dazed. She'd been so free with her love and her body. He'd given her everything—his heart, his soul, his virginity…

Enough. He didn't want thoughts of Cassie's betrayal fucking up his summer.

Bill propped himself up on his elbows as a car passed by. He'd lived in this house since the second grade. He could barely remember his other house back in Los Angeles anymore. Sitting up completely, he looked down the street. It didn't seem that long ago that he, Todd, and Zack had raced their bikes here, traded baseball cards, and camped out in his tent, and—

His thoughts were cut short when a light in the top room of the Huff house flicked on. He stared at it, watching the silhouette of someone moving around up there. Over the years, he'd wondered about Juliet. Was she still trapped in that house? He'd never seen her again, but for the past nine years, he gazed up at that upper window, hoping to catch a glimpse of her.

But by the time he'd started high school, he'd let his boyhood theories about the Disease Girl down the street fade into distant memory. For all he knew, the Huffs moved away years ago. The light flicked off again, and Bill lay back down in his truck, searching the night sky for constellations and shooting stars.

Summer in Southern California… He couldn't ask for much better.

JULIE-EIGHT BLEW OUT her birthday candles, clapping her gloved hands together with a wide grin. "Hope my wish comes true!"

"I'm sure it will, perfect girl." Their mother nodded, reaching for the plates.

Juliet forced a smile as she watched her younger sister pluck the candles off her cake. Smiles were tough to come by lately. Juliet would be eighteen in less than a month, and while age meant freedom for characters in her books, she knew the milestone wouldn't matter for her. Nothing would change. She would still be her parents' prisoner.

Julie-Eight hadn't realized it yet, but wishes didn't come true in this house.

Her sister still believed their parents stories about protecting them, but ever since Juliet's ninth birthday when she'd opened that door to the outside world, she'd been unable to hide from the truth any longer. They were "keeping" them like dolls on a shelf.

That night had not only changed *her*. Her parents had added a security system on every door, not to keep people out but to keep her in. All the exits that led outside were locked with keypads, and only her parents knew the combination.

A few years later, after her fifteenth birthday, Juliet had tried to climb out a window, but before she could get completely out, her mother had carefully lifted her back inside. She'd spent nearly a week in the closet for that incident. When she'd finally been allowed back into her bedroom, all the windows had been barred. There would be no escape.

With each day, her desperation to get out grew. She was practically a grown woman, and she'd never set foot outside her own house. What could they possibly think they were protecting her from?

And along with her yearning for freedom, a pit of dread festered in her belly. There were similarities between her and her sister that seemed…strange.

When Julie-Eight had turned seven years old, Juliet had realized that she and her little sister had the same voice. Not just similar tones but the *identical* inflection and the same rate of speech. Sometimes when they read books together, Juliet wasn't sure where she left off and Julie-Eight started.

That wasn't all. The chart that hung on the wall of her father's exam room and tracked their heights began to show a strange pattern. Julie-Eight was the exact height Juliet had been at the same age. Their growth rates were identical. They also looked exactly alike. Seeing Julie-Eight was like looking into a mirror and finding a younger version of herself staring right back. In the photos of the two of them that covered the walls downstairs, it was impossible to tell them apart.

They were identical twins, and yet, that shouldn't be possible. Twins couldn't be born years apart, or at least not in the books and magazines she'd read.

"Juliet, go get the scissors," her father barked. "I don't want your sister hurting her fingers trying to break the ribbon on her present."

His voice jarred her from her thoughts. "Yes, Papa."

Juliet went upstairs to the room she shared with Julie-Eight and flicked on the light. She found the scissors on her desk and stared at them for a moment. Julie-Eight wasn't allowed to touch them yet. Scissors were sharp and very dangerous to "perfect" children. Juliet sat down and pulled off her glove, reaching out to run her finger over the cold metal. What would a cut from scissors feel like? Her skin had never been broken in her entire life. In fact, she'd never seen her own blood until the day she'd started menstruating when she was thirteen.

She'd thought she was dying, but apparently, it was expected for a girl, even a perfect one, to bleed once a month, as her mother later explained. According to her father and the other doctors who sometimes examined her, the bleeding came right on schedule, furthering her perfection in their eyes.

Even so, she'd never actually seen herself bleed or experienced the pain of any injury. Dark thoughts whispered in the shadows of her mind. She slipped her glove back on with a sigh.

She'd never really *felt* anything. Except the night she'd kissed Billy's cheek on her doorstep. For that single moment, she'd been alive, but he was normal and she was perfect. She'd never seen him again.

That wasn't strange in her world. She never saw anyone other than her parents and sister, and an occasional research doctor who worked with her father. Even then, they wore masks and gloves around her, and none of them were much for conversation. They were only there to get their questions answered, not to be her friends.

Pushing the thoughts from her head, Juliet picked up the scissors and went back downstairs to clip the ribbons on Julie-Eight's gifts.

Once the presents were opened and her sister was happily reading her new book, Juliet realized her father was missing.

"Where's Papa?" she asked.

Her mother gave her a dismissive glance. "He left for his business conference. He'll be back next week."

Her father had been going out of town more often lately, and her curiosity was eating her up inside. Until this past year, he'd always been home, working at all hours in the basement laboratory, but now he attended more conferences and had more appointments outside the house.

"He must be selling a lot of his special vitamins."

Her mother looked over with a nod. "Looks like it."

"And if it's selling," Juliet cautiously probed, "then pretty soon Julie-Eight and I will be able to go outside, right? He'll have all the proof he needs about the vitamins working and we won't have to stay perfect anymore."

Her mother shot her a look that could kill, her lips pursed as she rose to her feet. "Why do you insist on fighting with me over this? Do you *want* to get the world's dirt and filth on your perfect hands? You're not going out there, Juliet, not ever, so get it out of your head. You and your sister are staying right here where you belong, and I won't have you filling little Julie-Eight's head with any nonsense about leaving." She stepped closer, looming over Juliet. "Do you understand me?"

"Yes, Momma."

But peering up at her mother didn't frighten her as

much anymore. They couldn't hurt her physically. They needed her to be perfect. And the closet couldn't contain her imagination.

Suddenly, a thought crystalized. Their threats were empty.

And if her father's research on her and her sister proved his proprietary vitamin regimen worked, why did they have to stay perfect? It didn't make sense.

But she was going to find out.

IT WAS NEARLY midnight before Juliet risked sliding out of her bed. Part of her still couldn't believe she was doing this. Getting out of bed wasn't against her parents' rules, but where she planned on going was forbidden.

She tiptoed across the room and stopped for a moment at her younger sister's bedside. Juliet pulled off her soft sleeping mittens and reached out to brush Julie-Eight's hair back from her forehead. It was silky and looked exactly like her own, dark-chocolate brown with a gentle wave of curl. Maybe if Juliet could discover the reason behind her parents' need to keep them perfect, she could persuade them to reconsider. If she was successful, she could free both her and her sister.

With a sigh, Juliet straightened and replaced her mittens with her rubber gloves. The mittens were more comfortable to sleep in, but they made it impossible to grip anything.

She wanted to leave the gloves off completely, but she couldn't bring herself to take that risk. Just six months ago, she'd lost another baby sister, Julie-Ten, and her death was still fresh in Juliet's memory. She had only been a week away from her first birthday when a diaper rash began to form, and once the redness became welts, it wasn't long before Juliet found her littlest sister in her crib, cold and no longer breathing.

Julie-Eight had been too young to remember Julie-Nine's death, but when her mother carried lifeless little Julie-Ten out of their room, she'd been inconsolable. Their parents had drilled into them the importance of perfection, but Julie-Eight hadn't truly understood.

Juliet sat with her, embracing her while she cried. Their mother rarely touched them, and comfort wasn't something she ever offered. Juliet had raised her little sister, understanding the challenges of their existence better than anyone else in the house. But until her little sister died, Julie-Eight hadn't recognized how final the punishment for imperfection was in this house.

For days, nightmares had plagued her younger sister until, thankfully, the morbid memory faded. But it never went away, not completely. It was always there, lurking in the shadows, reminding both of them that their lives depended on staying perfect.

Like the porcelain dolls in her mother's glass display case.

Juliet pushed the thoughts from her head and carefully opened their bedroom door, listening for any sign of her mother. Silence. She held her breath and stepped out into the darkness of the hallway, closing the door behind her.

There was no turning back now.

Her new slipper socks made it easy to pad silently toward the stairs without slipping, but every noise made her tense. Gradually her eyes adjusted to the dim light as she walked down the stairs. Her heart pounded in her ears, but something else bloomed inside her: determination.

Tonight, she would find out what her parents were hiding.

She wasn't a little girl anymore, and she refused to stay locked up in her parents' house forever. Just the thought of it soured her stomach. She couldn't keep living like a caged bird, watching life pass by outside her window. She needed answers.

Over the years, her parents had explained that her father's special vitamin formula kept her free from ever having an illness, cut, acne, or bruise. She was, in her mother's words, perfect, just the way God intended all his creations to be.

Her father's invention would save the world's children, she'd been told, and she was his living research. Her sacrifice would change the world, her parents would say. But in the past few years, she'd started questioning everything. She was almost eighteen years old. She'd stayed inside and remained perfect, proving his vitamin formulation worked. But if that was true, why couldn't she leave now? They had what they needed.

It didn't make sense.

Besides, if the vitamins were really a success, then why didn't all her siblings survive? They all had been taking them. Why were she and Julie-Eight the only ones to remain perfect? Juliet also wondered if her father was being honest in reporting his research findings. Only two of the ten girls had responded properly to his vitamin formula. Eight hadn't been so lucky. And she was old enough to know those weren't good odds.

Juliet went through the kitchen and down the next flight of stairs to the exam room in the basement where she had been inspected, given cognitive tests, weighed, and measured once a week for her entire life. The room was bathed in an eerie green light from the exit sign over the door. She flipped the switch and studied the door across the room. In all these years, she'd never seen what was on the other side.

But that was about to change.

Tonight, her mother had made it perfectly clear that Juliet would never be allowed to leave this house, and she wanted to know why. The answers must be down here somewhere.

For the last few weeks, she'd been memorizing her father's every move during her exams, and she knew the key to the other door was in the middle drawer. She held her breath as she slid it open. The shiny silver key tempted her.

Answers.

Her father was out of town. This might be her only chance.

With a determined breath, she reached out with her gloved hand and took the key. Her fingers trembled as she fumbled to get it into the lock. Finally, it slid inside. She swallowed the lump in her throat, burying the fear, and grasped the knob. She turned it slowly.

Her eyes widened as she took a step out onto a metal platform overlooking an expansive laboratory. The temperature dropped in the cavernous space, and a chill shot down her spine. This was bigger than a workspace for just one man.

A banner with a large green insignia hung from the ceiling and spanned the distance across the large room. The logo was simple. The Earth with a green infinity symbol emblazoned across the middle.

The block letters below spelled out, *The Genesis Foundation.*

CHAPTER 6

SHE WASN'T SURE how long she stood on the platform, but when she finally forced her feet down the steps, the oppressive silence threatened to drown her. She pressed her lips together.

No turning back.

Her gloved hand slid down the thin railing as she took in her new surroundings. Pictures of her from a baby until now lined the walls with her vital statistics at the time of the photo. Everywhere she looked, her own eyes stared back at her until she ached to run back up the stairs and try to forget she had ever gotten out of bed.

But she'd come too far to go back now. Her father would be home in two days, and her mother would be awake in a few hours. If she wanted answers, she needed to find them while she had the chance.

The chill of the cold concrete floor soaked through the fleece of her slipper socks with every step. She wandered toward a dark computer screen, unsure where to start.

What was all this hidden beneath her house? And

what was the Genesis Foundation? A slip of paper was taped to the bottom of the screen. She recognized her father's rushed penmanship scrawled on the paper.

Perfect – Free from any flaw; faultless

Perfection – The state of being perfect; a perfect person

I have crafted perfection.

Juliet blinked, staring at the haunting words. It didn't make sense. Her father invented a vitamin pill to help people stay healthy from the day they were born. He might have invented a means to stay perfect, but he hadn't *made* a perfect person. That was impossible.

Frowning, she pulled open a drawer in the filing cabinet next to the desk and thumbed through its contents. There were so many papers, graphs, and printouts, and most of it was covered in symbols and numbers she didn't understand. She could search through the maze of this underground lab for days and still be without any answers. Shifting her attention to the desk, she gently lifted more papers and sifted through files until she found a worn, leather-bound book with her name embossed on the cover.

She sat in the chair and opened it. Her pulse raced as she skimmed the pages. This was her father's research journal, and it dated back to the day she was born.

Although the notes had been scribbled by hand, the

details were meticulous. Apparently, the doctor who delivered her, Dr. Turner, had taken it upon himself to run tests without consulting her father first. He was livid that the doctor had pricked the bottom of her foot for a blood sample.

> *I've been examining her heel every few hours for any sign of bruising or bleeding, but her skin remains flawless. She might be the perfection we have been striving to achieve; however, if she exhibits any outward signs of imperfection, she'll have to be destroyed like the others. I am doing all that I can to avoid this. I don't have time for the gestation of another fetus. Our funding depends on her survival. I need this research to be successful. Juliet must be Perfect.*

A chill shot through her as she finished the entry. She skimmed it again, her fingers trembling. She didn't want to believe what she was reading. It couldn't be true.

Her father wasn't worried for her safety. The only reason he cared if she lived or died was because he didn't have time to *gestate another fetus.*

She put her gloved hand to her mouth, sorting through her jumbled emotions. Her father had never hugged her or told her he loved her, but he'd always professed he was protecting her, keeping her safe. He was the only man she'd ever known, and…she'd loved him.

She shook her head. This was an early entry. Maybe he had grown to love her over the years.

Her heart raced as she flipped chunks of pages. Whatever his research was, she found no mention of his vitamin formula anywhere. When she went even further into the journal, the dates started to skip months at a time. Finally, she stopped on the day Julie-Eight was born.

The surrogate gave birth today without complications. My hope is to raise the subjects together as "sisters," making either one of them dispensable should an imperfection occur. Juliet is nearly ten years old now. If she retains perfection through her eighteenth birthday, my research will be concluded, but if she is flawed in some way, Julie #8 shares the identical DNA, making her a perfect replica and replacement should we need it. If the funding comes through, we will bring in two more surrogates. The cloned embryos are viable and frozen, should the opportunity arise.

Our dream is becoming reality.

Juliet closed the journal, her vision blurring with tears. Her chest tightened as she read the note again. She'd only been ten when her parents had carried Julie-Eight into her room. It never occurred to her back then that her mother hadn't been pregnant. Momma was heavyset, and even though she'd mentioned a surrogate, and back then, Juliet hadn't known what they were, and she never asked again. She only knew now because her father had introduced aptitude tests to her regiment of measuring statistics. He'd said he needed to be sure her cognitive abilities were perfect, as well. She'd loved school, even if it was at home. All the books and reading and writing had eased some of her ache to be outside.

But now she wondered if any of it mattered. They were never going to allow her to leave this house. She and Julie-Eight were "dispensable" to their parents. Just subjects in their father's experiment.

And her observations about Julie-Eight being her twin made sense now. Julie-Eight was identical to her all the way to her DNA.

Juliet flipped to the back of the journal. The final entry was from two days ago, and it seemed…cryptic.

Juliet's birthday is next week. We will be the first pod to cross this milestone with a Genesis child. Our portion of the research will be complete. Utopia is within our grasp. Funding for the Genesis Foundation is gaining momentum, too. The ceremony will be a triumph.

She read it one more time. His research would be *complete*. So why did her mother still seem intent on holding her prisoner?

Juliet got up from the chair and quietly wandered around the empty lab, looking at the strange equipment and test tubes that lined her father's worktables. No sign of the vitamins she and her sister took every day—not a single pill bottle. Her entire life they'd told her she was perfect because of the vitamin supplements, so how could that be if there wasn't a single pill to be found down here? Microscopes and specimen jars with unidentifiable substances inside were neatly lined up on the stainless steel tables and countertops, and at the far end of the room was another door.

It didn't have a security pad, but the lab was underground. It couldn't lead outside, so where did it go? Maybe the vitamin inventory was stored inside.

If not, at least she'd know it was all a lie.

Juliet went to the gray metal door and turned the knob. The door creaked, but it wouldn't budge. She tried once more, tugging until her arms shook with tension, but still the door remained closed.

Maybe it was for the best. If it suddenly burst open, she probably would have given herself a black eye or stubbed her toe, and it was obvious from her father's notes that she was expendable. They had Julie-Eight to replace her if she had to be "destroyed."

Her eyes welled with tears again. Although her parents were never outwardly loving like the ones she'd read about in books, they were the only parents she'd ever known. Knowing they could just destroy her like a lab rat not only terrified her, it also hurt.

But living like this, caged in this house, was destroying her, too, minute by minute, day by day. There was no hope of ever feeling the sunshine on her skin or the warm hug of a friend. Her only hugs were from Julie-Eight. She didn't know how she would have survived until now without her younger sister. Caring for Julie-Eight and helping her stay perfect had given Juliet a purpose, a reason to get up every day.

She'd never have any friends, not that she'd know how to make any anyway. And even if she managed to get out of the house, she wouldn't know where to go or what to do. She'd seen her mother use a cell phone and work on her laptop, but Juliet had never touched either one. The list of things she'd never experienced—riding a bike, sitting in a car, driving, going to a party—She sighed, cutting off the train of thought. The more she thought about all the things she was missing, the angrier she got.

The rage simmered in her belly. So many secrets. She was sick of it.

She tore off the rubber gloves and grabbed the door handle again. The paint on the doorframe cracked as she tugged, but it didn't give. Neither did she. Grinding her teeth, she pulled and jerked until her arms ached with the effort.

Suddenly, a loud crack broke the silence as the door flew open.

Juliet lost her grip on the knob and flew backward,

landing hard on her back. Her head hit the cold concrete floor and stars danced on the edge of her vision. She was too stunned and terrified to move. She'd never fallen before. Ever. She couldn't breathe. All the air had left her lungs. Panic gripped her. Was she going to suffocate?

She winced. This was pain. She wanted to scream, but she couldn't make a sound. She rolled onto her side and sucked in a breath, then coughed it out. She slowly pushed up to her knees. Her hands trembled as she brushed her hair out of her face.

She looked around, frantically searching for any sign of blood or broken skin. Even without cuts and scrapes, she was almost certain to have a bruise or a bump on the back of her head. She collected her latex gloves and put them back on as anxiety sank its claws into her. She'd be eliminated.

Wincing as dizziness threatened to topple her, Juliet stood up. The fresh paint fumes coming from the next room choked her, bringing back memories of her mother repainting the cradle after another imperfect baby had stopped breathing. She always repainted it before a new Julie came home.

But this was no cradle.

Juliet took a tentative step inside the freshly painted room. The walls and ceiling were light green, and the emblem of the Genesis Foundation covered the wall opposite the door. Unlike her father's lab, this room had recessed lighting and plush, forest-green carpeting. The only furniture was a long, slender glass case in the center of the room. The lights overhead accentuated the emptiness of the display. Maybe they were going to fill it with her father's vitamins.

But pictures of her hung all over the walls again. She passed by them as she made her way to the far wall. Below the Genesis Foundation emblem was a bronze plaque. When she got close enough to read it, her heart hammered in her chest.

Juliet Huff
Perfect DNA Specimen

What did her DNA have to do with vitamins? She stared at the final word. *Specimen.* She'd done something none of her siblings had: she'd stayed perfect her entire childhood. Yet she was still only a *specimen* to them when all she ever wanted was to be their daughter. To be loved.

Even being perfect wasn't enough.

She wiped her nose and stepped back, suddenly eager to get out of the room. The cold glass case impeded her progress as her back pressed against it. Juliet turned around and noticed that this end of the case had a small pillow in it. In fact, the entire length of the glass box was padded on the bottom. Like a coffin…

Her pulse pounded in her ears as she ran from the room. No. That couldn't be right. There had to be some other explanation. She scrambled back to her father's desk in the lab. With shaking hands, she reached for the journal bearing her name and turned back to the last entry again. It mentioned a ceremony but not what would happen.

There had to be something else.

She riffled through the drawers until she found a stack of papers she hadn't looked through yet. Most were from utility companies asking for payments, but in the middle was a handwritten note.

Dearest Martha,

We have done the impossible. It took decades, but our struggle has yielded the potential to change the world.

On Juliet's eighteenth birthday, the entire Genesis Foundation board will be here to share in our triumph. The first success. The first step in our ultimate mission.

I've hesitated to give you this news. I know you spend more time with the subjects, blurring the lines between scientific objectivity and human connection, but I hope you'll understand. The board has made the decision to entomb Juliet's body in the shrine in its current state of perfection.

This will insure she will never wither with age like the rest of the world, and she will never leave us.

Juliet will be perfect forever.

She covered her mouth to silence her scream. They were going to *kill* her. Next week.

Tears rolled down Juliet's cheeks as she got to her feet. She paced the room, the rush of adrenaline making coherent thought difficult.

One thing was clear, though: she had to get out of this house.

It seemed impossible, but the only other option would end with her dead inside the glass case. She had no intention of being preserved forever in a box. No. No way.

Freedom or die trying. It seemed that death would be paying her a visit either way.

She stuffed the letter into the journal bearing her name and tucked the book under her arm before she raced for the stairs. There had to be a way out of the house. She just needed to calm down so she could think clearly.

But right now, calming down seemed more improbable than escaping the house. Anxiety taunted her with unanswerable questions every step of the way. *Where will I go? What if they find me? How will I live?*

As she slipped back into the house and closed the door to the exam room behind her, she looked at the staircase leading up to her room. Her chest heaved for air as she checked the clock on the wall. She let out a relieved breath. Her mother wouldn't be up for another two hours, and their morning inspection was at least three hours away.

After quietly climbing the stairs, she ducked into her room and shut the door. Julie-Eight was buried under her quilt. For now, Juliet had made it.

She carefully went to her bed, where she stuffed the journal under her pillow. She stared out the window, willing her breathing to slow. The sky was just beginning to color outside, the stars twinkling into oblivion before the sunrise. Was it cold out there?

She raised her pale hand, removed the latex glove from the other, and pressed her bare palms to the glass. What did morning dew feel like when you stepped in the grass? She'd never been out in a rainstorm or touched snow. She wanted to live, not be turned into some twisted version of Snow White in a glass case.

This wasn't a fairy tale; it was her life.

She dropped her hands into her lap and removed her other glove before putting her sleeping mittens back on her hands. Maybe she wouldn't have a bump on her head or a bruise from the fall. But there was too much riding on a *maybe.*

A soft moan came from Julie-Eight's bed. Juliet got up and crossed the room. She sat beside the lump of blankets that hid her little sister and stroked her back. As Juliet soothed Julie-Eight, she realized her escape was going to be even more complex. Leaving Julie-Eight behind wasn't an option, not now that she knew what was in store for them. Once they finished growing, the research was complete. They were only specimens for the Genesis Foundation.

Who knows what they might do to her if they find out I'm gone?

She didn't want to think about it. Somehow, she had to take Julie-Eight with her. But it wouldn't be easy. Her sister still thought of the house as a home, not a prison. Juliet wasn't sure Julie-Eight would be willing to leave. She believed the stories about the outside world being filthy and dangerous. She thought their parents were keeping her safe by locking her up in the house. But Juliet had to get her out, even if Julie-Eight wouldn't go willingly.

I'll cross that bridge when I come to it.

First, she needed to find a way outside.

CHAPTER 7

"JULIET...WAKE UP. MOMMA'S coming."

"What?" Juliet blinked, trying to remember how she had gotten into Julie-Eight's bed.

"Inspection." Julie-Eight tugged at her arm. "Momma will be mad if you're still sleeping. Come on. You have to get up."

Juliet nodded and rose from the bed to stretch as memories from the night before filtered into her consciousness. Her head snapped over to her pillow. Her father's thick, leather-bound journal was under it. If her mother tried to make the bed... Juliet rushed across the room as the doorknob squeaked. She straightened.

Momma breezed into the room. "Morning, girls."

"Good morning, Momma," Julie-Eight replied like a trained parrot.

Juliet turned to face her mother, praying her nerves wouldn't show on her face. "Hi, Momma."

The longer her mother stared at her, the more her stomach knotted and tightened.

"Why are you sweating?" her mother asked.

"Just a little hot, that's all."

"It's not too warm in here." Martha spun around to Julie-Eight. "Are you hot, Julie-Eight?"

Her little sister's eyes volleyed between Juliet and their mother before she finally answered. "I'm all right now, but it was warm under all my covers."

Their mother faced Juliet again with a frown. Distrust shone plainly in her eyes. "What are you up to, Juliet? You aren't..." For the first time, concern flickered in her eyes. "Are you...sick?"

The word itself carried a mortal terror. Juliet shook her head quickly. "I'm not sick, Momma. I promise, I'm fine."

"We'll see about that." She disappeared into the bathroom, no doubt for the thermometer. Usually, their father documented their temperatures down in the exam room, but her mother kept one in the bathroom as a backup.

She returned and held it up to Juliet's mouth. "Under your tongue."

Juliet sighed and did as she asked.

Her mother went to the vanity, and Julie-Eight sat down in front of the mirror. Momma picked up the brush and ran it carefully through her sister's hair, then started braiding it.

Juliet stared at her pillow, struggling to think of a way to smuggle the journal out of her room. If her mother found it, she'd know Juliet had been inside the lab.

Her younger sister jabbered away about the new book she got for her birthday, and Juliet's eyes welled with unwanted tears. She didn't want to think about birthdays. Hers would be her last if she didn't find a way out of this house.

"Juliet? Did you hear me?"

She flinched with surprise and nodded.

"Then get over here so I can check your temperature."

Juliet stopped at her mother's side and opened her mouth.

Momma took the thermometer, squinting to read the numbers. Her frown softened. "Perfect. Good girl." She looked at Juliet. "Go brush your teeth and get dressed for inspection. I'll braid your hair as soon as I finish looking over Julie-Eight."

Juliet nodded and tidied her quilt on her way to the bathroom, hoping it would keep her mother from making the bed. It was the best she could do. She couldn't move the journal with Momma in the room.

After closing the bathroom door, Juliet carefully removed her sleeping mittens and put on a fresh pair of latex gloves. She winced as she undressed. Her muscles ached. She straightened and looked at her reflection in the mirror with a curious stare. Was this how the normal people in the outside world felt?

She stretched, leaning from side to side, drinking in the tightness in her muscles. Every twinge was a new sensation. She was sore all over, but she also felt more alive than ever. Gradually, the thrill mutated into terror as she pulled off her shirt.

A patch of her skin was…purple. She stared in the mirror, lifting her shaky hand to touch the black-and-blue mark on the back of her shoulder. A bruise. She'd seen pictures of them in books but never had one in her entire life. It must have happened when she had fallen the night before.

She pressed her fingers into it and gasped as pain radiated through her. This was a physical sensation she'd never experienced before, and the sudden sting shook her out of her trance.

This was bad. She had to hide it somehow.

As silently as she could, Juliet searched through the cupboards and drawers for anything that might help save her life. She didn't have time to analyze it right now. Survival had to come first.

I'm not perfect anymore.

If only she owned some of the makeup she saw in the magazines. But cosmetics, like many things, were for the normal people. She'd never had any blemishes to mask.

"Juliet, hurry up in there," her mother shouted.

"Coming, Momma!"

What am I going to do?

Her hands trembled as she reached for a tin of talcum powder. She put some over the bruise and took an anxious peek into the mirror. It didn't cover it. She'd never pass her mother's inspection. Panic wove its way through her until her palms were damp with sweat. Dazed, she pulled on her clean turtleneck and sweatpants.

Maybe she won't even look.

It was possible. Since Juliet had become a teenager, her mother's inspections weren't quite as invasive. And her father wasn't home so there wouldn't be a physical exam today. She just had to hope. She picked up a brush with her gloved hand, took a deep breath, and opened the door.

"About time." Her mother rolled her eyes. "I have better things to do than wait for you to get dressed, you know. I'm expecting a package to be delivered this morning. Now get over here so I can fix your hair before the driver shows up."

"I can do it myself." Juliet brushed her hair with slow even strokes, praying her mother would leave the room.

"I wasn't asking you a question, young lady. I was *telling* you to come here so I can braid your hair." Her eyes narrowed into a glare.

The flat tone in her mother's voice was a warning. If Juliet pushed back, she'd find herself locked in the closet, and she couldn't risk her mother finding the journal.

"Sorry, Momma." She handed her mother the brush. "I just wanted to help."

She sat in front of the mirror, and her mother started running the brush through her long brown hair. Juliet stared at her reflection, willing herself to sit still. The sooner her mother finished, the sooner she could hide the journal and think. She had to make a plan if she was going to survive her eighteenth birthday.

And she had every intention of surviving.

"Help?" Her mother scoffed, taking the brush out of from Juliet's hand. She dragged it gently through Juliet's hair. "You could *help* by staying put and not worrying your perfect head about—"

Her words cut off as her fingers explored Juliet's scalp. "What's this?"

Her mother's fingertips pressed firmly against a lump on the back of her head until Juliet winced in pain. "Ouch!"

Her mother's eyes widened in the mirror. "Ouch?" She tightened her hold on Juliet's hair while she searched for the imperfection again. "You have a *bump* on your head!"

Juliet tried pull away, but her mother's merciless grip on her hair made it impossible. "No, Momma, I couldn't. I just woke up."

"Liar!" she screamed, pulling Juliet to her feet by her hair and turning her around. She pushed her backward until her back pressed against the wall. "I told you *never* to lie to me."

"Momma, don't." On her bed, Julie-Eight pulled

her knees up to her chest. "You'll leave a mark. She won't be perfect anymore."

"She's already ruined." Momma didn't take her eyes from Juliet's face as her hands moved along her shoulders to the base of her neck. "Completely ruined."

Tears ran down Juliet's cheeks as she struggled to keep her mother's hands from closing around her throat. "No, Momma, please… I'm sorry."

"Too late for sorry. You've wrecked everything, you selfish little bitch!" She slammed Juliet's head into the drywall.

The room blurred, and Juliet coughed as her mother squeezed her hands tightly around her neck. Adrenaline shot into her veins as the pain and panic hit her. Somewhere in the distance, her little sister screamed. Juliet tried to shout, to tell her to run, but she couldn't breathe. The cold rage in her mother's eyes and the determined set to her jaw made it plain that Juliet might not take another breath.

Julie-Eight raced over from her bed and tugged at their mother's shirt, crying. Time seemed to slow as her mother released one hand from Juliet's neck. Juliet took a sip of oxygen as her mother backhanded her younger sister, sending Julie-Eight to the floor, squealing in pain.

Juliet's eyes widened as instincts she never realized she possessed took over. Protecting herself hadn't come naturally, but seeing her sister being hurt was too much. Somehow, she was going to get them out, or she would die trying.

When her mother brought her hand back to her throat, Juliet caught her wrist, clawing at her mother's face with her other hand, fighting for air. Her mother stumbled backward. Juliet coughed, barely pulling in a single breath before her mother was on her again, painfully crushing her tender throat.

"You're so selfish," her mother hissed as blood trickled down her face. "We sacrificed our lives for this calling. You're weak. Just an imperfect piece of garbage."

Juliet's vision blurred further, and an odd metallic taste burned the back of her throat. With the last of her strength, she slapped her mother's injured face, then closed her fist and hit her again.

Momma yowled, releasing Juliet's neck to cover her wounded face.

Sliding down the wall, Juliet wheezed and coughed, fighting to breathe again.

"Look out!" her little sister screamed.

Juliet turned as her mother lifted a marble bookend over her head. Momma swung, and Juliet dove forward, barely escaping being smashed in the head. She started to crawl for the shelter of her bed, but her mother dropped the weapon and bent over, grabbing her ankle and yanking her back. Juliet clawed at the floor with her gloved hands and kicked her legs, struggling to break free, but she was losing.

There was a hollow thump behind her.

Juliet rolled over to see her younger sister standing with the bookend still clenched tightly in her hands. She followed her sister's gaze to the floor. Momma lay quiet, a silent heap.

Dragging herself up onto her bed, Juliet pulled her sister into her arms.

"I'm bleeding, Juliet." She sobbed. "I'm not perfect. I'll die, just like Julie-Ten did!"

Juliet looked down into her eyes and shook her head slowly. "We'll be fine. I promise. I won't let anything happen to you, but we have to get out of here, okay? We need to leave now."

Little Julie-Eight nodded, her swollen bottom lip quivering as she whispered, "Is…is Momma…dead?"

"No," Juliet answered without hesitation, but truthfully, she wasn't sure and didn't want to risk checking. They had to go. "Come on. We've got to hurry."

Her sister got up while Juliet retrieved her father's journal from under her pillow.

"What's that?"

"Papa's book, but it's ours now." Juliet took her sister's hand and hurried downstairs to the back door in the kitchen. The security keypad taunted her. They were so close to the outside world.

"Where are we going?" Julie-Eight asked.

"I don't know, but we'll find someplace." She looked at her younger sister and took her hands. "It's not an awful place out there like they say, I promise."

"How do you know?"

Juliet's ninth birthday popped into her head, the

night she'd met Billy Manning. She could still hear his voice like it happened yesterday. But there was no time to reminisce.

"I just do, okay? Trust me."

Her sister nodded, sucking on the cut on her lower lip. Juliet faced the keypad again. She didn't know the code, and she wasn't sure if an alarm would sound if they tried to break it open. Juliet glanced at the windows, wondering if there might be some way to unhinge the bars on the outside when her sister shrieked.

Juliet spun around, and Momma came at her like a freight train, blood oozing from her nose and her swollen eye. Juliet raised her arms up to protect her face just as her mother slammed her back into the door.

"Where do you think you're going?"

"Away!" She wrestled, trying to push her mother back. "You said we're ruined. Just let us go."

Her mother slapped her again, and stars ignited on the edges of her vision.

"You think I can let you walk out that door?" Momma shook her head. "You're too stupid to be perfect."

"I never wanted to be perfect, anyway." Juliet bit back tears.

"We don't need you, anyhow. Julie-Eight only has eight years left. Ed will be disappointed, of course, but all's not lost."

"She's not perfect anymore, either, Momma." Juliet's hands trembled. "You hit her."

Her mother's eyes flashed with rage. She snatched a knife out of the butcher block and pointed it at Juliet. "She'll be fine by the time Ed gets back." She looked over at Julie-Eight with her good eye and smiled, exposing bloody teeth. "We won't tell Papa a thing will we, Julie perfect love?"

She spun around toward Juliet, pointing the knife at her. "But we've got no use for you anymore." She closed the distance between them, raising the blade. Juliet grabbed her mother's wrist as she pushed the sharp edge closer to Juliet's neck.

"Momma...no!" Juliet's arms trembled under the strain as her mother pressed harder. Every second the blade got closer.

Julie-Eight cried. "I love Juliet! Please don't hurt her!"

"I've loved every single one of you, and over and over you break my heart." Momma spat. "But this is bigger than all of us. Besides, I'd rather give you up than see you imperfect. No one else will ever know."

The cold blade pressed against Juliet's skin until something warm trickled down her neck. Another dose of adrenaline coursed through her veins, and Juliet shoved her mother back a step.

But she didn't let go. "Julie, go wait for me in the other room."

"No, Momma," Julie-Eight cried. "Don't do this... Please!"

"In the other room," her mother ordered. "*Now.*"

Before little Julie-Eight could move, the doorbell chimed.

"Damned UPS man." Their mother grumbled, stumbling back from Juliet with a threatening glare, knife still firmly in hand. "Don't take a single step, or Julie-Eight will die, too." She waved the knife as she spoke. "I'll bury you both. Don't think I won't. I love you girls enough to do just that."

Juliet held her hand over her bruised and bleeding neck, and watched her mother calmly wipe the blood off the knife and her face before going to answer the front door.

Julie-Eight rushed into Juliet's arms, clinging to her. Juliet lifted her up as she crept forward, trying to see her mother enter the security code on the keypad, but her mother's shoulders blocked it from view.

Juliet's hope for escape evaporated. The knife was behind her mother's back in a tight grip, but as the door opened, a plan began to form.

"Julie," she whispered. "I'm going to have to do something awful. You need to be ready to run. Understand?"

Her sister nodded, and Juliet pried herself free of Julie-Eight's arms. With her heart in her throat, she quietly moved closer to her mother. She'd never be able to do this. But if she didn't get Julie-Eight out now, both their lives would be over. Her mother would see to it.

The UPS man hurried back to his truck, but before her mother could close the door, Juliet leaped forward, reaching around to cover her mother's mouth with one hand and the other hand gripping her mother's wrist, pressing the knife against her back.

"Run, Julie! Run!"

"But—"

"Just go!"

Her little sister ran to the door and hesitated. Juliet understood completely. Neither one of them had ever stepped outside that front door. But they had no other choice.

"Go!"

Julie-Eight bolted as their mother bit Juliet's fingers. She screamed, shoving her mother forward. They both fell to the floor. Momma uttered a guttural cry as Juliet crawled to her feet. The knife was embedded in her mother's side.

Juliet had never seen so much blood.

Don't look at it, just run!

Juliet stumbled toward the door.

The journal...

It was the only proof she had of her parents' plan and the Genesis Foundation. She couldn't leave without it. She raced to the kitchen and picked it up from the floor. Clutching the book in the crook of her arm, Juliet sprinted past her injured mother and out the front door.

CHAPTER 8

BILL WANTED DONUTS from the moment he woke up. It was odd. He didn't usually crave sweets, but he couldn't get it out of his head and nothing in his parents' pantry looked good, so he hopped in his Toyota and drove to the Yum Yum Donuts a few miles down the street.

The rich scent of sugar embraced him as soon as he stepped inside the donut shop. He stared through the glass case at the deep-fried delicacies and realized he wasn't even sure what type of donut he wanted. Since the donut shop didn't have a "try before you buy" program, he bought a half dozen assorted donuts. He'd never eat them all, but he figured he could taste them and find at least a couple he liked. Donuts were also well within his starving college student's budget.

Normally he wouldn't need to forage for food, but with his parents out of the country and the house all to himself, grocery shopping hadn't been high on his priority list. And now the milk sitting in the fridge was a little chunky for his taste.

His stomach growled as he drove home, and he

reached into the bag and pulled out a maple donut. He took a bite just as he made the right turn onto his street. Although he'd been at UCLA for most of the past year, this street still felt like *his*. It seemed like just yesterday that he was speeding by the creepy Victorian house on his bike with his head full of monsters.

He dropped the rest of the maple donut back in the bag and poked his hand inside for another one to try when someone screamed. He jerked his head up and swerved to the right. His truck lurched, the bed fishtailing as he jammed his boot on the brakes.

"Dammit!" He fought to regain control of his pickup.

He pulled over and shut off the engine. His legs were like rubber as he jogged over to the woman and little girl huddled in the street.

Oh shit, did I hit them?

He slid a shaky hand back through his hair as he ran toward them. "Are you guys all right?" His stomach knotted more and more the closer he got.

Please let them be okay...

The woman looked up at him, her face swollen on one side and her neck black-and-blue...and bleeding.

"I'm so sorry." He knelt beside them, shaking his head. "I didn't see you. Is your daughter okay?"

The little girl tipped her head back, and his heart stopped. "Juliet?"

It wasn't possible. She hadn't aged a day. She was

the exact same nine-year-old girl who had kissed his cheek that night. As impossible as it seemed, he had no doubt this was Disease Girl. But it couldn't be…

"Billy?"

He shifted his attention to the young woman, his eyebrows pinching together as he frowned. She seemed familiar, but at the same time, he knew he'd never met her before. "How do you know my name?"

"I'll explain later. Just help us get out of here, please?" She looked over her shoulder at the creepy Victorian house.

He nodded and helped them up without any further questioning. It was the least he could do after hitting them with his truck, right? They hurried to the pickup, but they didn't open the door. They just…stopped.

Bill rubbed the back of his neck. "I thought you needed to get out of here."

Something was very wrong with them. It was almost as if they'd never seen a car before. They stared at each other. Did they have concussions?

Bill shook his head and opened the passenger door for them. "Better get in…"

"Thank you." The woman sat inside and lifted the girl up onto her lap.

They made no move to close the door so Bill slammed it shut and hurried around to the driver's seat. Once the engine was revving, he looked over at them, getting a chill again when he looked at little

Juliet. It was like she was frozen in time, trapped forever in a nine-year-old body like some bad, late-night sci-fi movie.

He forced his attention straight ahead, trying not to notice her big brown eyes staring up at him. "I should get you two to the hospital." He hoped he sounded calm and responsible, but he was pretty sure the panic and confusion were bleeding through.

"No!" The woman held the girl a little tighter. "We can't go there."

"Why not?" Bill asked.

"Long story." She peered over her shoulder out the back window. "Can we go to your house?"

She seemed *so* familiar.

"Sure." He drove down the street. This had to be a bad dream. How was he going to explain to his parents that he'd hit two people with his truck and instead of taking them to a hospital he'd brought them home with him? His dad's only rules had been no parties and no houseguests.

Shit. After I run them down with my truck, all bets are off, Dad.

He wished the woman would stop twisting around to look behind them. It made his nervous stomach churn. Why had they been in the street anyway? Was someone after them?

By the time he pulled into his driveway he was sweating.

When he reached for the key, she said, "Can you park in the garage?"

He gave a tentative nod and pressed the opener. Once he parked and closed the garage door behind them, he turned to her. "Okay, we're here. Now tell me how you know my name, and how—" He stared at little Juliet again. "How can you still look exactly the same as you did nine years ago?"

The little girl looked up at the young woman, and Bill followed her gaze, nearly flinching when the older girl smiled at him.

"You remember," she said.

"Remember what?"

"My birthday."

Bill studied her face, and bewilderment gave way to disbelief. Underneath the swollen face, split lip, and badly bruised neck was Juliet Huff. "Juliet? Then who is—"

The carbon copy of Juliet said, "I'm Julie-Eight."

"Juliet?"

"No," grown-up Juliet answered. "Julie-*Eight*."

"Julie-*Eight* as in the number eight?" He frowned, glancing from one set of big brown eyes to the other. "What kind of name is that?"

"She's my eighth little sister named Julie," Juliet said. "You know, like Henry the Eighth."

He couldn't stop staring at little Julie. "So your parents named all their kids Julie?"

Juliet nodded.

"But why?"

"I don't know." Juliet's smile faded. "Is that…strange?"

"A little, yeah." He looked at each of them, not quite believing what he was seeing. They were like identical twins but nine years apart. He met Juliet's eyes. "She looks exactly like you did. How is that possible?"

"I'm not sure, but I think the answer could be inside this book somewhere." She showed him a leather-bound journal with her name on the outside.

"What's that?"

"My father's journal."

He raised a brow. "With your name on it?"

"It's all about me."

"Like a baby book?" He had to be dreaming. This couldn't be real.

"I've never seen a…baby book." Juliet shrugged. "This has a lot of my dad's research notes in it."

"Is your dad a scientist?"

The little girl in her lap sighed. "Can we go inside?"

"Sure." Bill nodded and got out of the truck, but Juliet and Julie-Eight didn't move.

He went around to the passenger side and opened the door.

"Thank you." Julie-Eight hopped out with Juliet close behind.

He stepped in front of her, keeping his voice down.

"You guys have never been in a car before, have you?"

Juliet lifted her battered face, studying him. "We've never been outside before."

Bill blinked, trying to put himself in her shoes. He was a writer, so stepping into another character's skin wasn't a big leap. He couldn't remember the exact date the night he and his friends had hopped over the Huffs' fence, but Juliet had to be almost eighteen now. And she'd *never* left that house? How was that possible? And why?

Little Julie-Eight came back to her sister's side and raised a gloved hand to her swollen lip as she looked up at her sister. This had to be overwhelming for them.

"Wow." Bill forced a smile, hoping to lift the mood a little. "I guess you both have some catching up to do." Juliet smiled, and his memories of that dark night when she'd kissed his cheek came rushing back. Now she was bruised and bloody. What the hell had happened to her? "Come on, I have a first aid kit inside."

"What's a first aid kit?" Julie-Eight asked.

He knelt to her level. It still unsettled him that she looked exactly like Juliet had when he'd met her nine years ago. Maybe his memory was just foggy, playing tricks on him now. "It has medicine and Band-Aids and ice packs for fat lips." Her brow pinched in confusion. Bill added, "We have to clean the cuts and scrapes to keep them from getting infected."

She stared at her socks. "I've never had a scrape before."

He hadn't noticed that neither of them had shoes on.

"It's okay." Juliet took her sister's hand. "We're normal now. That's not so bad, is it?"

Juliet looked up at Bill, her eyes prodding him.

"No," he stammered, not quite sure what she wanted him to say. "I've always been pretty normal. It's not half-bad."

Juliet knelt by her sister. "See? We'll be fine. I promise."

She gave her sister a little squeeze and followed Bill into the house.

JULIET HELPED JULIE-EIGHT onto a stool at the counter. Billy called it a breakfast bar. She kept her arm around her younger sister's shoulders and scanned the room. They were free. Her heart raced at the thought.

Billy came back and opened the first aid kit, pulling out all sorts of tiny packets, rolls of tape, a blue squishy pillow, and a few other things she'd never seen before.

"Okay, who's first?" he asked.

Julie-Eight quickly pointed to Juliet.

Juliet chuckled, shaking her head. "I guess I am."

He nodded and tore open one of the little packets. "This might sting a little. It's an alcohol pad to clean the cuts so they don't get infected."

Juliet held her breath as he came closer. No one

other than her parents and her sister had ever touched her. She wasn't sure if she was scared or excited. Maybe both. She'd secretly borrowed a few romance books from Momma over the past couple of years, and she'd imagined being touched.

But having a boy clean her bloody wounds wasn't anything like what she'd been fantasizing about. It was probably the first of many things that would be different from how she'd envisioned. She was just grateful she didn't have to dream about it anymore. She was on the outside, living.

"Hey." He covered her hand with his. "It's not going to hurt *that* bad. You don't have to be scared."

She hadn't realized she was holding her breath. Taking in a slow inhale, she readied herself. "Sorry. I'm just a little nervous."

Billy smiled, and for a minute, he was the same boy who had come to her back door years ago. But he'd changed quite a bit in the past nine years. He was tall and lean now with broad shoulders. His face was thinner and his large, curious green eyes seemed wiser somehow, but his grin was familiar and it lit up the room.

He dabbed the cool, wet square against the cut on her neck, and she gasped, her hand popping up to grab his. The touch sent an equally unsettling twinge through her, nearly as strong as the burning ache on her raw neck.

"Sorry." He pulled back, concern written all over

his face. "I'm trying to be careful of the bruises."

"No, I just wasn't sure what a 'sting' felt like." She managed a smile and released his hand. "Now I know."

"Oh-kay." Billy chuckled, raising one brow. "All right… Almost done."

Once he finished cleaning her wounds, Billy smashed one of the small, blue, plastic pillows against the counter and handed it to her. "This will be icy in just a second. Hold this to your cheek. It'll bring the swelling down."

Juliet nodded, wincing as the instant cold prickled her throbbing skin. She turned to Julie-Eight. "See? It's not so bad."

"You're next." Billy smiled.

Julie-Eight sucked her sore lip right back into her mouth.

Billy set the first aid supplies back into the little white box and showed her his empty hands. "You're not going to let me see your lip?"

She shook her head.

"It won't hurt," Juliet tried to reassure her. "Try putting one of these cold pillows on your mouth. It'll just cool it off, okay?"

"Uh-uh." she muttered, still not exposing her lower lip.

Juliet reached for her sister, tugging her over to her lap. "Come on. Billy's trying to help."

Julie-Eight shot her a pouty glare.

Juliet sighed, shaking her head. "It's not going to

hurt."

Gradually Julie-Eight's injured lip started to reappear. "You promise it's not gonna hurt?"

"It'll just be cold." Billy smashed the other blue plastic square and gently pressed it to her swollen lip. "Not too bad, is it?"

Julie-Eight didn't look convinced, but she didn't fuss. She reached up and held it to her mouth. Juliet breathed a sigh of relief.

For now, they were safe.

AFTER SETTLING JULIE-EIGHT in the living room with some cartoons on the television, Bill grabbed a couple of sodas and followed Juliet onto the back porch. She set her father's research journal on the table and started flipping through the pages.

"She learned how to use that remote pretty fast." He chuckled as he pulled out a chair.

"Julie-Eight is very bright." Juliet stared at the soda can.

He hesitated for a second. "You two have never seen a television before, have you?"

"No." Juliet sank into a patio chair. "We read about them in books and magazines, but Papa was worried television and computer screens would hurt our eyesight. We had to be perfect. Nothing else was tolerated."

She looked straight ahead again, her gaze going distant. Despite the cuts, bumps and bruises, she held her head up. This was a fish-out-of-water story no one would believe. She was battered and lost, but she hadn't fallen apart.

He wished he had a clue what to do to help her. If everything she'd said was true and their parents had kept them locked up like prisoners in that house, he should be taking them to the police, not hiding them in his parents' house. He looked over his shoulder at her little sister through the sliding glass door. She stared at the television with the ice pack on her lip and wide eyes. A shiver racked her shoulders, reminding him of a frightened puppy who wakes up one day in a cold cement kennel at the dog shelter.

The police station could wait a little bit. His parents were in Europe right now anyway. If the Huffs showed up looking for them, he'd tell them he didn't know they had kids. Problem solved.

He looked at Juliet again. She was still holding the sealed can of Dr. Pepper. He took it from her, cracked it open, and handed it back to her. "Haven't ever had a soda, either, huh?"

"No." Her lips curved into a hint of a smile, but when she turned toward him, she seemed…haunted. "We're not perfect anymore."

Bill wasn't sure what to say, but this felt like one of those "do these jeans make me look fat" kind of things when no matter what he said there wasn't really a "right" answer. He finally couldn't take the awkward silence any longer and tried to change the subject. "Those injuries didn't come from my truck, did they?"

"No." She stared down at her opened soda can without taking a sip. "Did you think you hit us?"

"It all happened so fast I wasn't sure." He let out a sigh of relief and took a swig from his soda can. "I'm glad I didn't hurt you guys."

She looked up at the sky, shaking her head. "I've dreamed of this day forever, but in my dreams, I was happy and free. Right now, all I feel is...lost and afraid." She gnawed at her swollen lower lip and winced as she glanced over at Julie-Eight sitting inside on the sofa. "I promised her we'd be all right, but I don't know how I'll be able to keep my word. Everything is so..." Her eyes brimmed with tears.

Bill set his soda down on the cement next to his patio chair and wrapped a comforting arm around her shoulders.

Juliet tensed.

He removed his arm immediately with an apologetic smile. "Sorry. You looked like you could use a hug."

"You just surprised me. I'm...not used to being...comforted." She met his eyes. "But I think a hug sounds great."

Bill opened his arms and let her make the first move this time. Tentatively, she leaned closer and settled against his chest. He embraced her gently, and it felt...right. One thing he had learned since he'd started dating was there were only certain people who really "fit" in your arms.

And no one had ever clung to him so tightly.

"Are the cuts and bruises from your parents?" he asked. She nodded against him, and he ground his teeth together as his gut clenched. It wasn't bad enough keeping them locked up like animals in the zoo for their entire lives? They had to beat the shit out of them, too?

Sick bastards.

He pulled back to meet her eyes. "We should go to the police, Juliet."

"What if they take us back?" Panic filled her eyes. "I read stories about runaways. They always take them back." She swallowed and set her jaw as she lifted her gaze to his face. "We're not perfect anymore. They'll kill us both."

He stared at her, trying to comprehend her words. This was unreal. People didn't get murdered by their parents in this town, let alone on his street. Then a memory came creeping back of the rows of sunken dirt squares in their backyard. What if they really were graves?

He would've laughed at the suggestion a couple of hours ago, but things were different now. The bruises on her face and neck made it all too real.

But what could he do to help her? All he could think of was to tell the police, but what if Juliet was right? She might be eighteen, but her sister was definitely a minor.

Juliet cleared her throat and flipped more pages of the journal before ushing it over toward him. "Read this."

He skimmed the words, faster and faster. He turned the page, his jaw slackening. He looked back at the little girl in front of his TV. She wasn't Juliet's sister.

She was a clone. That explained why he'd thought Juliet had never aged. Julie-eight was the same age Juliet had been when they met nine years before. He met Juliet's eyes. "How?"

She shrugged. "All my life I thought they were making some kind of supplement to keep kids perfect, but they were actually...cloning my DNA." She shook her head. "Julie-eight doesn't know. I'm not sure if she should. I don't know what to do, but we can't go back there. Ever."

"My parents are out of town. You and your sister can stay here tonight, and we can figure out what to do in the morning." It would buy them some time. They didn't have anywhere else to go, and he was out of ideas.

"I don't even know if my mother is alive." Her eyes welled with tears as she shook her head. "But if she is, she'll call my father and they'll be hunting for us." She picked up the soda can from the table. "I don't know what we're going to do, and Julie-Eight is counting on me."

A single tear slid slowly down her cheek. Something inside him sparked, smoldering in his gut. He'd never had any desire to be a hero. That was Todd's department. Bill was usually the communicator, the one who smoothed out arguments and made sure everyone walked away as friends. But seeing Juliet beaten, bruised, and crying was more than he could take, and for the first time in his life, Bill wanted to punch someone. It wouldn't solve anything, but he was pretty sure it would feel amazing.

Instead, he reached out to brush her tear away. "No one knows you're here. You guys can get some sleep, and tomorrow we'll make plans. You don't have to do this alone, okay? I'm right here."

She wiped her face and rested her head against his shoulder as they stared into his backyard. He patted her knee, unsure if he was talking to her or himself. "Everything will work out. You'll see."

This shouldn't have been his problem. He was a college student home for summer break. But if he didn't help her, who would? He needed to talk to Todd and Zack. They'd come up with something. The three of them always did.

The question was, would it work?

CHAPTER 9

"JULIET?"

She rubbed her eyes and squinted. Her younger sister's face was right in front of hers. Juliet frowned. "What's wrong?"

"I can't sleep," her little sister whimpered. "Everywhere hurts. I didn't know what normal felt like before. I want to be perfect again." Julie-Eight wiped her eyes, heaving a quiet sob. "Make it stop hurting…"

Juliet sat up and winced as the room spun around her. She blinked her eyes hard, forcing the dark room into focus. "Normal people get cuts and scrapes all the time. Remember the books we used to read?"

"Then I don't want to be normal. I want to go home."

"We can't." She squeezed her hand. "You heard what Momma said. We're ruined. You know what they'll do if we go back." Juliet pulled her sobbing little sister into her arms, rocking her slowly as she stroked her hair. She closed her eyes, wishing she had answers. "It'll be okay. I promise."

"But it hurts."

"Where does it hurt?"

She loosened her hold on the girl and watched helplessly as Julie-Eight pointed to scrapes on both her knees, a bruise on her forearm, the cut on her lip, and finally her right ankle, which was much puffier than her left. It seemed as if all her perfect skin was marred and aching now.

Juliet sighed and rose from the sofa bed with a stifled groan. She could relate to her sister's unhappiness. Scraped knees seemed much more romantic from her bedroom window when she used to sit and watch the other kids playing stickball in the street. She'd had no concept of real pain. And now that she did, she didn't blame her younger sister for being less than thrilled.

She took Julie-Eight's hand and carefully led her down the hallway toward Billy's room. The carpet felt good under her bare feet. She tried to focus on the new experiences instead of the loss and fear. They had a lot to learn about this outside world, but it wasn't all bad. She opened and closed her fingers on her free hand. She'd never miss sleeping in gloves, that was for sure.

She tapped on his door and eased it open. "Billy?"

It was too dark to see, and she had no idea where the light switch might be so she called to him again, a little louder. "Billy?"

"Just ten more minutes…"

The grumbled voice came from her right, and Juliet blindly followed it. "It's Juliet. Julie-Eight needs help."

The bed rustled, and suddenly the room was flooded in light. Juliet gasped, shielding her eyes.

"Sorry. I should've warned you I was turning on the lamp." He sat up and looked at them. "Is she sick?"

"No. Well," Juliet quickly corrected herself, "I don't think so. We've never been sick before."

Billy swung the blankets back and strode toward them. Heat flushed her cheeks. Was she blushing? She stepped back as he knelt in front of her little sister. Juliet wasn't sure where to look. Until tonight, she'd never seen a boy in just boxer shorts. Billy's chest and abdomen were toned with a dusting of dark hair in the center. His legs were muscular, too, more defined than her own. She was tempted to touch his tan skin but thought better of it. Right now, she should be paying attention to Julie-Eight, not the way Billy's muscles tensed every time he moved.

"Is she going to be okay?" Juliet knelt on the other side of her sister.

"I think so, but I'm no doctor. I think she's just sore. Nothing looks infected or broken." He stood up and offered his hand to Julie-Eight. "Come on. I think we've got some Bactine and Advil in the bathroom."

Julie-Eight snatched her hand away from him. "Will it hurt?"

He shrugged. "It might sting a little, but it won't *hurt.*"

She tentatively placed her hand back in his, and Juliet followed them to the bathroom. He lifted her up onto the edge of the counter by the sink while he opened the medicine cabinet.

"What's a sting feel like?" Julie-Eight asked. "Seemed an awful lot like it hurt Juliet when we got here."

Billy had a white bottle with a green lid in his hand. He popped it open and smiled. "You know, I've never really thought about it. I guess a sting just kinda hurts for a minute, and a real hurt goes on for a long time afterward."

Julie-Eight cringed. "So a sting *is* a hurt…"

"Only a little, temporary one." He reached for a cotton ball. "But it'll make the scrape hurt less if you let me put this medicine on it."

She sighed. "I don't like being normal."

Juliet draped her arm around her sister's shoulder and gave her a little squeeze. "This will be much better than staying locked away trying to be perfect."

Julie-Eight squealed when the moist cotton touched her scraped knee and kicked out at Billy, her toes connecting with his bare stomach.

"Okay, okay… I'm all finished."

He blew on her wound, and she let out a sigh of relief. "That makes it feel lots better."

He grinned, putting the Bactine away. "It's an old trick my mom showed me."

"Thanks." She inspected her red knee with the curiosity of a scientist. "Will it be like this forever?"

Billy frowned. "No way. It'll heal up under the scab and be good as new. You'll never know you scraped it."

"Really?" She smiled up at him. "I'll be perfect again?"

A crease formed in the middle of Billy's forehead, but he quickly recovered and lifted her down to the ground. "A banged-up knee doesn't make you any less perfect. It just makes you a kid."

Juliet took her sister's hand and led her back to bed. "Now you should rest so your body can get better."

"Okay." She crawled into bed and snuggled in. "Good night."

Juliet leaned down to kiss her temple. "'Night, Julie-Eight."

BILL LAY IN his bed staring up at the ceiling. He couldn't fall back to sleep. What was he doing? He was house-sitting for his parents while they toured Europe for the summer. How had he gotten himself tangled up in all this?

He raked a hand back through his hair. Hell, he didn't even know what "this" was. Strange, that was for sure. This was all strange. *Very* strange.

"Billy?"

Juliet stood in the doorway.

"Can't sleep?" he asked.

"Not really." She hesitated. "Can I sit with you?"

"Sure. I wasn't sleeping anyway." He moved over on the bed. "Make yourself at home."

Juliet sat beside him with her hands in her lap, looking much younger than almost eighteen. Ever since that night when he and his friends had snuck into her backyard, he'd never forgotten the sparkle in her eyes, her soft kiss on his cheek. Every time he passed her house, he'd glance up at her window and wonder if Juliet was still caged up there.

It had never really occurred to him that she might want to get out.

"Want to talk about what happened today?" he asked softly.

She turned toward him, and the haunted look in her eyes made his gut clench. God, what had he gotten himself mixed up in?

"I don't know where to start," she said.

"How about with your little sister. Do you think she'd mind if I just called her Julie? Calling a little girl Julie-Eight seems kind of…off."

"Julie?" She looked as though she were tasting the word, trying it out in her mouth.

"It won't draw as much attention. People will ask questions if she starts telling them her name is Julie number eight. It's like she's a lab experiment or something."

"I think we both were." Juliet sighed and then nodded slowly. "I'll talk to her about it in the morning."

He sat up beside her and reached over to brush her hair back from her temple so he could see her bruised eye. The swelling had gone down a little, but she definitely had a shiner going. “Does it hurt?”

She shrugged. “It doesn’t *not* hurt. I’m still getting used to all this.” She turned her head, meeting his eyes. “In a weird way, it almost feels good, if that makes any sense. I’ve spent my whole life in gloves and socks while you and your friends played on the street. I’d see you falling off your bikes, and I’d wonder what it would feel like if I didn’t have to be perfect.”

He frowned. “I don’t understand this whole ‘perfect’ thing.”

“I’m only just beginning to understand it myself. I’ve never known any other way to live until today.”

He waited for her to go on, but she just stared into the dark.

“Tell me why you think your parents would kill you if you go back.”

“Because we’re not perfect anymore.” Her eyes welled with tears. “Our skin has been broken. We’re useless to them, ruined. My father would never accept anything less than perfect for his research, Billy.”

He frowned. What kind of research was he doing over there?

Then Bill took her hand in his, trying not to notice the zing of electricity shooting through his body. He almost asked her to call him Bill. No one had called him Billy since he’d graduated from elementary school, but something about the way Juliet said it… He sort of liked that she was the only person who called him by that name.

"You two are his daughters, not his research. I bet they're just overprotective. Right now, your father is probably really worried about you and your sister."

"Worried he'll lose his funding." She brushed a tear from her cheek. "I ran away because I found out my parents are going to kill me in a few days, on my eighteenth birthday."

Bill frowned. "That doesn't make any sense. They've been so overprotective your whole life. They must love you."

"I don't think they do. They *require* me. There's a difference." She met his eyes, no longer looking like a lost deer. Instead, he saw a spark of defiance that could ignite a forest fire. Determination. "If I stayed perfect until I was eighteen, my father's research finally would be complete, or at least my part of it. They wouldn't need me anymore."

"What?" He shook his head. "Of course they'd need you. You don't stop being their daughter because you become an adult."

"It's not that." She shot up from the bed, wringing her hands together. "I saw my coffin today. It had my name on it."

He fought to keep from pinching himself. This could not be real. A coffin? Memories of the sunken square plots of dirt in the Huff's backyard filled his head. The graves…

He wished he were dreaming.

Juliet's hands gradually slid down her sides. "The

room had pictures of me everywhere. It looked like a shrine or something." Moonlight sparkled on her wet cheeks when she walked past the window. "And I might have killed my mother during our escape."

"Wait. You said earlier you weren't sure if she was alive, but…what happened?"

"She had a knife. And I was trying to get Julie-Eight out… And I… We fell." She let out a sob, covering her face.

Bill was at a loss. He didn't know what to say or do. Quietly, he climbed out of the bed and went to her, then carefully embraced her. This time she didn't tense. She melted against him, crying. It broke his heart, and at the same time, his legs felt wobbly.

Think, man. Keep your head.

What if her mother really was dead? Would they take Juliet to jail? When he'd found them in the street earlier, Juliet had a cut on her neck. If her mother had been holding a knife, had she been attempting to slit Juliet's throat before they'd escaped?

This was some sick and twisted shit he'd just stepped in.

Juliet was talking about murder. No, not murder. An accident. Self-defense. But what if no one believed her?

Bill helped her back to the bed. He was afraid he wouldn't be able to stand much longer. He was in way over his head.

She sniffled and looked up at him. "Even though I

wanted to get out, I didn't want to hurt her."

He believed her. "If we can't go to the police, who can we trust? We can't hide you here forever."

"I've been thinking about that, too." She met his eyes. "My father works for the Genesis Foundation. I thought they made vitamins. That's what my parents always said, but that journal I found doesn't even mention supplements. If we can find proof of what they were doing, or planning to do to me, maybe then we could make the police believe us. I don't know what else to do."

Bill didn't know what to do, either. "First, let's try to get some sleep. I'll call Zack and Todd tomorrow. They can help."

"Who are they?"

"Friends. We can trust them."

"I've never met other people before."

Bill smiled in spite of himself. "They're gonna love you."

He lay down and moved all the way over to the other side of the bed. He'd never slept with a woman in his bed before. He and Cassie had had sex at college. Many times. But it had been a dorm-room thing. Sock on the door, sweat, grind, and then run back to your own room so your roommate could get some sleep.

He wasn't sure where to lie, or what to say, or how to sleep, but he didn't want to creep her out, either. Juliet curled up beside him. Her breathing gradually evened out, slowing down, and finally, she dozed off.

He kept watch over her battered body, wishing like hell he was the hero she needed him to be. She deserved that. He stared at his ceiling again. Genesis. Tomorrow he'd read through the journal. Maybe he'd be able to make sense of some of the notes, and if he couldn't, he could call his dad. Sure, they'd probably lecture him about having someone over while they were on vacation, but it wasn't like he was having a party. This was a fucked-up, life-or-death situation, and suddenly, he had two people counting on him to keep them safe.

He groaned. He might never sleep again.

CHAPTER 10

BILL WOKE UP, wincing at the morning sun coming through the edge of the shades. He rubbed his eyes and rolled onto his back. What day was it? He was waiting for the fog in his head to clear when laughter echoed from the kitchen.

He sat up in bed, reality slamming into him like a Mack Truck. Juliet Huff was real, and she was in his house. He climbed out of bed and yanked on a pair of sweats over his boxers. All the peace of sleep evaporated. Yesterday had really happened.

And he still had no clue what to do next.

He walked down the hallway and stopped when he saw them in front of the stove. Juliet and her little sister were cooking. Or *trying* to cook was a better description. He smiled. It was amazing how alike they were. It wasn't just their faces, which seemed identical, but even their laughter was the same.

Could that happen when you lived together cooped up in a house with no one else to talk to? It was the only explanation he could think of.

They had their hair braided down their backs, and

both of them had oven mitts on their hands, even though it didn't look like they were picking up any hot dishes.

Pancake batter was splattered all over the counter, and little Julie wiped a lock of hair out of her face, spreading more batter along her cheek and the top of her ear. They each had a spatula gripped tightly with a mitt. Instead of cooks, they looked more like mad scientists eagerly anticipating the perfect moment to flip a pancake. He couldn't swallow the chuckle that escaped him.

Juliet looked up and grinned. "Morning, Billy!"

"You two are—" he glanced around the kitchen again and raised a brow "—cooking?"

"Yes!" Julie squealed. "We've never cooked before. We're making you pancakes!"

He nodded, leaning against the island. "I can see that." He smiled at Juliet. "Those mitts are usually for taking hot dishes out of the oven."

She shrugged, plopping the next pancake onto the pile of misshapen pancakes. "We're used to wearing mittens and gloves. Just habit, I guess."

"I don't want any more stings." Julie turned the stove knob to the "off" position.

If his mom could see the disaster area that her kitchen had become, she'd blow a fuse, but he didn't care. Juliet and her little sister were scratched and bruised, but they seemed happy. He could clean it later.

"It looks delicious." He took three plates out of the

cupboard.

Juliet smiled at him. "Hopefully it'll taste good, too."

They set the table, and Bill flipped on the television before sitting beside Juliet. He wasn't really interested, but it was a morning ritual for his dad to run through channels and watch the news, and since he was out of the country, Bill seemed to be taking over where his dad had left off.

Julie—yeah, there was no way in the world he was going to call that little girl Julie-Eight—happily munched on her lumpy, not-quite-round pancakes. She grinned at him, watching him take his first bite.

Okay so they weren't the best pancakes he'd ever had, but the expectant smiles on their faces made this one of those times that would be ruined by complete honesty.

"These are amazing." He forked his next piece. "You two are pancake wizards."

Julie smiled at her big sister and grabbed her glass of orange juice. Before it reached her lips, her hands started to tremble and her face went pale. The glass slid from her fingers and crashed onto the floor. She didn't seem to hear it or feel the cold juice that had just splattered all over her. Her right hand came up slowly, and she pointed at the television screen.

He and Juliet both turned.

"Oh my god," Juliet gasped. "It's Momma."

JULIET COULDN'T TAKE her eyes off the television. Billy turned up the volume.

Her mother and father were huddled together in front of a bundle of microphones. "Please help me find my babies." Her mother sputtered. "Our elder daughter is a little touched in the head. She babbles on about imaginary things, and she can't take care of herself, let alone her little sister." She dabbed her eyes and quieted her sobs. "I just want my babies home."

A chill shot up Juliet's spine when pictures of her with Julie-Eight flashed on the screen alongside a bunch of numbers and a plea to call to report the missing children. She couldn't look away. Her mother had been careful to make Juliet sound unstable, hinting that she'd kidnapped her sister.

No one would ever believe her now.

Billy flipped to another channel only to find her parents again with the big Victorian house behind them. Her mother sniffled into a handkerchief while her father put his arm around her, offering comfort he'd never shown either of his daughter's. It was the first time Juliet had ever even seen him touch her mother. He seemed uncomfortable, not distraught.

When Momma lowered the handkerchief, she allowed the cameras to bear witness to her bruised and swollen face. "My Juliet didn't mean to hurt me. She was frightened. I tried to stop her and get her to take her medication."

"That's not how it happened." Julie-Eight's voice snapped Juliet from her sick fascination with the television screen.

Juliet's chest tightened. "They want to make it our word against theirs."

Her little sister shook her head. "Lying is wrong."

Billy clicked the TV off. "That circus was probably to keep us from going to the authorities. If we try to go to the police now, they'll give Julie back to your parents and put you in a psych ward for observation."

Juliet stared at her hands. She'd been so focused on getting out of their house that she hadn't considered what they'd do afterward. Going back wasn't an option. Neither of them was perfect anymore, and failed experiments ended up buried in the backyard. Destroyed.

"I'm sorry I got you mixed up in this." She looked into Billy's green eyes. "Do you want us to go?"

"Where would you go? You don't know anyone, and the police are looking for you."

He was right. She struggled to steady her voice. Julie-Eight was depending on her to be strong. If she panicked now, her sister would be inconsolable. "This isn't your problem. You were kind helping us last night, but..." She glanced at Julie-Eight. "We'll figure something out."

Billy sat beside her and took her hand. His touch lit

an awareness in her that she didn't recognize. "If you leave now, you're walking right into their trap. They went on TV to scare you out of hiding. My parents are out of the country, but they're not unreachable. I can call their hotel and fill them in on what really happened. Maybe they can help us find an attorney to get you both some protection."

"They'll believe my parents, just like the police. My mother just told everyone I gave her all those injuries."

He shook his head. "My folks are in Europe. There's no way these local news broadcasts traveled all the way over there. We can tell them before they see anything else. They'll help us."

Hope danced just out of her reach. "You really think that'll work?"

"Yeah. I do." He squeezed her hand and got up. "I've got the emergency number in here—" A knock at the door interrupted him. His voice dropped to a whisper. "Take Julie and go back to my parents' room. There's a lock on the door."

With her heart in her throat, she went to the other side of the table. Taking her sister's hand, Juliet walked her down the hallway until she found a large bedroom. She closed the door and set the lock. Julie-Eight wrapped her arms around Juliet's waist, pressing her face into her abdomen. She stroked her sister's hair and wished she could see who was at the door.

Until a couple days ago, the worst punishment her parents could threaten her with was time in the closet, but now that they were ruined…

Death was on the table.

BILL TOOK A breath and blew it out before cracking open the door. "Can I help you?"

His pulse jumped at seeing Juliet's parents fresh from their press conference. Her father narrowed his eyes. "We're looking for our girls."

"Your…girls?" He shook his head. "Sorry, I just got up for breakfast. I haven't seen anyone."

"They couldn't have gotten far." Juliet's mother crossed her arms, no sign of the tears she'd turned on for the cameras. "She can't drive, and she doesn't have money or a phone."

"Mind if we look around?" Her father reminded him of a creepy vulture with his beady eyes and hooked nose. Never in a million years would Bill have guessed this man was related to Juliet. "They might be hiding out back."

Bill didn't budge. "I don't think that's a good idea. I'm house-sitting, and I've never met you before."

Her mother pressed her lips into a crooked grimace. "We can tell the police we saw them run in here. They'll get a search warrant."

"I haven't seen your kids, but you're not getting in here without a warrant." Bill looked at each of them. "Good luck finding your daughters."

He shut the door and turned the dead bolt, his heart galloping in his chest. From the frosted sidelight window, he peered into the sunshine. Their shadows grew as they walked away.

But they'd be back. He knew they would.

He went to the master bedroom and tapped on the door. Juliet opened it, worry lining her face. Now that he'd met her parents face-to-face, he was sure they couldn't be related to Juliet and her sister. Her mother had blunt, wide features—nothing like Juliet's—and her father's thin, sharply angled bone structure didn't fit, either. Her mother may have carried her for nine months, but it hadn't been her DNA that made this refined girl or her matching sister.

Or maybe his imagination was running away with him again.

"It was your parents."

Her eyes widened as she stepped into the hallway and closed the door. She kept her voice low so her sister wouldn't hear through the door. "We've got to get out of here."

"Not yet. First, we need a plan. Without a warrant, they can't force their way in here so we've got some time." He pointed at the door. "My parents have a walk-in closet in there. You could find something to wear. She has some hats in there, too. My folks left me some money for emergencies. We could stop at Walmart on the way out of town to grab something for Julie."

Juliet caught his hand, her gaze locked on his. "You don't have to do this."

Without thinking, he brought his other hand up to her soft cheek, hating every bruise on her skin. He swallowed the lump in his throat. "I want to."

A crease formed between her eyebrows. "Why?"

That was a good question. How many times had he sat in this house and imagined himself as some kind of superhero rescuing his school? But those were kid dreams. Her cuts, her bruises, her little sister—this was real, not some heroic fantasy.

"Because you're special to me." He leaned closer, his voice dropping to a whisper. "You were my first kiss."

Her lips curved into a tentative smile. "That night on my birthday."

"Yeah." He nodded. "I never told anyone that I saw you."

"Why?"

He looked at his hands, deciding not to reveal that they'd all believed she'd had a highly contagious disease. "Just…" He shrugged. "I guess I wanted to protect the memory and you." He met her eyes again. "I didn't want to share it."

Juliet rose on her toes, her warm breath caressing his lips. Her gaze never left his eyes as she brushed her lips to his mouth. His heart pounded in answer as he slid his arms around her. When he straightened, her eyes sparkled. She took his breath away.

"Sorry." Her face flushed with color. "I always wished I'd kissed you on the lips, and I may never get another chance." She cleared her throat and turned to the door. "I guess I'd better get changed."

He fought the urge to reach for her. If he was going to help them, he needed to focus. "Yeah, I'll call my dad and let him know there's trouble. Maybe they can find a lawyer who can protect you from the police and your parents."

"I'll get Julie-Eight ready, too, and we can go."

"About that." He waited for her to look at him. "I don't want to hurt your feelings, but you can't call her that anymore. Not out here. It'll attract too much attention."

"Can't call her what?"

"No one has siblings with the same names and a number after them, remember?"

Realization dawned in her eyes as she nodded slowly. "Just Julie."

"Yeah."

"I forgot to talk to her."

He took her hand and gave it a squeeze. "I know it's hard right now, but we'll figure it out, okay?"

She didn't reply. He let go of her hand and went back to the front room to grab the cordless phone off the base. His parents' emergency cell phone number was on the fridge. He stared down the hall as he punched the buttons.

His mom finally answered. "Bill? Is everything

okay?"

"Hey, Mom. I need some help."

"Are you out of money?"

Hearing her voice settled his pulse. His mom was one of the smartest people he knew.

"I still have money." He paced around the kitchen island trying to figure out where to begin. "Remember the weird Huff place down the street?" He didn't wait for a response. "Turns out they've been keeping their daughters locked up like prisoners, and yesterday, the girls broke out. I know this sounds like I'm making it up, but it's real. I need to get them out of here, but I'm in a little over my head. I think they need a lawyer."

"Whoa. Slow down. How did you get involved?"

"That doesn't matter right now. Do you know a lawyer I could take them to see so they'll be safe? They can't go back there."

"That's not your decision to make, honey. You should take them to the police station and let them sort it out. This isn't your problem."

"I realize that, but the police will just give them back." Bill sucked in a breath and tried to keep from raising his voice. "Their mother beats them, Mom. And after they escaped, the Huffs went on television with some lame-ass story about their older daughter being unstable and kidnapping her sister."

"Bill, this is important." Her voice sounded clipped now like she was in a rush. "I need to know how they ended up with you."

"When they bolted out of their house, I almost hit them with my truck."

"Stay there. I'm changing our tickets, and we'll be home tomorrow."

"That might be too late." I ran my hand back through my hair. "They've already come by here looking for them. They could make up a story seeing them here and the police could get a warrant."

She cursed under her breath, and his eyebrows popped up. His mom usually saved them up, and when she let one go, it was only when things were reaching shitstorm levels. "You don't know anything about their family. Those girls could be lying. Please, honey, just send them home."

"It's a little more complicated than that." He decided against mentioning the whole perfect-or-else thing. His mom already sounded like she thought he was being irrational. He kept his voice even. "They're keeping Juliet and her sister against their will."

"According to *them*. These are kids, not adults. Don't get involved."

"She has proof. She brought her father's research journal out of the house with her. They can't go back. They need a lawyer."

"We'll be home tomorrow." She lowered her voice. "This isn't a game. Don't tell anyone what you've seen, and take those girls home. I mean it, Bill."

What the hell was happening? "Look, just forget I called."

He hung up, pulse pounding in his ears as he pulled in a slow breath. He should've called Zack and Todd instead of his folks. Seeing the Huffs at his door had startled him. Staring at the phone, an idea started to form.

He opened his messages and sent a text to both of them.

Meet me at the Cove. One hour. It's important. Can't discuss in writing.

CHAPTER 11

JULIET FLIPPED THROUGH the hangers, overwhelmed by choices. After spending most of her life in sweats and furry socks, seeing so many colors and styles—sweaters, long sleeves, short sleeves, tank tops—how could she decide?

Julie-Eight sauntered into the walk-in closet. "What's taking so long?"

Juliet held a bright-blue blouse under her chin. "Will this look okay?"

Her sister shrugged. "I guess." She wandered into the corner and started peeking into the plastic bins on the shelves.

Juliet pulled her shirt over her head and put the new one on over her sports bra. She turned around. "What do you think?"

Julie-Eight crossed her arms, pondering. "It's okay. But if we go outside you should have long sleeves so you don't get sunburned. You could get freckles."

"We don't have to be perfect anymore." She knelt to her sister's level. "And since we're hiding from Momma, we can't tell anyone our last name."

Her little sister swallowed hard. "All right."

"And from now on, you're just Julie."

"Why?" Concern flooded her eyes. "I'm Julie-Eight."

"I know." Juliet nodded, praying her sister would accept changing her name. Julie-Eight had a stubborn streak. "But Billy says other families don't name their children with a number. We'll attract attention."

Her sister sighed with a frown. Juliet braced herself for an argument, but gradually, her younger sister nodded. "Fine. Just Julie."

"Someday you'll understand." Juliet wrapped her arms around her sister, closing her eyes. "It was wrong for them to keep us trapped in that house. They shouldn't have forced us to be perfect. We're never going back there."

She had no idea how she'd keep her word, but there was no way she would ever set foot in that house again. They'd have to kill her first.

Of course, that was their plan all along.

She boxed up her fear and her anger, and focused on getting changed. As soon as Billy got off the phone, they'd be leaving. She would be ready. There would be time to fall apart later.

His mother's pants were a little big on Juliet, but she found a plain black belt hanging on a hook by the closet door. In the bathroom, Juliet stared at her reflection as she brushed her hair. She could count the times she'd been allowed to brush her own hair on one hand. Fumbling with a hair tie, she managed to get it contained in a ponytail.

She washed her face and peered into the medicine cabinet for mouthwash. When they stopped at for clothes for Julie-Eight—*Julie*—she needed to get toothbrushes, too. Scanning the bottles and boxes inside, her gaze fell to an enamel pin in the right corner of the cabinet.

Her heart stuttered. She'd seen that symbol before. It couldn't be. Her fingers trembled as she reached for the tiny lapel pin. The Earth with an infinity symbol across in the middle.

Genesis.

"WHO DOES THIS belong to?" Juliet came into the living room with his dad's lapel pin in her hand.

"It's my dad's. Why?"

All the color drained from her face. She set the pin on the table and took Julie's hand. "Thanks for everything, Billy, but we need to go."

He frowned. "What's wrong?"

"That's..." She pointed at the pin. "That's the logo in the lab underneath my house. The Genesis Foundation. Your dad works for the company that—" she glanced at Julie and back at Bill "—that pays our parents to do their research on us."

"That's impossible." He stared at the pin. Though it would explain his mother's reaction when he'd mentioned the research journal.

Dread twisted in his gut. His parents couldn't have been involved in this. No way had they known about Juliet and her sister being locked up in that house. They never would have looked the other way.

And if they had… No, he couldn't believe it. There had to be some other explanation.

He picked up the pin and shook his head as he lifted his gaze to her face. "You can probably guess how much help my parents were on the phone."

She backed away, eyes wide like a deer in headlights. "I'm sorry I got you involved. We'll go. Just please don't tell them we were here."

He rubbed his hands down his face. "Too late for that. They're coming back from Europe right now. They'll arrive tomorrow."

"What?" Juliet put herself between him and her sister. "We need to get out of here."

"I swear, I didn't know who my dad worked for." Bill jammed his hand in his pocket, trying to figure out what to do. If they walked out that door, their parents would find them. Juliet didn't have any money or a phone. She probably didn't know how to use one, for all he knew. "My dad is a scientist. He used to work for UCLA. I don't understand what he does exactly, but something with mapping DNA. We moved here after my brother died. They told me it was for a fresh start. I didn't even know he'd switched jobs."

She didn't look super convinced, and he wasn't sure why he was trying so hard to earn her trust. It would be easier if they left.

But if his parents really had looked the other way while these girls had been locked up and treated like prisoners, how could he do the same damned thing? He couldn't.

"Juliet, I can help you. Todd and Zack are going to meet us at the Cove. We'll come up with a plan." He took a step closer. "We can figure this out."

"I have to protect my sister. I'm all she has."

Julie looked up at her sister. "Where will we go?"

Juliet sighed. "I don't know." She lifted her gaze to Bill's face. "I wish we had some other option."

"But we don't." Bill handed the pin back to Juliet. "Put this back where you found it. For now, it's probably best if my parents don't realize we know who my dad works for."

Juliet took it and vanished down the hall, leaving him alone with little Julie. With their eyes locked on each other, he sat down, keeping his gaze on hers. "You're going to be all right."

Tears shone in her eyes. "How? They're all grown-ups."

"That doesn't give them the right to keep you locked up."

A tear spilled down her cheek. "We were perfect."

"That's the thing." Bill's mouth curved into a sympathetic smile. "You still are."

Juliet came back, and he went into the kitchen and grabbed the envelope of emergency money out of the drawer. He stuffed it in his pocket as he hustled them into the garage. "Let's get out of here."

Bill helped them into the truck and instructed them to keep their heads down so no one would see them. He opened the garage door and held his breath. The driveway was empty. Good. He started the engine and pulled out onto the street. He gripped the wheel so tight his knuckles ached. He couldn't reconcile his parents being involved with the Huffs. Did they know Juliet? Had they met her and left her imprisoned in that house?

Once they were a few miles away from the neighborhood, Bill looked over at his passengers. "You can sit up now."

Julie straightened on the bench seat between them, her legs on either side of the gear shift, and Juliet stared out the window, her father's journal clutched in her hands. He wanted to ask what she'd discovered in it, but not with Julie there. She was scared enough.

When they reached the aging strip mall parking lot, relief swamped him. They'd made it. He pulled into a spot and turned off the engine.

Juliet looked around and frowned. "This is the Cove?"

He pointed to the last store at the end of the strip mall. "It's the arcade down there."

"What's an arcade?" Julie asked.

He did his best to keep his jaw from hitting the floor. He kept forgetting how sheltered they were. "It's a place with lots of video games inside for you to play. It's usually loud and full of kids. Perfect place to hide out from your folks while we make a plan."

They got out, and he scanned the parking lot while they walked to the arcade. No police. That was a good sign. He opened the glass door and let them in first, then followed them inside. The Cove was dimly lit, and the scents of body odor and bubble gum lingered in the air. A few kids were scattered at the machines.

Bill finally noticed Todd and Zack seated in the *Sega Racing* game. He led Juliet and Julie over and leaned on the frame, watching his friends, and just for a second, the normalcy made him almost forget why he'd set this meeting.

Todd looked up as he made a turn on the virtual track. "Hey, Bill. Good to see you, man." He focused on the screen again.

Zack's car flipped over the barrier on the screen. "Dammit."

The screen flashed for him to insert more quarters to continue his game. He got out and came over to stand with Bill. Zack was no longer the chunky kid in their group. He'd grown to about six feet tall, a couple inches taller than Bill, but he was lanky and bony, the opposite of Todd.

After Todd finished, he stood up and smiled. Since

he started playing football for USC, Todd had been working out, and it showed. His Trojans T-shirt could barely contain the muscles in his chest and arms.

Bill shook his head with a chuckle. “Too bad Trojans football gave you a shirt two sizes too small.”

Todd flexed his biceps with a grin. “You’re just jealous.” He sobered as he looked past Bill. “You brought…friends?”

“This is Juliet and her sister, Julie. Come on.” Bill led the group to the back corner of the arcade near the vending machines where they could be alone. He lowered his voice. “They escaped from the Huff place last night.”

Todd raised a brow. “Escaped?”

Juliet nodded. “Yes.”

“Disease Girl?” Zack asked.

Bill cringed inwardly. “Her name is Juliet, and she’s healthy.”

Zack studied her for a second, then focused on Bill again. “What do we have to do with this?”

“I’ll fill you in later.” Bill fished out a twenty-dollar bill from his pocket and handed it to Zack. “Julie has never played a video game before. Can you show her while we talk?”

The concern vanished from Zack’s face as he grinned and looked down at Juliet’s sister. “Never?”

Julie shook her head.

“We should fix that right away. Come on.” They headed for the flashing lights.

Juliet grabbed Bill's hand. "Are you sure about this?"

He nodded, meeting her eyes. "Zack's a good guy. I just wanted to keep Julie distracted. I don't think it's a good idea for her to hear the plan. She's scared enough, you know?"

Juliet looked over her shoulder as Zack scooped the quarters out of the change machine. He and Julie went to the *Dance Dance Revolution* game, and Juliet faced forward again. "Okay."

Bill turned to Todd. "Any chance Cindy could watch Julie for a few days?"

Juliet's brow furrowed. "Who is Cindy? I can't just leave my sister."

"Just hear me out." Bill hadn't had time to discuss this plan with her alone, and all the pieces were just starting to fall into place organically. "My parents aren't going to pay for an attorney and we don't have the money, so the way I see it, we need to dig up more evidence on the Genesis Foundation and take it to the press." He paused. "We can't do that with Julie tagging along. It's too dangerous. If people see you two together, they're going to call the police."

Todd crossed his arms over his chest. "What the hell is going on?"

"You didn't see the news this morning?" Bill asked.

"No." Todd frowned. "What'd I miss?"

Bill sighed. "Her parents work for a company called the Genesis Foundation. They kept them locked in that house so they could keep them perfect."

Todd's eyebrows shot up as he looked at Juliet. "So you didn't have a contagious disease, they just wanted to be sure you didn't catch one from us..."

"Yes." Juliet nodded. Her voice sounded a little tentative at first. "I bumped my head, and my mother found the lump yesterday." She cleared her throat and lifted her chin. Bill couldn't help but admire her. Everything was new to her, including speaking to strangers, but here she was doing what she had to in order to protect her sister. She was so damned strong. "Now that we're flawed, she tried to kill me."

She tugged her collar back to expose the bruises on her throat. The sight of them cemented Bill's decision to do whatever it took to keep her away from the Huffs. "Today she was on the news with the police telling everyone that I'm unstable and kidnapped my sister."

Bill nodded. "So we can't go to the police. They'll hand them back to their parents." Bill looked over at Zack and Julie stomping on the dance pad. "And we found out today that my dad works for Genesis, too."

"No way." Todd's eyes widened as he dropped his hands to his sides. "Your parents wouldn't let them keep kids locked up."

Bill stared at his shoes. "Yesterday I would've agreed, but now..." He raised his gaze. "When I talked to my mom on the phone this morning, she said I should take the girls to their parents and not tell anyone I'd seen her father's journal."

"His journal?"

Juliet pulled it out of her bag. "Yeah. He's got all his notes on my growth and my DNA and my *usefulness* to the Genesis Foundation." She lifted her eyes from the book. "It also talks about a ceremony where I'll be preserved and stay perfect forever."

A crease formed between Todd's eyebrows. "They're going to want that back."

Bill nodded. "They want Juliet and her sister, too."

Todd ran his hand down his face. "This is too much, man. How can we help them? We can't go up against the police."

"We won't have to if we can get the evidence we need and take it to the media. If you can get Cindy to take care of Julie for a day or two, that'll help. They're looking for two girls on the run." Bill cleared his throat. "Once Julie's safe, we can figure out what exactly they were doing over there so we can take it to the newspaper."

"Shit, Bill. This isn't a game." Todd shook his head as Zack and Julie wandered back over. "We could get arrested."

"Arrested?" Zack tensed. "What did I miss?"

Bill looked over at Zack. "I'll fill you in on the details outside." He glanced down at Julie and back to Zack. He seemed to take the hint they weren't going to get into details with Juliet's little sister present and followed him out the back exit. He filled him in about Genesis and his parents' connection, ending with

Juliet's mom trying to kill her.

Zack shook his head. "That's messed up." He looked back at the arcade. "What did Todd say?"

"He hasn't committed either way." Bill held his breath. "But I can't do this without you both."

Zack rubbed his forehead. "What do you want me to do?"

"Let's get back inside first. Come on." They found Todd and Juliet in the back corner of the arcade. Her little sister was sitting at a Ms. Pacman tabletop game, pretending to run through the demo screens.

Bill stopped beside Juliet and faced his friends. "Zack knows what's up. If we're going to help Juliet and her sister, we need his hacking skills to find a money trail. Without it, it's our word against theirs."

Zack cracked his knuckles. "That's something I can do. I'm always up for a firewall break."

"Dude, this is serious." Todd nudged Zack's shoulder. "If there's cash involved with whatever research they were doing on these girls, they're going to want them back. And who knows how far they're willing to go to get them." He tipped his head in Juliet's direction. "She's got bruises on her neck from her own mother. If these people catch us, we might *wish* we were going to jail."

Julie's head popped up from the game screen. She raced to Juliet's side, wrapping her arms around her big sister's waist.

Bill narrowed his eyes at Todd. "Enough. Are you

guys in or not?"

Zack shrugged. "I've got your back."

Todd groaned and looked skyward. Finally, he leveled his gaze on Bill. "If I get tangled up with the police, I could lose my scholarship."

"The last thing the Genesis Foundation is going to want is the police snooping around. They won't risk a police investigation." At least Bill didn't think they would.

Todd looked at Juliet. "You said your parents were on TV. The police are probably already investigating."

"I don't know." Juliet sighed. "Their lab and computers are all in the basement. For all I know, they cleared them out before they called the police." Her gaze wandered over their group. "This is a huge risk." She looked at Bill. "I never should have gotten you involved in this."

"Too late for that now. I'm already in." He took her hand and focused on his friends. "I won't hold it against you if you need to walk away, Todd. I understand."

The silence stretched out between them. Bill's heart sank, but he couldn't blame him. He just needed to come up with a new plan.

"See you around." Bill started to turn back toward the exit with Juliet and her sister in tow.

"Wait."

Bill stopped and looked back at Todd. He came to his side. "I'll call Cindy." He looked down at Julie and cleared his throat. "Cindy's got a little sister your age. Maybe you guys can be friends."

Julie sniffed. "I've never had a friend before."

"Then you're way overdue." Todd's eyes shifted to Bill. "Friends are the best."

Bill smiled, but his stomach twisted in knots. He was putting his best friends in danger. They were college kids up against who knew how many adults in this Genesis thing.

He turned to find Juliet staring at him. He gave her hand a squeeze. "We can do this."

He had no idea *how* just yet, but adding Zack's hacking skills was a step in the right direction.

It had to be.

CHAPTER 12

JULIET DRANK IN the sun beating on her shoulders as she sat on the park bench beside her sister. After spending her entire life inside, sunshine was still novel, a treasure. Julie-Eight wasn't as thrilled.

"I'm hot."

"Feels good, doesn't it? Maybe we'll sweat." Juliet smiled at her sister, dreading the upcoming meeting with Todd's girlfriend.

They'd shared a bedroom since the day her younger sister was born. They'd never been separated unless Juliet was locked in the closet for some infraction or another. She'd held her breath as Julie-Eight passed each milestone, praying her sibling would remain perfect—and safe. And while their parents rarely offered them any physical contact, the girls had learned to comfort each other. Juliet had rocked her sister to sleep after nightmares, and Julie-Eight had often gotten Juliet's punishments lightened by pleading on her sister's behalf.

Now Juliet had freed them both, but at what cost? With no money, no friends, no family, and no place to go, they were dependent on boys she'd watched from her upstairs window.

Billy jogged across the grass, smiling as he got closer. Her heart fluttered in response. He was the only bright spot in this mess. Even if her parents caught her in the end and put her into that glass case with her name on it, she wouldn't leave this world without experiencing that jolt of excitement the moment she'd kissed him on the lips. Reading about it in books didn't even come close to the real thing.

He sat beside her on the bench. "I checked out the park and the lot. No sign of the police or your parents, and Todd sent me a text that he and Cindy were on their way. They should be here in a few minutes."

Juliet glanced at her sister and back to Billy. "If Julie doesn't like her, we'll make another plan. She doesn't have to go, right?" She silently patted herself on the back for leaving the "Eight" off her sister's name.

"Right." He shifted his focus to her sister. "You won't have to stay away long anyway. Maybe a couple days while we dig up more information to protect you guys."

"What if they find me?" Julie-Eight asked.

"They won't." Billy shook his head. "They're looking for Juliet. They think *she* has you. This way, you'll be even safer. There's nothing to connect you to Cindy."

Juliet put her hands on the edge of the bench on either side of her legs. "What about us? Where are we going to go?"

He rested his elbows on his knees. "That's a little trickier. I'm still working on that part. I'm assuming Genesis doesn't have a website, so we need to find something else that might be connected to them. They must have a fake business front, especially if they need to pay employees like my dad. If Zack can find a way to hack into their records, we might not have to hide long."

"Maybe the vitamin supplements." She didn't have money or a phone, but she had her wits. That had to be worth something. "The bottles said Eden, Incorporated."

She half expected Billy to brush her off, but he surprised her, straightening up. "You could be onto something. I know where all the tax records are at home. We could see if Eden is paying my dad. That's a great place to start."

Hope blossomed inside her.

Bill looked over at her. "Any chance you have other names we could give to Zack? He could work those angles while I try to find a connection to Eden?"

Her heart sank. "The few times my father had other doctors in to see me, he never told me their names."

"Then we'll start with Eden and see if we can find a connection there. Maybe Zack can dig into them while we check the tax records." Billy got up as a silver car pulled into the parking lot. Todd waved. Bill looked over his shoulder at them. "Come on. Let's go meet Cindy."

Julie-Eight gripped Juliet's hand. "I want to stay with you."

"You heard Billy. They're looking for me. You'll be safer if you're not with me right now." She gave her hand a squeeze. "Just meet Cindy. If you don't like her, we'll figure out something else."

"If we're not perfect anymore, then why do they want us back?" Before Juliet could answer, she mumbled, "They just want to find us so they can…"

She didn't finish. They both knew what would happen.

Juliet clenched her jaw, digging deep to keep her voice even. She was finished being afraid. "What they're doing in that house is wrong, and they don't want us to tell anyone."

"But you're going to anyway?"

Juliet stopped and knelt, her gaze locking on her sister's identical eyes. "We're going to make sure they don't do this to any more kids. Never again."

Julie-Eight wrapped her arms around Juliet's neck, clinging to her. "When I grow up, I'm going to be brave like you."

Juliet closed her eyes and hugged her sister. When Julie-Eight stepped back, she wiped her eyes and sniffed. "I'll go with Cindy."

Her sister turned and walked over to Todd and his girlfriend without looking back. Juliet struggled to hold herself together.

She'd read enough of the journal to know that Julie-Eight wasn't really her sister, not genetically at least. Julie-Eight *was* Juliet. Identical DNA. Cloned. They were the same. All the Julies, the babies, were all clones of Juliet. But despite the laboratory, the imprisonment, the forced perfection, little Julie-Eight was still her own person. They liked different foods, and when their father played his classical music recordings, Juliet favored Mozart while Julie-Eight loved Beethoven. She wasn't just a carbon copy.

Juliet lifted her chin. She would fight with her last breath to keep Julie-Eight safe, even if it meant letting her go.

Billy came over. "Ready to meet Cindy?"

Juliet nodded, although she was shaking inside. "Sure." She cleared her throat. "What's she going to tell her family when she brings a little girl home to hide?"

"She won't have to say anything." Billy turned toward his friends. "Cindy's got a trust fund."

"A what?"

He shrugged. "Her parents have lots of money, and they set some aside for her. After she turned eighteen, she started getting a monthly allowance. It pays for her own apartment. Her parents are on a cruise for another week, and she's watching her younger sister."

Almost on cue, a willowy, blond girl got out of the car.

"What's her sister's name?"

"Vanessa." He touched Juliet's elbow, and she slowly let her hands drop to her sides. "The sooner we do this, the sooner we can go to the media and this will all be over."

She nodded and cleared her throat. "I'm ready."

They had barely taken a step when a police cruiser rolled through the lot. Billy moved in front of her and pulled her into his arms, fusing his lips to hers. She gasped into the kiss. This wasn't tender and slow like last time. It was intoxicating, making her heart race and her toes curl in her shoes. She tilted her head, bringing her arms up around his neck.

He tightened his hold on her, coaxing her mouth open. His tongue brushed past her lips and her pulse pounded in answer. He tasted sweet like the pancakes. Her body warmed, heat pooling low in her belly as time slowed and the world around them faded away.

Gradually, he pulled back resting his forehead against hers. "Are they gone?"

The police. She'd forgotten…everything.

Juliet stayed close to him, scanning the parking lot over his shoulder. No sign of the police car or Todd's. She stepped back. "They're gone."

Billy turned around. "Good."

"No, it's not." She grabbed his elbow, pulling him to face her. "My sister is gone, too. You said we'd give her a choice. I promised her. I didn't even get to say goodbye."

"She's safe." He shook his head. "If they had stayed, the police might've taken her. Both your faces have been all over the television today."

The realization sank in. "That's why you kissed me."

He cleared his throat, color creeping up his neck. "Sorry about that. I didn't want them to see you. I panicked."

She wanted to smack herself when she realized that a tiny part of her was disappointed. Her sister was with virtual strangers, and the police were hunting her. She had more important things to worry about than why he'd kissed her.

But she couldn't turn off the heat he'd stoked inside her. After sneaking her mother's romance novels into her room and reading them long after lights out, she thought she understood love and passion, but no amount of words on a page could've prepared her for the rush of desire that had flooded her when he'd pressed her tight against him and their tongues had tangled.

She'd missed so much while being a lab rat for her parents. No more. Even if they caught her in the end, she would live these days of freedom fully. She had eighteen years of catching up to do.

"Don't be sorry." Heat burned in her cheeks, but she pushed back against the self-consciousness. There was a good chance her life would be much too short to waste time being bashful. "I… It…" She groaned and met his eyes. "I liked it."

The corner of his mouth curved into a lopsided smile that made her heart stutter. "I did, too." He took her hand. "We better get out of here."

"What about my sister?"

"Todd's taking her back to Cindy's apartment."

Juliet and Billy walked to his pickup. "Can we stop over there to check on Julie?"

He shook his head. "Not a good idea. But we can call her once we get the new cell phones from Zack."

"I don't know how to use one."

He squeezed her hand. "You'll catch on fast."

She smiled, his confidence in her bolstered her resolve. Cell phones, computers, maybe she'd even get him to teach her to drive.

BILL PARKED AROUND the back of Zack's place. His parents had renovated their garage to better serve Zack's computer obsession while in high school. It was like his own personal apartment. All that was missing was a kitchen.

Bill rapped his knuckles on the side door and waited.

Zack cracked open the door, grinned, and freed the security chain to let them in. "About time you guys got here."

Inside the dimly lit room, three computer screens glowed. One had streams of data flowing while the other two were stationary.

"What's that?" Bill pointed to the moving screen.

"I used your phone log in and now I'm scanning your dad's cell phone records and recording any repeat numbers." He chuckled. "You watch, someday they're going to require everyone to use two-factor authentication for log ins."

Bill wasn't sure what that meant, but there wasn't time. He and Juliet sat in folding chairs Zack had set up to the right of his workstation as Bill watched the numbers scrolling. "What are you hoping to find?"

Zack plopped into his seat and took a sip of his Dr. Pepper. "I've scoured all the search engines and even some of my favorite conspiracy sites for Genesis, and I keep coming up empty. If I can find some frequently called and answered numbers could give us other leads." He tipped his head in Juliet's direction. "On the plus side, your girlfriend here is completely off the grid. Did you know she's legally dead?"

"I'm what?" Juliet scooted to the edge of her chair.

"Yeah. According to your death certificate, you were six months old. And there's no record that Julie was ever even born." Zack crossed his arms over his chest. "Calling the police was a mistake on their part. I'm sure the authorities are going to have *lots* of questions for them. They could probably blame the death certificates on a data-entry mistake, but they must *really* want you two back to risk the police sniffing around."

Bill stared at the ground, still mystified about how

his dad could be mixed up in all this. Seeing all the data on the computers made this even more real. He was knee-deep in something he didn't remotely understand.

He reached for a yellow legal pad and a pen. He wrote Eden Incorporated on the page and slid it to Zack. "Juliet said her parents told her they were working on supplements and the bottles said Eden. It could be a front for Genesis. I'm going to check the tax records at home and see who has been paying my dad."

"Solid. I'll start on this angle next." Zack rolled closer to his desk and handed each of them a phone. "These are prepaid burner phones." He looked at Bill. "You need to turn yours off and use this one until we nail these guys."

"You think they'll track my phone?"

He nodded. "It's still on a contract with your folks, right?"

"Shit." Bill pulled out his phone.

"Exactly. Even when you're not using it, it's pinging the cell towers to keep a signal. They might not be able to get your exact location, but they'll have a good idea."

Bill started to press the power button, then stopped. "I better power this down someplace else. Otherwise, when they see my last ping it could lead them to you, right?"

"Good plan, buddy." Zack clicked a couple of links on another screen. "And go empty out your bank account. You can't have them tracking your debit card transactions, either."

"Oh shit. You're right." Bill shook his head. "I need to watch more detective shows."

Zack shrugged. "Hopefully I can find something soon, and once you expose them, you won't have to hide anymore. Until then, though…"

"We have to be careful." Juliet sat back in her chair, worrying her lower lip.

Bill was beginning to recognize the tells of guilt settling on her shoulders. He reached over to pat her knee. "This is *their* fault, not yours."

Her dark eyes flicked over to him. "I don't know how to thank all of you. Julie and I have nothing to give you in return."

Zack chuckled and glanced at us. "If we can bring these guys down, it'll be national news. I'll probably get job offers, Bill will get a book deal to write the story, and Todd will be a media hero." He paused, basking in the glow of his fantasies.

Bill gave Zack's chair a gentle kick. "What we get out of it isn't the point."

Zack flinched and added, "Oh…oh yeah, you and your sister will be free of those bastards, too. We're good, Juliet."

She laughed, and for a second, Bill forgot all about the threat. Beautiful didn't begin to describe this woman. She'd had her life stolen for no other reason than some faceless company's gain, and instead of bitterness or crippling fear, she was sitting with him in

Zack's garage laughing.

He wanted to laugh with her and his friends again without having to look over their shoulders.

And the next time he kissed her, it wasn't going to be because he was trying to hide her face from the police.

CHAPTER 13

Julie-Eight dried her eyes in Cindy's bathroom. She had to be brave like her sister. But she didn't know how. She'd spent her whole life locked in the house with Juliet.

"Julie?" Someone tapped at the door. "Are you all right?"

Cindy. Julie-Eight struggled to sound cheerful and called out. "I'm okay."

"If you come out here, we can call Juliet on the phone."

Her eyes welled with tears again. She missed her sister so bad she ached all over. Juliet would tell her to stop crying and think of something good.

But nothing about locking herself in a stranger's bathroom was good.

She turned on the sink and cupped her hands under the water. The cool water calmed her nerves a little, and splashing it on her face soothed the redness in her eyes, cheeks, and nose. Juliet said they didn't need to be perfect anymore, but Julie-Eight didn't know any other way to be.

Her new scabs were a reminder that, so far, being "normal" hurt.

After drying her face, she inspected her reflection in the mirror. Better. If she got to talk to Juliet, she needed to hold herself together. She wasn't a baby.

She grabbed the knob and opened the door.

Cindy looked over from the couch and smiled. "There you are. I saved you a seat."

Julie-Eight did her best to keep her head up and shoulders back as she walked over to sit down with Cindy. She didn't feel brave yet, but she could pretend.

Cindy's little sister, Vanessa, sat on the floor watching the television. She didn't seem to notice Julie-Eight existed.

Cindy touched her Julie-Eight's knee. She flinched, and Cindy retracted her hand with sympathy in her eyes. "You've had a rough couple of days."

Julie-Eight nodded, gnawing at the inside of her cheek. She was done crying. "Can we call my sister?"

"Yeah." She glanced toward the kitchen and raised her voice. "Todd, do you have the number Zack gave you for Juliet's new phone?"

His shoulders took up the entire hallway. Julie-Eight had never seen such a tall, muscular man before. Her father was skinny. Todd smiled a lot, too. It made him less scary—more like a friendly giant.

"Hey, Julie." He winked and focused on his cell phone, touching the screen. Finally, he lifted it to his ear as he approached the couch. "Juliet? Hey, it's Todd.

Got a minute to talk to your sister?"

He nodded and held the phone out to Julie. Her pulse raced as she brought the little device to her ear. "Hello?"

"It's me," Juliet replied, and Julie-Eight's lips curved into a smile. Just hearing her sister's voice lifted some of the fear she'd been carrying since they had driven away from the park. "Sorry we didn't get to say goodbye." Juliet paused. "Are you all right with Cindy and Todd?"

"Yeah." Julie-Eight nodded, wishing her sister was in the room with her. "They're nice."

"Good. You can call this number anytime you need me."

"Okay." Julie looked at her hand in her lap and added, "I'll be brave."

"You're very brave. I love you. And I'll see you soon."

"I love you, too." She couldn't quite keep the wobble out of her voice, but she didn't cry. She handed the phone back to Todd.

He lifted it to his ear and said, "Everything is cool over here. Try not to worry, okay? And tell Z–Man I'm heading back his way."

He ended the call and put his phone in his pocket. "Zack is a wizard on a computer. You'll be back with Juliet really soon. You'll see."

Julie-Eight nodded and hoped he was right.

She wasn't sure how much courage she had left.

THE GENTLE HICCUP at the end of Julie-Eight's words broke Juliet's heart. She stared at the ceiling, struggling to keep from crying.

Zack glanced her way. "Everything all right?"

"No." She wiped her nose and set the cell phone aside before wrapping her arms tightly around herself. "But hopefully it will be."

Hearing Julie-Eight's voice had flooded Juliet with relief. She was safe. Now Juliet could focus on exposing the people who had been using them from birth.

Billy had been gone about a half hour. He'd left her with Zack while he went to empty his bank account, check his parents tax records for any connection to Eden, and leave his cell phone. They figured it'd be safer for her to stay out of sight in case her parents showed up at Billy's place again.

Sitting still wasn't helping the dread building inside her. "Is there anything I can do?"

Zack had gentle eyes, like an old soul, a dreamer. His lips curved into an awkward smile. "Sure." He picked up the cell phone. "You need to learn how to work this thing. We showed you how to answer a phone call, but you should be able to text, too. You can add our numbers into the contacts, then press on a name and send a message." He wrote a few numbers on a slip of paper and slid it to her. "Once you master using the cell, then you can help me look for patterns in these phone records so I can focus my efforts on a target."

He spoke English, but she wasn't sure exactly what he meant. Patterns of what? But he was already facing the screens again. She gripped the cell phone and started experimenting, pressing the screen over and over until she found the spot to add a contact. After entering Billy's number, she clicked the "message" button and typed. After a few frustrating mistakes and autocorrections she pressed "send."

Testing…

She waited with no idea how long it would take for a response. When the phone chimed, she almost hit the ceiling.

Got it. This is?

She grinned and feverishly typed, then touched "send" again.

Juliet.

His reply came back fast.

You're texting!

She nodded, then rolled her eyes realizing he couldn't see her.

I am! Zack told me to learn to use the phone.

A few seconds later the phone chimed again.

You're a quick study.

She had no business being so proud. But she couldn't help it. She'd watched people focused on their cell phones as they walked down her street, but this was her first time. And she had figured it out.

Thank you.

Zack peered over his shoulder. "You're already addicted to texting, I can tell."

She chuckled and shrugged. "I never knew what a cell phone was like."

It chimed.

On my way back now. No sign of your parents.

"Do I need to say goodbye or something when we're finished?"

Zack shook his head. "Nah, you just stop texting."

Juliet kept busy with the phone, trying to familiarize herself with all the functions and apps. She was the one who had gotten Billy and his friends into this mess, the least she could do was become a valuable member of the team.

BILL COULDN'T STOP checking his rearview mirror. He

used to imagine that being a spy like James Bond would be exciting, but now that he wasn't sure who he could trust, it wasn't thrilling. It was stressful—and scarier than he wanted to admit.

His wallet bulged with just over $950. All his savings from his part-time job at Starbucks on campus and what was left of the emergency cash his parents had left would have to be enough to sustain them until Zack found evidence they could share with the media. The prepaid cell phone was beside him in the passenger seat. His iPhone was turned off, and he'd left it sitting on the dresser back in his bedroom. They wouldn't be able to use it to trace him to Juliet.

He wiped sweat from his brow at the light. His phone beeped, and he grabbed it, way too eager to see the text from Juliet.

Zack said these are emoticons. He also says I've mastered the cell phone.

The message was flanked at both the beginning and end with happy faces, hearts, and every other emoticon she could find.

He chuckled, setting the phone aside as the light turned green. How was it that she could make him smile when he was so tense that his knuckles ached on the steering wheel? Until now, he'd thought finals at UCLA were stressful. But school pressure was nothing compared to finding out his dad was paying for his college education with money from a company that was cloning girls and holding them prisoner.

Perfect girls.

He still couldn't believe it. He shook his head and made a right turn.

His mom had called his cell right before he powered it down. They were in New York. She tried again to persuade him to give Juliet and her sister back to their parents. And this time, she'd sounded scared.

That was the only reason he'd agreed to meet her tomorrow morning. Nothing she could possibly tell him would make him hand Juliet and Julie-Eight over to their evil excuses for parents, but he wanted to understand how his dad had gotten involved in this foundation and, more importantly, *why*.

If he got lucky, maybe he'd get some information that might help them expose Genesis to the world.

A guy could hope.

He pulled into Zack's place and parked. Juliet came out the side door as he slammed the truck door. He frowned, scanning the street. "Juliet, you can't be out here. Your picture has been all over TV. Someone might see you."

Her smile faded, and she slipped back into the garage.

Bill rubbed his nose, sighing as he stepped inside. "Sorry. I didn't mean to bite your head off. I just don't want…"

"I know." Her arms were wrapped around her middle. "I get it. Being out of that house makes me forget I'm still not really free."

"Not yet, but you will be."

She didn't look convinced, and he couldn't blame her. He was a nineteen-year-old undergrad with no superspy experience attempting to take down a corporation that was secretly cloning humans and trying to achieve some twisted perfection. This was way above his pay grade.

"How's it going, Z-Man?" He clasped his friend's shoulder.

Zack looked up from the screen. "Getting closer. I have a list of frequently called numbers, and one has an out-of-state area code." He stopped typing, his hands dropping from the keyboard. "You left your cell?"

"Yep. It's back in my room." Bill held up the new burner phone. "I'm only using this one."

"Did you dig around your parents' tax records?"

His chest tightened as he pulled an open envelope out of his back pocket. "These were in my mom's tax bin from last year." He laid *two* W-2 forms on the table. "My mom works for Eden, Incorporated too."

Both of his parents were mixed up in human cloning. He couldn't reconcile it. They'd always been good parents to him. How could they have turned their backs on Juliet and her…sister?

Zack slid the papers over and shook his head. "Damn." He looked up a Bill. "I'll see what I can find with Eden. This is a good lead."

"Let me know if there's other info that you need.

I'm meeting my mom for coffee tomorrow morning. Maybe she'll tell me something we can use." Zack and Juliet stared at him as if he'd sprouted two heads. Bill shrugged. "I'll be fine. We'll be at the busiest Starbucks in town during the morning coffee rush. Plus, she's my mom. She's not going to hurt me. She thinks she's protecting me."

Zack raised a brow. "Being overconfident never ends well. I'll drive you and wait in my van just in case."

Juliet nodded. "I'll go, too."

Bill turned to Juliet, shaking his head. "Bad idea. You're the one they want."

"But if something goes wrong, I can protect you."

"By giving yourself up?" Bill pulled a chair over and sat down. "No. They'll kill you."

Her arms tightened around her middle. "They were going to do that anyway, perfect or not."

Zack whistled. "This is messed up."

"Yeah." Bill nodded. "But if my mom lets some information slip that could incriminate Genesis or hands over any proof of what they're really up to, then meeting with her is a risk worth taking." He met Juliet's eyes. "And you're my insurance policy. As long as I'm their only link to you, they can't take me out. They need me, or they'll never find you."

A car pulled up outside. Bill peered through the slats of the mini-blinds and smiled. "It's Todd."

It was stupid, but having Zack and Todd on his

team made him feel invincible. They'd been the three musketeers since elementary school. If they stuck together, they could get through anything.

And right now, he was betting his life on it.

CHAPTER 14

JULIET TOYED WITH her cell phone while Billy made plans with Zack and Todd. This wasn't how she'd pictured her life in the real world. It would've been naive to think she'd fit right in, but she sure hadn't imagined she'd be hiding again. The cage was bigger now, but it was still confinement.

For years she'd watched these three guys from her window and yearned to go outside, to make friends. She'd witnessed games, fights, and best of all, unity. They were part of a greater whole.

Billy's logic for leaving her behind in the morning made sense, but it didn't make it hurt any less. Maybe she was never destined to be normal, to go on dates, to get a job, or even try for college like they were doing.

Her destiny had been a glass box in her parent's' basement.

Todd separated himself from Zack and Billy. He stopped beside her, but his gaze lingered on his friends. "Your sister is a trooper. Sorry you didn't get to say goodbye."

"I'm glad she's all right." She swallowed the lump

in her throat. "Thanks for letting me talk to her."

"Everything's going to be okay. Between Zack's brain and Bill's plotting, they're going to figure this out."

Juliet looked up at Todd. "And what's your job?"

He grinned and lifted an arm, flexing his bicep. "I'm the muscle."

An unexpected burst of laughter bubbled from her lips, and all conversation quieted. Billy and Zack turned her way, and her cheeks flushed with heat. She hadn't meant to interrupt everything.

Todd lowered his arm and chuckled. "It's okay. They're not jealous…much."

Billy rolled his eyes and Zack groaned, but the back-and-forth banter with Todd lightened her mood. But it was only for another moment before Billy told her the plan for the morning. Todd would stay with her at Zack's place while Zack drove Billy to the meeting with his mother.

Her stomach soured at the thought. If anything happened to him, it would be her fault.

Todd said his goodbyes and left, and Zack disappeared into the main house. He returned with rolled-up blankets under his arms. "Here are a couple sleeping bags. The couch pulls out into a bed. It's not very comfortable, but it's cheaper than Motel 6."

"Thanks, man." Billy took the sleeping bags. "Let's plan to leave by eight tomorrow morning, okay?"

Zack nodded. "Will do." He sheepishly met Juliet's

eyes. "Um…nice hanging out with you."

"Thank you for letting me stay."

"No problem." He almost smiled, then seemed to stop himself and backed toward the door. "I guess I better get some sleep."

Billy started moving the sofa cushions. "'Night, Z-Man."

After Zack closed the door, the awkward silence ate at her. Billy tugged on a bar on the couch, and a large, folded piece lifted from out of the frame.

The springs screeched, and he cringed. "Sorry about that."

Juliet came a little closer. "Need any help?"

He unfolded it to reveal a thin mattress. "Did you have one of these at your house?"

She shook her head. "No."

"Nothing to get excited about. They're pretty uncomfortable."

He handed her one of the rolls that Zack had brought in, and she mirrored his movements, pulling the elastic bands free and unrolling it until it was flat on the mattress. She'd never used a sleeping bag before, either, but she kept that to herself.

She was grateful for something to do. This wasn't the first time she'd shared a bed with Billy, but that had been before the hot kiss in the park.

She bit her lip, struggling to push the memory away. Nothing had to change. He'd been trying to hide her from the police. Nothing more.

"Is everything all right?"

His voice interrupted her thoughts. She cleared her throat and sat at Zack's card table. "Yeah, I'm fine."

Billy came over and sat in the chair beside her. "I guess that's kind of a dumb question, right? With the police after you and your sister over at Cindy's, I know things could be better."

Juliet nodded, staring at her bare hands. "I always slept in gloves."

"What?"

She glanced his way. "My mother kept our fingernails trimmed, but we couldn't risk getting scratched in our sleep, so we wore fleece-lined gloves and slipper socks to bed." She dropped her hands into her lap. "I'm probably just exhausted, but when I used to dream about going outside, this wasn't what I pictured. I'm still not free. Not really."

"You will be." He hesitated. "Juliet?"

She lifted her gaze. He had beautiful green eyes, much brighter than she'd imagined from her bedroom window. "They had no right to keep you and your sister locked up. This is wrong, and people need to know. What if Genesis has more houses like yours out there?"

Her breath caught at the thought. It hadn't crossed her mind that her father might not be the only scientist obsessed with perfection. Genesis could be in other towns, too. Could there be more copies of her out there? Clones like her sister?

She didn't want to think about it. One step at a time. She stood up and glanced over at the noted Zack had written and the pages of phone numbers he printed out. "When you came to my door that night, after my birthday, I spent lots of time day-dreaming about when I'd get to go outside and we could be friends." She shook her head and stared up at the ceiling. "It never looked like this." She sighed and met his eyes again. "I'm sorry I got you mixed up in this."

Billy got up and came closer, raising his hand like he might touch her cheek. He paused and slowly lowered it to his side. "You had no choice." The corner of his mouth twitched. "I was the one who almost ran you over with my truck."

She laughed as a tear spilled down her face. He wiped it away with the pad of his thumb. His tender caress tied her stomach in knots. She wished she had more experience—okay, *any* experience—with guys.

Standing there like a frightened rabbit wasn't really the message she wanted to send.

Clearing her throat, she forced a smile. "Whatever the reason, I don't want anything bad to happen to you."

"Can I tell you something?" His voice was soft, his gaze intense.

She nodded, holding her breath.

"My whole life I've been the storyteller in our group, the writer. Hell, I'm getting a degree in English lit with the dream of writing the great American novel someday." He rolled his shoulders back with a nervous chuckle. "Telling someone this out loud is harder than I thought it would be."

His eyes met hers again. "Until you ran into the road, I'd spent my life watching the world, taking notes, writing stories about it, like an observer. Right now—" he pointed to the printout of phone numbers on Zack's desk "—I can make a difference. I'm in this." Billy paused and slowly turned toward her. "I'm not leaning on my folks or witnessing a conflict. I'm living this story, Juliet. With you. So no more apologizing. I chose to be involved, and so did Zack and Todd."

Her pulse thrummed as she sat on the edge of the sofa bed. The fire in his eyes and the determination in his tone made her knees rubbery. Again, she wished she had a clue how to relieve the tempest of unfamiliar emotions he conjured inside her. All she could think of was to change the subject.

"What's college like?"

He shrugged and pulled a chair over. "It's all right. I like living in the dorm on campus. The freedom of not having my parents watching over my shoulder or a curfew is nice. The term papers and final exams aren't fun, but overall, I like it."

"I've only read about it in books. Do you have many friends there?"

Billy nodded. "Yeah. My roommates are cool, and I have some friends in the English department now."

"Do you have a girlfriend?" She almost gasped

when the question came out of her mouth. Could she have been any more obvious? And what if she didn't like his answer? Her cheeks warmed. No doubt her pale skin was bright red.

Billy glanced at his hands. "I did." He looked at her again. "We broke up."

"I'm sorry." She backpedaled. "It's none of my business."

"No." He reached forward and touched her hand. "You didn't upset me. It happened before we finished this last semester. I feel more foolish than hurt."

"Why?"

His fingers slipped away from her hand. "Her name was Cassie. She's an actress, and she played *me* pretty well."

Juliet waited. While she didn't have any real-life experience, she'd read enough books to have an idea of what he probably meant.

"She liked having me around when she wanted to go to a movie or something, but after a few months, she was tougher to pin down for a date." He rolled his eyes. "She started seeing a guy that she was performing with in one of her plays. She hid it behind my back. I should've seen it coming, but…" He leaned back in the chair, his green eyes locked on hers. "I didn't have much experience with women. I kept giving her the benefit of the doubt and ended up feeling like a total ass when I caught her with some other guy's hand up her shirt."

Juliet frowned. "She was the fool."

He smiled, setting off a hundred butterflies in her belly. "Thanks." He glanced at the sleeping bags. "I guess we should get some sleep."

She nodded, crossing her arms around her middle. "Okay."

His brow furrowed. "What's wrong?"

Juliet released one arm, running her fingers along the zipper of the sleeping bag. "I don't know."

It was an honest answer. She wasn't sure what was happening inside her, but she didn't want to turn out the lights and sleep.

Billy came and sat on the edge of the fold-out bed beside her. Fire smoldered under her skin as he lifted her chin so she'd meet his eyes. "Do you want me to sleep on the floor? I won't touch you, I swear. You're safe with me."

She searched his eyes and whispered, "I want you to touch me."

Confusion lined his brow. "What?"

"I..." She wet her lips. "When you kissed me this afternoon I...I know you were just trying to hide me from the police." She took a breath. Life was short, especially for her. She rested her hand on his. "But I can't stop thinking about it."

He leaned in a little closer. "I'll take that as a compliment."

"How many girls have you kissed?"

"Does it matter?"

She shrugged, every nerve tingling, her skin aching for attention as if her body was its own entity and she was at its mercy. "You know how many guys *I've* kissed."

"I should've mentioned this before but…" He smiled, whispering, "You're a natural."

His lips brushed hers slowly, parting her mouth until the tip of his tongue caressed her lower lip. She moaned into the kiss as their tongues twined together. Unlike earlier in the park, this time she savored every second, memorizing every sensation. Her physical desires had been dormant, imprisoned for years just as she had been, but Billy's touch set her free.

His fingers slid into her hair, pulling her closer. She reached out, allowing her fingertips to explore his chest. She'd never touched a man before, and he groaned against her, tilting his head to deepen the kiss. Her pulse hammered in her ears, and her breasts were suddenly heavy, nipples hardened and straining against her soft, cotton sports bra.

Juliet gasped for air, and Billy slowed, caressing her lips over and over. Finally, he rested his forehead against hers. "I could kiss you all night."

Juliet grinned as she lost herself in his bright-green eyes. "I wouldn't complain."

"When this is over—" he laced their fingers together and leaned back "—would you go to a movie with me?"

She nodded, staring at their joined hands. "I've

never seen a movie or been on a date before."

"So you're due."

She laughed. "I have a lot of catching up to do."

Billy sobered. "Can I ask you something?"

"Sure."

"Once this is over, do you know what you'd like to do?"

She didn't. No high school diploma, no computer skills, no work experience. She shrugged. "I like to draw."

"Nice." He smiled. "I can't even do stick people justice."

She got up and grabbed a pen and paper from Zack's desk. "Just hold still."

Glancing up every few seconds, she sketched the shape of Billy's face, then started shading in the variances in his eyes and the angle of his jaw. Once she was happy with her work, she turned the paper around and held her breath.

Billy's eyes widened as he reached for the paper. "Wow." Taking a closer look, he shook his head. "You're really good." He chuckled. "And fast, too. You're amazing."

She soaked up the praise. It wasn't something she ever got at home. She set the pen on the table and took her seat beside him again. "Lots of time to practice. One of the doctors who sometimes helped my dad used to sneak me comic books and graphic novels. I thought after I turned eighteen, I'd get to go outside and maybe take some art classes. If I worked at it, maybe I could illustrate comics."

"No way." His face brightened. "I love them, too. I have a storyline about three high school kids who battle dark forces. They call themselves the Triad."

Juliet's pulse pounded again but not from a physical yearning this time. She grinned. "Maybe I could read it sometime."

"You might be able to draw up some cool characters for them."

"I'd love that."

He took her hand, smiling. "This is incredible."

She nodded, unable to verbalize the joy of actually considering a future outside that horrible house. Instead of sleeping, Billy logged into his "cloud" storage. She had no real concept of what that was, but inside were some files and he shared his writings and ideas with her—like an equal, a friend.

And if she died tomorrow, at least for one amazing day, she had really lived.

CHAPTER 15

JULIET BLINKED, SQUINTING as the morning sun peeked through the window shade. For a moment, she was completely disoriented. Where was she? She started to move and found an arm around her waist.

Billy.

She turned her head and smiled. He was sleeping behind her, his arm holding her close. They were both still fully clothed on top of the sleeping bags. When had they finally fallen asleep? All she could remember were their big plans for a new comic series.

She rested her hand over his and started to lift his arm to slip out, but his grip on her tightened. She peered over her shoulder at him.

He almost smiled, but his eyes were still closed. “Going somewhere?”

She laughed. “I think you’re the one going. I have to stay here and hide, remember?”

“My mom.” He let go of her, reached for the cell phone, and groaned. “Shit. It’s almost eight. I’ve got to get ready.”

While Billy rushed around grabbing clothes out of

his duffel and brushing his hair, she sat up, staring at her hands. No gloves. There was an imprint of the sleeping bag's zipper in her skin. An imperfection.

For a split second, adrenaline dripped into her bloodstream before she remembered her days of being perfect were behind her.

She got up and retrieved the hairbrush and toothbrush they'd bought yesterday. Without realizing it, she counted the brushstrokes, just like Momma. When she finally noticed, she set the brush down, repulsed. How long would it take for a lifetime of programming to wear off?

Her reflection in the mirror reminded her of the danger. The bruises on her neck had shifted from purple and red to black-and-blue. Pretty. She frowned and walked away.

Zack came around the corner with a white bag in hand. "Brought you some donuts."

"Donuts?"

His brow creased, and gradually, his eyes widened. "Oh my god. No. This can't be. You've never had a donut?"

She shook her head sheepishly. "Are they good?"

He pulled out something fluffy and round. It looked like a bread roll topped with chocolate. He handed it to her. "Food of the gods!" He plucked out another braided one for himself. "Careful. Yours has a surprise in the middle."

She took cautious bite and let out a euphoric groan.

"Wow."

Juliet had tasted chocolate before. Her mother coaxed good behavior from them with little squares of Hershey's bars. One square per week. She'd said they couldn't risk more. One pimple and they wouldn't be perfect anymore.

But Juliet had never bitten into a cream-filled donut with chocolate frosting before. The single square of a chocolate Hershey bar wasn't even in the same league as this.

Zack licked the sugar off his fingertips and raised a brow. "Well?"

She grinned. "Delicious."

"Right?" He dug into the bag. "Here, try one of these. It's an old-fashioned."

It didn't look old-fashioned to her, but she took it anyway, humming in delight.

Billy walked in and chuckled. "Your first donuts?"

She nodded. "They're amazing."

Billy pulled a slender rectangular donut with chocolate frosting from the bag and nudged Zack. "We need to get going."

The door opened, and they all jumped.

Todd laughed, shaking his head. "Oh yeah, you guys have this undercover thing down. Nerves of steel."

"Screw you, Todd." Zack bumped his shoulder as he pushed past him to go outside.

Billy came toward her with his hands in his pockets. He cleared his throat and met her eyes. "We'll be back soon. Hopefully she'll tell me something that might help us."

Juliet nodded and moved a little closer. He made no move to touch her. Maybe she was expecting too much. She didn't know anything about relationships, but the kiss last night had her thinking he liked her, too. She'd even woken up with his arm around her.

But it was broad daylight now, and they weren't alone.

She forced herself to say something. "Be careful."

He nodded. "I'll be fine." For a moment, he leaned in, staring into her eyes, but he turned away at the last second and went to the door. Billy glanced at Todd. "You've got my number, right?"

Todd patted the pocket of his jeans. "Yep." Billy's gaze shifted to her and back to Todd. "Keep Juliet safe."

The door closed leaving her alone with Todd. "How's my sister?"

"I haven't talked to Cindy yet today, but Julie and Vanessa were getting along okay last night. Cindy said they were introducing Julie to Pixar movies."

Juliet smiled, even though she didn't have a clue what a Pixar was. "I hope Billy finds something we can use to expose Genesis."

"He and Zack will find something, and you and your sister will be together again before you know it."

And what would happen then? They had no money, no job, and no place to live. Julie-Eight didn't have a birth certificate, and according to Zack, their parents had declared to the government that Juliet had died before she'd turned one.

All this worrying and waiting was making her antsy.

She sat at the desk, skimming the pages of Billy's Triad stories. Snatching a piece of paper from the printer, she escaped into her sketches and hoped for the best.

ZACK PARKED AT the back of the lot. Bill didn't see his mom's car, but that didn't mean she wasn't here someplace.

"Be careful, man."

He nodded at Zack. "I'll be fine."

Zack pulled out his laptop. "I'll work in here so we can be ready to roll fast." He glanced up. "Just in case."

"Okay." Bill slammed the door. His palms were slick. Until now, he hadn't been nervous. This was his mom, not some stranger. She arranged the meeting because she wanted him to be safe.

But his muscles didn't relax. Something wasn't right. He kept scanning the lot for his mom or her car as he sat at one of the outdoor tables in the corner.

"Bill."

He spun around toward the whisper. A woman in a large floppy hat with big sunglasses and red lipstick motioned him to sit. His mom rarely wore more than mascara, so her bright-red mouth distracted him. She didn't remove the dark glasses.

"Did anyone follow you?"

She was still whispering, too.

"No." Bill followed her lead keeping his voice down. "What's with the disguise?"

She sat across from him and leaned in closer. "This research, Genesis…it's more important than my life or yours. That's why you need to take those girls back. They won't stop until they have them."

Bill gripped the edge of the table, straining to keep quiet when he wanted nothing more than to shout bullet questions at her. "I know you're both involved with these people. Did you know they kept these girls locked up like lab rats for their entire lives. And the others…" He whispered. "Mom, they killed the other babies."

"You don't understand." She pressed her lips together, but he couldn't see her eyes behind the dark glasses. "This is a chance to make sure no more boys lose their big brothers."

Bill sat back for a moment, stunned. He opened his mouth and closed it again before leaning forward again. "This is about David?"

How many years had it been since he'd said his brother's name out loud? It seemed foreign on his lips now. Leukemia had taken him right after his tenth birthday, and gradually, his name had vanished from family conversations. At first, Bill had figured it was too painful for his folks, but as time went by, they'd moved to the suburbs and he'd found Zack and Todd. Day by day, the grief had faded.

But maybe his parents had never recovered.

His mom reached out to squeeze his hand. "Bill, Genesis has a vision. A world with no more disease or deformities. Our children will be healthy. They'll be *perfect*. We can change the world. They're so close."

"Is that what they told you?" He recoiled, frowning. "Can you hear yourself? These aren't rats in a cage or cloned sheep. These are human beings with hopes and dreams, and according to Dr. Huff's notes, if one of those babies got so much as a snotty nose they were terminated."

"It's not that simple." She scanned the lot. "They aren't normal children. They're test subjects. We created them. Every aspect of their growth is being monitored. This project is expensive, and since the FDA is decades behind in approving cloning research, they need to acquire private funding. Positive results are vital for financial backing."

He winced, shaking his head. Suddenly his mother was a complete stranger to him. "Results? Mom, they killed defenseless children. Some of them weren't even babies anymore." He leaned in closer, whispering, "They're planning to kill Juliet on her eighteenth birthday and preserve her body in a glass case. Did Dad sign off on that?" His stomach roiled at the thought.

He shook his head. "Jesus, is he the one who'll shoot her up with a drug cocktail to stop her heart so she can be some kind of twisted sales brochure for more funding?"

His mom reached across the table, grabbing his hand and squeezing it—Tight—stunning him into silence. "You don't have to understand, but this isn't a game." She glanced around and back to him. "Please, Bill. I can't lose you, too."

"Are they going to kill me like they did their test subjects?"

"I don't know—" A hollow thud, and she slumped in her chair, her hat hiding her face.

"Mom?" Bill ran to her side. "Mom?" Kneeling beside her, he lifted the wide brim. Her glasses hung at the end of her nose. She stared up with lifeless, empty eyes. Blood trickled from a tiny hole in her forehead.

Bill fell backward. "Shit! Call 911! She's been shot."

Chaos erupted. People scattered, screaming, and running away. Bill caught her as she slipped from the chair. "Mom?"

Rationally, he knew she was gone, but he couldn't allow that to be true. It couldn't be. It had to be a dream. His mom was alive.

Zack's voice cut through the noise. "I know this is all kinds of wrong, but we can't stay here."

Bill's eyes widened. A silent sob strangled his throat, stealing his voice for a second. He looked up at Zack. "I can't leave her. Not like this."

Sympathy shone in his friend's eyes, and he tugged on Bill's arm. "Sorry, man. Come on. Let's get out of here before we're next."

Bill jerked his arm free as rage burned through numbness of the shock. "Those fucking bastards. They shot her."

"Keep your voice down. We need to get out of here. You can't be here when the police arrive." He helped Bill to his feet. "Did you hear a gunshot?"

"No." Bill stared at the red halo growing around his mother's head.

"Shit." Zack pulled him toward the van. "Then they've got a silencer, and we could be in the sights right now."

Bill struggled to keep from screaming. "My mom is…"

"We can't help her now." He shook his head. "But we can still protect Juliet."

Her name jerked Bill into the present, away from the abyss of shock. *Juliet.*

They'd kill her, just like they did his mom. And if they got him now, he'd never be able to bring them down.

He'd make them sorry.

"Fuck." He ran for the van with Zack right behind.

Zack jumped behind the wheel and turned the ignition. The tires screeched as Zack punched the accelerator.

Burning rubber stung Bill's nostrils, but he welcomed the unpleasantness, anything to ground him to this moment, to stop his mind from replaying that strange hollow thud of the bullet. Bile rose in his throat. "I'm gonna be sick."

"No time for that now." Zack gripped the wheel tightly as emergency vehicles passed by in the other direction, lights flashing.

Bill stared into the side mirror. No one was following them. Yet. He shifted his eyes forward. His mom was gone. A split second and now his life would never be the same. If he had known this would be the last time he heard her voice…

He couldn't think about it right now.

His chest constricted as he forced back tears. Zack slowed the van. They were back at his place. Already. Bill had missed the entire drive.

His friend turned off the engine and turned his way. "We weren't followed."

Bill nodded, unsure if he could speak.

"This is bad…" Zack's face shone with sweat his skin pale. "Maybe we should call the cops after all. This was murder…" His voice drifted off as he clasped Bill's shoulder with misty eyes. "I'm so sorry, man."

Bill got out of the van before he lost it completely. They couldn't get the police involved, not yet. What he'd just witnessed proved beyond a doubt that Genesis would kill Juliet and her sister if they found them. The police would return them to their parents, and it would be a death sentence.

The side door opened, and Juliet peered out. "Is everything okay?"

"No." He walked past her into the garage.

Inside, Todd was on his feet, but Bill raised his hand to silence him. "Zack can tell you everything. Outside."

Todd frowned and quietly stepped out to the driveway, closing the door behind him. Bill sat on the edge of the sofa bed, staring at his tennis shoes. There were red speckles on them now.

Juliet came to sit beside him, her voice barely audible. "What happened?"

He lifted his head to meet her eyes, his throat constricting. "My mom…" He struggled to breathe. "She…" Tears blurred his vision. "Those bastards shot her."

Shock lined her face, but she stayed quiet.

"In the middle of a crowded coffee shop, they put a bullet in her head to silence her. Forever."

He swiped a tear and stared at the ceiling. He hadn't cried in front of another person since elementary school. But there was no holding it back anymore.

She rested her hand on his thigh, not tentative, firm. "I'm sorry."

"My mom was talking and then…she was gone." His gaze met Juliet's, and her dark eyes seemed much older than her years.

"My sisters—or clones, I guess—they killed them, too. Any imperfection, even just a cough or runny nose, and in the morning, I'd find them too quiet."

He hated these people. "Why even leave them for you to find? Why not just hide the bodies and tell you they sent them to a relative or something? It's fucking cruel."

She shrugged, but her expression was anything but uncertain. "When I was younger, I thought they were accidents, that the babies just stopped breathing in their cribs." She swallowed and went on. "But Julie-Three made it to five years old. I loved her so much. My first sibling who lived long enough to play with me. We shared a bedroom, and for the first time, I wasn't alone anymore."

Her eyes shone with tears, but she went on anyway. "I tried to protect her and keep her safe, but one day, she stumbled on the stairs and hit her knees. We iced them, and I prayed it wouldn't leave a mark. The next morning, she was cold and stiff in her bed. Gone. I cradled her and cried, but I realized at that moment that they'd left her there for me to find on purpose. Her body was a warning. They wanted me to understand how important it was to stay perfect."

She broke eye contact with Bill and gazed down at her lap. "I dried my tears and cleaned myself up before Momma came. If my nose ran too long or my skin got raw from wiping it, I'd be next, and I already had another baby sister to watch over. Julie-Five needed me so I had to survive." She lifted her head again. Tears shone in her eyes, but she held them back, her tone even. "I know it hurts, and it's the hardest thing to do, but you have to go on. You have to live, or they win. At least that's what I always told myself. I'm never going to let them win."

Bill stared at her for a moment. He'd misjudged her from the second they'd met. He mistook her naivety about the world for weakness, but the shadows in her gaze told a different story. She'd lived her entire life with death on her shoulder and lost seven siblings before little Julie. Hell, she probably lost a few after Julie-Eight, too.

Losing his brother, David, had been a long journey. Slow. They'd had time to make peace, to tell him he was loved. In Bill's final moments with his mother today, she'd been angry with him, terrified Genesis would kill him.

He reached over to cup Juliet's cheek. His voice wobbled, but he didn't give a shit anymore. This was trauma, and he was clinging by his fingernails. If anyone in the world understood, it was probably Juliet. "We're going to expose them and show everyone what they've done. We're going to make those bastards pay."

CHAPTER 16

Julie-Eight watched the digital clock on the desk. Eight o'clock and Cindy's apartment was silent. And Julie-Eight was still in bed, in borrowed pajamas with messy hair.

How late did normal people sleep?

She got up from the futon and padded down the hall to the bathroom. The door to Vanessa's room was still closed. Julie-Eight shut the bathroom door as quietly as she could and then flipped on the light switch. On the edge of the sink, her new toothbrush rested on a white hand towel. She grabbed it and squeezed some toothpaste onto the tip when something caught her eye.

Small, framed pictures lined a shelf on the wall above the toilet. She balanced the brush on the edge of the sink and closed the toilet so she could stand on it for a closer look. There was a picture of a grown-up couple, probably Cindy's parents. Beside it was a portrait of Cindy and Todd, all dressed up with crowns on their heads. The name of their school was on a sign behind them.

She carefully picked up the last frame and stared at the photos. Two pictures and two girls. Her gaze shifted from one to the other and back again. Identical. Like she and Juliet were.

But one photo was discolored, and the clothes were…older. She glanced at the door and back to the frame. Turning it over, she slid the hooks free and lifted the back.

The pictures had writing on the backs. One Vanessa and the other…Cindy.

Julie-Eight had overheard Billy and her sister talking the first night they slept at his house. He'd said it was impossible for them to be twins. And there was another word—*clone*—but she didn't know what it meant.

Did Cindy?

Her hands trembled as she rushed to get the frame back together and placed it on the shelf again. If Cindy and Vanessa were just like she and Juliet were, then why didn't they have to be perfect, too?

It didn't make sense.

And it wasn't fair.

She got down and lifted the lid on the toilet. At the sink, she brushed her teeth, counting the seconds for each side and top and bottom, just like her momma had trained her, but inside, something burned, bitter and hot. Vanessa played video games and had friends. She slept late without morning inspections. She went to school. *Real* school, not at home with her mother.

Julie-Eight tightened her grip on the toothbrush, anger bubbling in her belly. Juliet would tell her to calm down, tell her to be grateful they have each other.

But Juliet wasn't there.

JULIET GOT OUT of her sleeping bag quietly, leaving Billy sleeping. Yesterday he'd insisted on staying busy. They'd spent all day combing through phone numbers and bank accounts until well past midnight. They found names to cross-reference for Zack, but for now, they were still empty-handed.

She sat in front of one of Zack's computer screens and started flipping through the digital photos he'd compiled for her from social media surrounding Eden Incorporated. Her job was to see if she recognized any of them. So far no one looked familiar. Not that she'd seen many people in her life. There was the male doctor who brought her a few graphic novels, her father, and an older woman who only came by once or twice a year. That was it.

Juliet had never been introduced or even told their names, but the woman always made her father jumpy. Whenever she visited, Juliet's usually aloof father would trip over his words and rush through the exam. She'd mentioned the visitors to Julie-Eight a few times, but her younger sister never had visitors at her physicals.

Zack came into the garage, and Juliet startled, barely stifling a scream. He put his hands up, noticed Billy still sleeping, and whispered, “Sorry. Didn’t mean to scare you.” He pulled over another chair. “Recognize anyone yet?”

She shook her head. “There were only two other people I ever saw in my house other than my parents. I guess our chances of finding them is going to be slim.”

“Every lead can help.” Zack scrolled through a website that said *Facebook* at the top.

She flipped through a few more pictures and glanced over at his screen again. Her breath caught. “Wait. Go back.”

He looked over his shoulder. “What?”

She moved next to him, pointing at the screen. “Go up. I saw someone.”

Zack crawled up his newsfeed, and she tapped the screen. “Him. That’s the doctor who was in my house.”

“This one?” Zack pointed.

Juliet started to nod when the pull-out bed creaked behind them. She turned around as Billy stretched and came forward. “You guys should’ve woken me up.” He squinted at Zack’s screen. “Why are you looking at my pictures from my parents’ barbeque?”

Juliet looked at the photo again. “I recognized this man.”

Billy came closer, frowning. “That’s my dad.”

Now that she studied the man’s face, Billy and his

father had the same bright-green eyes, but the resemblance ended there. His father had pale, freckled skin with more angular features. Billy must have gotten his skin coloring and expressive features from his mother.

Juliet never would have guessed Billy and the doctor were related. "He's the one who brought me comics."

Billy pulled a chair over to sit beside her. "I still can't believe he's involved in this."

She glanced at Billy. "He was only at my exams a few times a year. Maybe he didn't know what happened to all my sisters."

He raked his fingers through his hair. "My mom said the research was more important than her life or mine." He met her eyes. "She wore a disguise to our meeting yesterday and whispered the entire time." He cleared his throat, looking at the screen where his parents smiled together. "I think she knew what had been going on inside Genesis, and she was risking her life by telling me anything. How could they rationalize raising kids in captivity and killing them if they…weren't perfect?"

Juliet's stomach twisted as he clicked through the photos. His mother was beautiful. He definitely had her smile. Had she known what was happening to Juliet and her sisters and looked the other way?

The final photo was his dad smiling in front of a grill. She couldn't believe he'd lived just down the street all this time. She used to look forward to his visits. Being trapped in a house with only her parents and sisters had turned any outsider into an exotic treat. She'd never really gotten to talk to him, but his secret gifts of comics and graphic novels had been treasured.

Did he know they were planning to kill her in a few days and put her body on display as an example of their genetic engineering victory? Like some kind of trophy?

She popped up from the chair and went to the door, aching to turn the knob and run. But where would she go? Her feet remained glued to the floor while she blinked back tears.

Zack mumbled something about donuts and vanished into the main house. The silence settled onto her shoulders like an invisible weight, smothering her.

Billy came up next to her, his voice barely above a whisper. "I had an older brother. His name was David. I was six when he started getting sick. He'd be so tired that he'd fall asleep doing homework. He didn't want to go to Little League practice or go out and play."

She glanced up at him, but he wasn't looking at her, just staring straight ahead.

"Then the headaches came. He'd cry because they hurt so bad. My mom took him to the doctor, but they recommended Tylenol and sent us home. Pretty soon his nose started bleeding. He'd lose so much blood, and they came more often every day. My dad is a researcher, not a pediatrician, but he knew it wasn't normal." Billy rubbed his forehead. "He took David to the emergency room, and after a bunch of tests, they diagnosed him with leukemia, and the fight began. I didn't really understand what it was, but it scared my parents, and that terrified me. My mom cried at night after she thought I was asleep, and my dad mostly stayed at the hospital with David."

Juliet worried her lower lip. "That must've been awful."

"Yeah." He met her eyes. "My dad could map DNA, but he couldn't save my brother. We celebrated David's tenth birthday in his room in the pediatric oncology ward. I'll never forget it because we all had to wear masks. None of us could blow out the candles." A sad smile curved his lips. He cleared his throat. "It was the last time I ever heard my brother laugh. He died a week later."

"I'm sorry." She took his hand, and he laced his fingers with hers.

"I'm not telling you this for sympathy. I just want you to understand. They weren't always like this. Losing David changed them. Until now, I never realized how much." He sighed. "For a while, my dad lost faith in science. He even quit his job at UCLA, but after a month, he found a new one. That was why we moved here. I didn't know it at the time, but he must've heard about Genesis and…" He gave her hand a squeeze. "My mom said they were on their way to ending childhood diseases and birth defects. My parents think they're saving other families from going through what we did."

"But the research is flawed." She swallowed the lump in her throat. "They killed any children who were anything less than perfect. A cold, a bruise, it didn't matter. Making more…copies of my DNA isn't going to keep children from dying."

"*We* know that, but they probably don't tell their donors anything about the failures. As far as the money people know, you and Julie are the only 'specimens,' and they may not even realize you were kept locked in that house."

"We have to tell someone."

"And we will." He nodded. "Once we have a few names other than your parents so we can back up your story. We have the journal, but they're not going to believe us unless they can corroborate it. We need proof."

ZACK CRACKED THE door to the garage and poked his head inside. "Hey, Bill." Regret lined his eyes. "They just had a news spot about your mom on television. The police are asking for witnesses to come forward."

Bill ground his teeth together. He'd sat right across the table from his mother and had heard nothing. With a long-range rifle and a silencer, the shooter could have been anywhere. "I hope someone saw the shooter."

Zack raised a brow. "You're not going to talk to

them? There's a hotline you can call anonymously."

"And tell them what?" Bill shook his head. "I didn't even realize she'd been shot until it was too late." He sat in Zack's computer chair, eager for something else to focus on. The grief sat on his chest like an anchor, ready to drown him if he stopped treading water. "Can I check my email on here?"

"Sure, just open a new window in the browser." Zack set a bag on the table. "Donuts are here if you want them. I've gotta run a couple errands for the folks, but I'll be back soon."

Bill opened a fresh window in Zack's high-tech Firefox browser, went to his email, and entered his password. "Later, Z-Man."

After the door closed, Juliet scooted back over to her computer screen, clicking through photos while he deleted spam messages from his inbox. The simple, hollow clicks seemed surreal. His mom had died yesterday, and yet the offers for male enhancement products and lottery winnings were still coming. The world moved on despite his unrealistic urge to stop it, to scream, to curse, and maybe even cry.

He wanted to call his dad, but after yesterday, he worried any contact might put his father's life in jeopardy, too. He stopped clicking and glanced at the pictures Juliet was flipping through. When this was over, would his father go to prison? How deep was his family tied to Juliet's?

She looked his way. "Are you all right?"

"Not really." He shook his head and focused on his inbox again. "But hopefully I will be."

A subject line caught his eye. It was only one word: *Iridescence.*

That was the safe word his parents had given to him on his first day of school in case of an emergency so he'd know it was safe to go with the person they sent to pick him up from school if they couldn't for some reason. After losing David, they were hyper-vigilant over Bill's safety. They worried someone might kidnap him from school and had multiple fail-safes to ensure that never happened.

Bill hovered the mouse over the email address and frowned. Neither of his parents used Hotmail, but he was too curious to delete it without opening it first.

His pulse sped up as he read the email.

Bill –

I never wanted you to find out about my research this way. Please understand your mother knew the risks of talking to you, but your safety meant more to her than anything in the world. I couldn't keep her away from you.

Your life is in danger. They are searching for you. Your mother and I set up an emergency fund in your name, just in case. The account information is attached. Go to the bank, withdraw the money, and get out of town. Hide. You're all I have left in this world.

Stay safe.

Love,
Dad

Bill stared at the screen. It could be a trap. Would his own father lead him to the slaughter just to protect his work? He didn't want to believe that, but he also didn't want to dwell on the fact that this email made it clear his father wasn't going to the police for justice for his mother's murder. How could he stay and support the people responsible for killing her?

Bill shoved the bitter thoughts aside. Maybe his father was trapped, unable to talk to the authorities. Or maybe this was all a trick to get Bill out in the open so the Genesis Foundation could grab him. After losing his mom in the middle of a Starbucks patio, he wasn't going to take any chances.

Bill grabbed his cell phone and started texting Zack.

"What's wrong?" Juliet asked.

He stopped, his eyes darting to her face. "I got an email from my dad, but I want to see if Zack can trace the email address or the IP address. Maybe it can help us find Genesis."

"You don't think your dad sent it?"

He shrugged. "I don't know. According to the email, my dad has a secret bank account in my name. He told me to use the money to get out of town, but it could be a trap. I don't know if I can trust him."

Saying those words out loud hurt, but he forced himself to press on. He sent the text to Zack and logged out of his email. If it really was from his dad, that money would be a big help. He could take Juliet to Los

Angeles. It'd be much easier to hide in a big city, and the longer they stayed at Zack's the more danger they put him in.

But what about Juliet's sister? She was safer with Cindy. There was nothing tying the Huffs to Todd's girlfriend. There would be no reason for the police to come sniffing around. If they brought her with them, there was a better chance someone might recognize the two missing sisters.

Bill ran his fingers through his hair. Juliet wouldn't like leaving Julie behind, but she was probably safest with Cindy. Todd's girlfriend had no ties to Genesis or Juliet. They'd have no reason to look there.

He just needed to convince Juliet.

CHAPTER 17

THE TELEVISION CAME to life in the other room and Julie-Eight lifted her head from the book she was reading. She'd never even seen a TV until a couple of days ago, but already it called to her like the Pied Piper. She closed her book and looked at the door. Since she'd found the photos on the shelf in the bathroom, she'd been trying to figure out what to do. She thought about talking to Todd. He was supposed to be coming over today.

But he probably wouldn't be able to keep such a big secret from his girlfriend, and they'd be upset with her if she told them they were like her. Or at least she thought they would. Vanessa already didn't seem to like her much.

What she needed was to talk to Juliet. But her sister wasn't here.

Julie-Eight sighed and slid off the bed, then wandered out to the living room. Cindy and Vanessa looked up at the same time as Julie-Eight walked in.

"Hi, Julie." Cindy smiled and patted the sofa next to her. "Come on over and watch *Beauty and the Beast* with us."

Vanessa kept her eyes on the screen as Julie-Eight came over and sat down. Just as she started to sink into the animated world, there was a knock at the door. Cindy tensed, her back suddenly straight and rigid.

She turned down the television and whispered. "Wait here. Don't make any noise. I'm sure it's nothing."

Julie-Eight's pulse raced. Cindy might've said it was nothing, but she sure seemed worried. Julie-Eight ran down the hallway to the guest room and closed the door.

Muffled voices from the other room relaxed her a little. They weren't loud or upset. Maybe it was a friend of Cindy's. Even so, Julie-Eight had no desire to venture out. These people were hiding her; they didn't care about her like Juliet did.

She gasped when the door opened.

Vanessa giggled. "Scaredy cat, it's just my grandma. You can come out and meet her."

"That's okay. I'll just play in here."

Vanessa frowned. "You don't like my grandma?"

Julie-Eight shrugged. "I just don't know her."

"Because you haven't met her yet." Vanessa rolled her eyes. "Come on."

Vanessa grabbed her hand and tugged her out. Julie-Eight tried not to smile as she groaned. This was the first time Vanessa had shown any interest in her at all. It was tough not to be happy about it.

In the living room, Cindy and her grandmother turned toward them. Julie-Eight had never met a grandparent before. If she had any, they'd never come to visit.

The older woman had pure white hair that curled under at the ends, just below her ears, but she didn't have any wrinkles. The only part of her that looked old was her hands. Big gemstone rings shone on a few of her crooked fingers, and the jewelry was held on by swollen knuckle joints.

Vanessa's grandma smiled wide. Her teeth were very straight and white. "Well, well, who is this?"

"This is Julie," Vanessa said.

"She's a friend from school," Cindy interrupted quickly.

Vanessa frowned at her older sister. "No, she's not."

Cindy narrowed her eyes at Vanessa and then smiled at their grandmother. "They weren't in the same class." She glanced at Julie-Eight. "This is my grandmother, Claudette Sutter."

Claudette held out a hand. "It's nice to meet you, Julie."

Julie-Eight swallowed hard and took Claudette's cool hand. Her twisted fingers tightened around Julie-Eight's hand. "You look so familiar. Maybe I know your parents. What's your last name, dear?"

Julie-Eight's pulse raced. Had she seen her picture on television? She couldn't say her real last name, but she couldn't think of another one, either.

Vanessa blurted out, "Cindy's boyfriend brought her to stay with us."

Cindy narrowed her eyes at her sister. Vanessa crossed her arms. "I was telling the truth."

Cindy chuckled, but she wasn't smiling as she straightened to meet her grandmother's eyes. "My parents were smarter than I thought by having the two of us so far apart."

Claudette's gaze was locked on Julie-Eight. "Sisters fight sometimes, right Julie?"

Julie-Eight lifted her chin. "I never fight with my sister."

Something in Claudette's expression, the way her eyes glinted in the light as her eyebrows pulled up in surprise made Julie-Eight uncomfortable. She'd said too much.

"Where is your sister?" The older woman scanned the room. "Is she here too?"

Cindy swooped in. "Her sister's at home. They're on summer break from school so Julie's staying with us for a few days. Slumber partying, you know." She caught Julie-Eight and Vanessa each by the shoulder. "You two can get back to the movie. I'm sure Grandma came over for a reason."

Julie-Eight wandered over and sat on one end of the couch. Vanessa plopped on the other end. Good. Julie-Eight didn't want to sit beside her anyway.

Behind them, Claudette and Cindy talked about

tickets to the symphony. Another thing she'd never been to. How many times had Vanessa gone to concerts with her grandmother?

"Goodbye, Grandma," Cindy called.

"I'll see you darlings soon."

Vanessa ran over to hug her grandmother and finally the door closed behind her.

"I'm sorry about that." Cindy sighed and took the center seat on the sofa. "I missed her texts on the phone so she dropped by."

"Well, she *is* our grandma." Vanessa rolled her eyes.

Julie-Eight leaned forward so she could see around Cindy. "You almost blabbed everything."

"She's my grandma. I don't need to lie to her. Ever."

"Give it a rest." Cindy patted her sister's leg. "I know you're not happy about giving up part of our sister summer, but Julie didn't ask for any of this to happen, either."

Julie-Eight crossed her arms in front of her chest. "If she saw my picture on TV and something happens to me or Juliet, it'll be all *your* fault."

Vanessa didn't reply. She just smiled.

The animation blurred as Julie-Eight blinked back tears. She would *not* allow Vanessa to see her cry. No way.

But she wanted her sister. Bad.

BILL'S PALMS WERE sticky with sweat. Todd swiveled his head as they walked the five blocks from Bill's truck toward the bank. Zack couldn't trace the source of the email, but he had been able to determine that the Hotmail account was new and the IP address came from a public library.

As far as he could tell, this wasn't a setup, but until they got there, he wouldn't know for sure.

"Loosen up," Todd said. "You can't walk in there sweating with a stick up your ass. If this *is* a trap, you look like you're ready to step into it without a fight."

"Screw you." Bill rolled his eyes. "I've never walked into a bank to make a withdrawal from a secret account. I'm nervous."

"It's just like every other account at the bank. Mellow out."

Bill grumbled but did his best to box up his worry and focus on his next move. Todd was right. No one in there would know this was a secret account or strange for him. He could do this. And once he had the money in hand, he'd go back and get Juliet and all their things out of Zack's garage. They could find a hotel in Los Angeles and lie low. He had his new MacBook Pro laptop, so they could help Zack remotely and keep the police away from his house.

Making plans settled the butterflies stirring in his gut.

Todd grabbed the handle to the oversized glass door. "Ready?"

"As I'll ever be."

They stepped into the lobby, and nothing changed. No one even looked in their direction. Bill took a breath and walked to an open teller window.

"Can I help you?"

He nodded at the young woman with perfectly coifed hair and a dazzling white smile. "Yeah. I need to make a withdrawal."

After he filled out a slip with the account number and showed her his driver's license, she disappeared into a back room. Across the bank, Todd raised a questioning brow. Bill shrugged a shoulder just as the teller returned with her high-voltage smile still in full force.

"Do you have a preference in bill size?"

"What?"

"The money."

"Oh. Twenties please."

She gave him a dubious look.

He glanced at Todd and back to the teller. "Maybe a few hundreds?"

She kept her voice down. "How about one hundred dollar bills for the first thousand and twenties for the rest?"

"Sounds good."

She smiled and counted out the currency. Until today, he'd never held three thousand dollars in cash before. As the stack of money grew, he realized the teller had been right to suggest larger bills. She offered him a debit card, too, but he wouldn't be able to use it. As long as Genesis was still searching for Juliet and her sister, he couldn't risk a paper trail.

He left the rest of the money in the account. His parents had set aside almost ten thousand dollars for him over the years in this secret account. It was proof that, on some level, they'd known Genesis was dangerous. And they'd turned a blind eye anyway.

The teller slipped the cash into two bank envelopes. "Is there anything else I can help with today?"

"No. Thanks." He slid the envelopes into the inner pocket of his jacket and walked over to Todd. "Let's get out of here."

They headed outside, and just as they stepped off the curb, tires started to screech.

"Run!" Todd shouted.

Bill didn't need to be told twice. They bolted through the lot and down the alleyway behind the bank, narrowly escaping a black sedan barreling through the busy parking area. They ducked into the back door of a restaurant, exited through the front, jogged across the street through traffic, and ran into a mall. They wandered through the mall, watching for anyone that might be following them, but other than shoppers, there didn't seem to be any people tailing them. They must've lost them.

After they exited the mall, Bill scanned the streets

over and over for the car that had tried to run them over. Thankfully, the walk back to his truck was uneventful. He got behind the wheel and pulled into traffic, watching his rearview mirror. "Think they're gone?"

Todd kept his eye on the side mirror. "For now. That was close."

"Too close." Bill agreed. "Do you think they found out about the bank account?"

Todd shrugged. "No idea."

"Dammit." Bill got on the freeway, thinking out loud. "If they knew about the money, they would've intercepted us before I could get to it. They must've followed us here. They probably know what kind of truck I drive." He should've thought about that earlier. There wasn't time to beat himself up. He was making this up as he went along. If his dad worked for Genesis, there was a good chance they'd watched Bill's family closely. "I need to rent a car." The blinker clicked in time with Bill's pulse rate. "No. Zack could rent a car. I'll pay him back with the cash. He can pick it up, and we'll catch a cab and meet him at a long-term parking garage in Los Angeles. I can ditch my truck at the house for now."

Todd looked over at him. "You're not really talking to *me* right now, right?"

Bill chuckled, tightening his grip on the wheel. "Sorry, dude, just trying to make a plan. Thanks for coming with me."

Todd nodded and went back to watching the passenger-side mirror. “No problem.”

“Juliet’s not going to want to go to Los Angeles without her sister.”

Todd straightened up. “Julie isn’t going to like that, either. She’s champing at the bit to get out of Cindy’s place.”

“I bet. Juliet’s been her only friend.”

“That’s not going to change anytime soon.” Todd sighed. “I think Vanessa wanted Cindy all to herself. She doesn’t seem happy to have Julie there.”

Bill sighed. “Hopefully we won’t need to hide much longer.”

Silence dragged out for a couple miles before Todd cleared his throat. “I should’ve said something earlier, but…you were nervous about the bank and I didn’t want to upset you.”

Bill looked over at him. “What’s going on?”

Todd sighed. “Zack told me about—”

Bill interrupted. “My mom.”

“Yeah, I…” He shook his head. “I’m sorry.”

Bill shoved the grief aside. He didn’t have time to grieve. He wanted justice. He just wasn’t sure how to get it. “Do you think I should tell the police what I know?”

He shrugged. “For what it’s worth, I get why you’re not talking to them.”

Bill gave the truck a little more gas. “I didn’t see anyone with a gun, so I’m not sure how much help I would be anyway. Until we have more evidence on Genesis, her parents, and mine, too, we can't risk it. Maybe I'll talk to them once we can back up Juliet's story."

"If you turn over the evidence, your dad could go down with Genesis. You ready for that?"

Hell no. Bill shrugged. "I guess I have to be."

"Z-Man and I will have your back no matter what."

Bill nodded, keeping his gaze on the highway. He couldn't risk eye contact right now. His emotions were too jumbled. He swallowed the lump in his throat. "I owe you guys."

"Nah." Todd nudged his shoulder. "You'd do the same for us."

CHAPTER 18

JULIET SHOOK HER head, her eyes widening. "I can't go to Los Angeles and leave Julie behind."

Bill sat in front of her and took her hands in his. "I know this sucks, but Genesis is already closing in. They'll find us if we stay here any longer. They followed me to the bank. If we stay here, it's only a matter of time until we lead them right to Zack's place."

He rubbed her knuckles with his thumbs, wishing he could give her a better option.

"What if they find Julie?" Her voice cracked. "We'll be too far away to get to her in time."

"Todd and Zack will be here." He glanced over his shoulder to his friend. "Tell her, Z-Man."

Zack stopped typing and looked at them. "You won't need to hide much longer. I tracked some money from Bill's folks' financials and it's connected to private charity foundations. I should be able to connect the dots and get some names now."

"See?" Bill hated pressuring her, but after seeing his mother gunned down in front of him, and being nearly run down by a car today, the threat to their lives was very real and front and center in his head. "I've got cash now. We can lie low, and in a couple days, when Zack has the information we need, we'll go to the media and this will all be over."

"I already put you in danger. I can't spend your money, too." Regret lined her eyes.

"You're not. I'm in this, too, now." Bill shook his head. "They took my mom from me, and I'm going to make them pay."

"Okay." She nodded slowly. "I still want to take Julie with us."

Todd came over and stood beside him. "They've been broadcasting a picture of the two of you together all over the news. Keeping you and your sister apart is probably the only reason Julie is still safe."

She sighed and looked down at their joined hands. Bill held his breath, praying she'd come around.

"I can talk to her on the phone?"

Bill squeezed her hands. "Every day if you want."

She lifted her head. "I've never been so far away from her." She turned her attention on Todd. "You'll keep Julie safe for me?"

"Of course I will." Todd nodded.

She took a deep breath, and her gaze locked on Bill's. "All right. Let's get out of here."

Bill released her and shot to his feet to gather up his tings and put them back into his duffel. The plan was to leave his truck parked at the mall. Zack would rent a car and swing by the food court to give him the keys, and Todd would take Zack home in his car. Then Bill and Juliet would take the rental, get a hotel room in Los Angeles.

But Juliet hadn't said a word since he'd pulled out of Zack's driveway to head over to the mall.

"You're pretty quiet over there. It's making me nervous."

She looked out the passenger window. "I figured you've got enough on your plate watching for anyone following us."

"So far so good." He stole a glance her way. "This isn't going to be forever."

"I know." She finally faced forward. "I just can't shake the feeling that she needs me."

"She needs you to stay safe."

Juliet sighed. "Tomorrow is my birthday. Since she was born, I've never celebrated one without her."

"When we get through this, we'll get a cake and candles and throw a real party, okay?"

She nodded and stared out the window.

The silence was going to kill him. Bill slid his hands down a little on the steering wheel. "Have you thought about what you want to do while we're away? Los Angeles is a huge city. We can hide in plain sight there."

Her shoulders relaxed a little. "I wouldn't know where to begin. There's so much I've never done." She adjusted her seat belt. "This is the first time I've ever been on a freeway."

Bill switched lanes. "Well, how do you like the highway so far?"

The corners of her lips twitched, and his pulse surged. He'd never wanted to make someone smile so bad before. The past couple of days had been a nightmare. It was easier to pretend none of it had happened.

"I thought being inside a car when it's going fast would be scarier, but it's not much different from driving on your street."

"All right, so we can cross 'being on a freeway' off your never-tried-before list. What else do you want to mark off?"

She shrugged. "I've never seen the ocean or played a sport."

The beach he could manage, but a sport? That was more Todd's area of expertise. Other than stick ball and catch on their street as kids, he never… Wait a minute. He tried to peek into the back of the cab, but he could see if his bowling bag was back there. During the school year, he'd been in a league with a couple guys from his dorm building. Bowling at the Bowlero once a week was fun. Less pressure than when he'd been more competitive in high school. "Is there a camouflage bag with wheels on the little seat behind us?"

She twisted around and then nodded. "Yeah, it's back there."

He smiled. "Good. I'll take you bowling."

"What's bowling?"

He tried not to gape. “Um. You’ve never heard of bowling?”

She shook her head. “No television. If it wasn’t in one of my mom’s books or the graphic novels your dad gave me…”

“Wow.” He watched the rearview mirror. No unmarked black sedans nearby. Good. “Bowling is a sport. You roll a ball down a lane and try to knock down these pins at the other end. My mom didn’t want me playing full contact sports in high school so she got me a bowling ball and lessons. I think you’ll like it.”

She almost smiled. “Sounds fun.”

“Good. Then we’ll go to the beach, and I’ll teach you to bowl. Anything else?”

“Maybe a movie?”

He chuckled. “You’ve never seen one on a big screen, have you?”

A sheepish smile curved on her lips. “No movies on any screen.”

“We can hit the movies tomorrow. For your birthday.” He reached over and took her hand enjoying the way it fit in his. “You’re going to love it.”

“I wish we could take Julie, too.”

“When this is over, we’ll take her everywhere.” And he meant it. They just needed to get rid of Genesis first.

ZACK CHUCKLED AS Bill put his bowling bag into the

trunk of the rental car. "You're taking your bowling balls?"

Juliet tried not to notice the way Billy's tan biceps pulled at his T-shirt sleeve when he lifted the heavy bag. He'd told her the balls were each for different lane conditions. None of it made sense to her, but seeing him fired up about his sport made her smile.

"I'm going to teach Juliet to bowl. I can't be using house balls and rental shoes."

Zack raised a brow and looked her way. "Did he tell you he won the city championship in high school? He's got a 235 average."

She smiled. "Is that good?"

He grinned. "Let's just say, you've got a great teacher."

Billy slammed the trunk closed. "Got everything?"

She nodded and Zack handed Billy the keys. "Be careful with this thing. I had to pay a bunch of underage surcharges to get it."

Billy took out some cash and gave it to Zack. 'Thanks for all your help, man."

"Happy to help." Zack gave Billy a tight hug. "Stay safe."

"We will." Billy released him and took a step back. "I have my laptop and we're ready to help, so if you get anything on Genesis—"

"I'll text you if I need you." His gaze wandered over to Juliet, then back to his friend. "Please show this girl a good time. She deserves it."

Juliet did her best not to blush. "We're not on a vacation."

"Maybe not." Zack chuckled. "But you slipped through Genesis's fingers and got out of Moonlight Cove. That's worth a celebration. Live a little."

Billy clicked small, black remote control, and the lights flashed on the rental car. "Thanks again, Z-Man. See you soon."

"You know it, buddy."

She got in the white car. "Prius. What's that mean?"

"Prius is the model of the car." Billy got in and pressed a button. The screen came to life. "It's a hybrid."

"A what?"

He grinned. "It uses both gas and electricity."

The world kept getting bigger. How would she ever catch up? "Sorry about all the questions."

He took her hand, and she lifted her gaze to meet his. "You don't need to apologize." He searched her eyes. "You remind me how amazing some of this stuff is. I take it all for granted. Being around you makes me see things for the first time again." He smiled. "It's actually pretty cool."

She leaned over and brushed a light kiss to his cheek. "Thank you, Billy. For everything."

LOS ANGELES OVERWHELMED Juliet's senses. She'd had

no concept that a city could contain so many people. The freeway slowed to a crawl, stopping for a few seconds, only to roll forward several car lengths and start the process over again. Billy pointed out the Hollywood sign on the hill and some kind of castle for a sci-fi church. Tall glass buildings were everywhere.

He merged onto another freeway—not that it went any faster. The setting sun blinded her for a moment. "Are we almost there?"

"Yeah, we have a room in Santa Monica at the Doubletree. It's not fancy, but they'll give us free cookies and free breakfast in the morning." He pulled down a flap of plastic from the ceiling of the car. "It's a visor. You have one, too."

She flipped it down, breathing a sigh of relief. "Momma used to bake cookies sometimes. She never let us help, though. Too dangerous."

"My mom wasn't much of a cook…" His voice tapered off.

Juliet regretted mentioning her mother. Guilt weighed on her shoulders as she placed her hand over his and gave it a squeeze. If she hadn't escaped, his mom would probably still be alive. But Juliet couldn't go back in time.

"I'm sorry about your mom. At least we're doing what she would have wanted. We're using the money to stay safe from Genesis."

"Not exactly." He laced his fingers with hers, sending a jolt of electricity up her arm. "She was trying to talk me into taking you and your sister back."

Keeping his attention on the slow traffic, he sighed. "I'm an English major, and there's a saying that 'every villain is the hero of his own story.' I can't stop hearing her in my head telling me that this research is more valuable than our lives, than your life. She believed in what they were doing. She thought their work was going to change the world." He shook his head. "It's all bullshit." He looked over at her for a second. "They lost their way. Killing anyone deemed less than perfect is far from heroic, no matter what your goal was in the beginning."

"You're right." She worried her lower lip, unsure what to say. She'd lost so may sisters. "But according to my father's journal, we're not really people. We were creations and test subjects."

"That's bullshit, too. Maybe they told themselves that to keep their distance from you, but you and your sister have your own minds. You're just as human as I am." He pulled off the freeway and stopped at a light. "It's pissing me off all over again. Let's talk about something else."

"Okay." She was drawing a blank, though.

He looked over at her. "Learning to drive didn't make the top three on your things-to-try list."

She shook her head. "Until I escaped from the house, I'd never even been inside a car. I don't think I'm ready to get behind the wheel of one just yet."

"Fair enough." He drove across the intersection.

"This is going to be your first time in a hotel, too?"

She laughed. "I'm pretty sure you can assume that everything from here on out will be my first time."

He stopped at another light and leaned over to kiss her cheek, his lips lingering near her ear. "Not everything."

Heat flushed her face, but she didn't care. This was the adventure she'd always dreamed of if she ever got out of that house, and she wasn't going to waste it being timid or afraid. No way. She turned her head, her lips caressing his. She liked kissing more every time she did it.

He hummed into her mouth and straightened when a car honked behind them. "To be continued?"

She grinned as he drove through the light and turned into the driveway labeled *Doubletree.*

TODD HANDED JULIE-EIGHT his cell phone. She pressed it to her ear. "Hello?"

"Julie? It's me," Juliet said.

"My name is Julie-Eight." She didn't mean to be bratty to her sister, but she was sick of people calling her by different names.

Juliet's voice softened. "I know, but we agreed—"

"I want to stay with you." Julie-Eight interrupted, unable to stop the whine from creeping into her voice. "Can you come get me?"

Her sister sighed. "That's why I called. I wanted to be the one to tell you."

Julie-Eight frowned. "Tell me what?"

"The people Momma and Papa work for tried to run Billy over with a car today. It's too dangerous for Zack to keep hiding me at his house." She paused. "We had to leave Moonlight Cove for a few days. Just until we find the proof we need."

Julie-Eight's heart pounded like an angry drum in her ears. Her grip tightened on the phone. "Where are you?"

"Billy took me to Los Angeles." Before Julie-Eight could ask where that was, her sister went on. "You can call me anytime, and I'll check in with you every day."

"I don't want to call you. I want to see you." She cleared her throat, struggling to blink back tears. "You left me."

"No." Juliet sighed. "You're safe with Cindy, and I'll be back as soon as I can."

Julie-Eight ran down the hall with the phone stuck to her ear and locked herself in the bathroom. She whispered. "Please come get me."

"I can't." Juliet's voice cracked. "Not yet."

Julie-Eight turned on the faucet to cover her voice. "I can't stay here. Vanessa and Cindy are…like us."

"They're sisters, too."

"No. That's not what I mean." Her words spilled out in a rush. "They're twins born far apart. Like you and me."

Silence. Julie-Eight waited, biting at her lower lip as she stared at the door. Her sister *had* to believe her.

Finally, Juliet asked, “Why do you think that?”

“Because there’s a picture frame with two pictures.” She looked up at the photo on the shelf. “The back of one says Cindy age eight and the back of the other says Vanessa age eight, and they look exactly the same. They’re twins.”

“That’s impossible.”

Her brow furrowed. “I’m *not* lying.”

“I didn’t say you were.” Juliet paused. “There’s got to be an explanation.”

“Come get me.” Julie-Eight closed the lid on the toilet and sat down.

“Let me talk to Billy. He and Todd can see if there’s any way Cindy and Vanessa could be…like us.”

“No.” Julie-Eight frowned. Why didn’t her sister believe her? “You can’t tell Todd. He’ll tell Cindy, and then they’ll know what I found out. They’ll take me back to Momma.”

“No one is taking you back there.” Juliet’s tone was firm. “I’ll handle this. You stay where you are for now, and I’ll be back with you soon.”

Julie-Eight blinked hard. She would *not* cry. “You *can’t* leave me here.” She lowered her voice. “Cindy’s grandmother was here earlier asking me questions. It’s not safe.”

Juliet sighed. “She just met you, of course she’s asking about you. If anyone sees us together, they'll call the police and we'll both be back in that house. You need to stay with Cindy, far away from me."

Julie-Eight's voice wobbled. "You *promised* you'd take care of me."

"I know." Juliet's voice cracked. "I'm trying."

"You are not!" She clicked "end" on the phone, turned off the faucet, and shot out of the bathroom before the hot tears could spill from her eyes. She tossed Todd his phone, sprinted to the guest room, and closed the door.

She fell onto the little daybed facedown on the pillow and screamed. Her emotions teetered between heartbreak and rage. Juliet was out seeing the world without her. Her sister had broken her promise.

Julie-Eight was alone.

After bawling into the pillow for a while, a knock at the door snapped her out of her thoughts. "Go away."

Cindy cracked the door open. "Want to talk about it?"

"No." Julie-Eight blinked back hot, angry tears. "It won't bring Juliet here."

"She'll be back soon." Cindy came in and sat on the bed. "Bill is trying to keep her safe."

"He is not!" She crossed her arms tightly over her chest. "I saw him kiss her when we left the park. She's outside, free with her boyfriend, and I'm trapped here hiding." Her emotions tipped from fury back into sadness as her voice cracked. "They're in love, and she forgot me. I just want my sister."

"She would never forget you." Cindy ran a hand up Julie-Eight's back. "Todd told me as soon as they have the evidence they need, Juliet will be right over to get you. You'll see."

Julie-Eight glanced around and frowned. "Where's Vanessa?"

"She went with our grandmother to the symphony. I told her I couldn't go."

"I don't think she likes me."

"Vanessa?"

Julie-Eight nodded. "Todd said to be patient, but I don't think that's it. She took me out to meet your grandma and then tried to spill everything. She wants me out."

"It's not you. Things with my sister are…complicated." Cindy sighed. "Can I tell you something? It needs to stay just between us."

Julie-Eight wiped her eyes and sat up beside her. "Sure."

"My parents butt heads with my grandmother a lot when it comes to my little sister."

"Butt heads?" Julie-Eight tried not to laugh at the mental image.

"It means fight, like mountain goats ramming into each other with their hard heads."

"Oh." She sobered. "Why?"

Cindy met her eyes. "Because when I was just a little older than you, I was diagnosed with cancer and the treatments to cure it were killing me. The doctors told my parents I needed a bone marrow transplant to make me better, but my parents weren't a match for me."

"So they had your sister?"

Cindy stared out the window. "It wasn't that simple. My mom couldn't have any more children. My grandmother—her mom—spent a lot of money and found a surrogate... Long story short, my sister was born, and she was a perfect match. They used her stem cells to save me."

"And that's bad?"

"No, but my parents decided Vanessa didn't need to know about the bone marrow transplant, at least not until she was older. Our grandmother took her out one day and told her everything against their wishes." Cindy tipped her head down. "Vanessa has never been the same."

"Why not?"

"Without my grandmother, Vanessa wouldn't exist." Cindy sighed, staring down at the floor. "She calls Vanessa her miracle, and my sister thinks our grandmother is the only person who really loves her."

Julie-Eight wasn't sure what to say. The photo in the bathroom popped into her head. Juliet had said it was impossible, but what if there were others like them? Others who *weren't* locked up in their houses and killed if they weren't perfect anymore.

"Vanessa is really angry." Cindy finally met Julie-

Eight's eyes. "She thinks the rest of our family only wanted her for her bones."

Julie-Eight pressed her lips together. Vanessa wasn't the only one who was angry.

CHAPTER 19

JULIET TOSSED THE cell phone onto the bed and covered her face. "I can't leave her there. We have to go back."

"We knew she wouldn't be happy about this, but it's to protect you both." Billy came over and embraced her. She didn't deserve his comfort. She'd taken her sister away from everything she'd ever known and then left her behind with strangers. She had every right to be angry with Juliet.

She stepped back and turned toward the window. "She's convinced herself Vanessa is Cindy's 'twin,' just like we are."

He sat on the edge of the bed. "There's no way. If Genesis is trying to attract donors, they wouldn't risk allowing one of their clones to go out in the world. It's too risky that someone might find out. That's why they want you back so badly."

She wanted to believe him. But what if…

"Juliet?"

She looked back at him. "Yeah?"

"Julie is in good hands." The determination in his

eyes reassured her. "Todd isn't going to let anything happen to her."

She sighed and sat beside him. "We've never been apart like this. I'd be mad, too. It's not fair."

"You can make it up to her later when you're both safe." He took her hand and laced his fingers with hers.

The connection between them still surprised her, surreal after so many years of daydreaming from her window.

Billy reached for her chin with his free hand, raising her gaze to meet his. "If we hurry, we can get to the beach in time to watch the sun setting on the water."

Her stomach twisted with guilt. "I don't think I can."

He frowned. "We're only a couple blocks from the ocean—walking distance."

"I shouldn't see it without Julie." She pressed her lips together. "She was trapped in that house, too."

Billy got to his feet, pulling her up with him. "I give you my word when this is over, I will take you *both* to the beach."

"When this is over…" She shook her head. "What happens then?"

"Honestly? I don't know." He looked at their joined hands. "Before my brother got sick, when we'd get nervous about a new school year, my dad would tell us to take each day as it came. One day at a time. We could worry about tomorrow when it got here." His gaze wandered over her face. "You and your sister are strong. You might not realize it yet, but surviving in that house and escaping the way you did... Most people would've given up. You never did."

"I wanted to sometimes, but then another baby would come and there'd be no one but me to protect her."

"And believe it or not, leaving Moonlight Cove *is* for Julie's protection. She doesn't have to like it, but Genesis tailed my truck. We couldn't stay there any longer."

Everything he said was true, but it didn't make her feel any better. The glass case with her name on it had shocked her and propelled her into action, but she hadn't thought beyond getting out the front door. Julie-Eight depended on her.

"Juliet?"

She lifted her chin, meeting his eyes.

"We're doing the best we can." He gave her a tentative smile. "Screwing up sometimes...it makes us human."

In that instant, a dam gave way inside her heart. The weight of perfection lifted, at least for the moment. Her sister could be mad at her, and mistakes were an option now. In fact, they were expected.

And forgiven.

The death sentence that had followed her as long as she could remember was gone.

A ball of emotion choked her. She wrapped her arms around Billy's neck and clung to him, allowing the tears to come. He didn't say anything, just held her tight.

He kissed her hair. "I didn't mean to make you cry."

She pulled back enough to see his face. "It's not your fault." She sniffled. "Now I can sob until my eyes are puffy and my nose runs. I can cough, and…" She wiped her eyes and noticed his cheeks were wet, too. She frowned. "What's wrong?"

He laughed and sniffed, shaking his head. "Everything." He swiped the tear from his face and blew out a breath. "This has all been…a lot. But we're still standing. That has to count for something."

"Definitely." She nodded.

He placed his hand on her knee. "All we can do is keep getting back up and trying again."

She smiled. "Sounds like heaven to me."

He stood and offered her his hand. "Come on. Let's go see the sunset." He stopped at the closet and yanked a baseball cap from his bag. "You should probably wear this. Just in case."

She took it and went into the bathroom. She wasn't sure if they'd brought a brush, but she did her best to pull her hair back into a ponytail, her fingertips instinctively checking for bumps or flaws. Would the inspections ever end? She put on the hat and tugged her ponytail through the opening in the back.

"Well…" She turned to face him. "How do I look?"

Billy smiled, and her body warmed. "You're beautiful."

Heat crept into her cheeks as she pulled the brim down a little. “I’ve got cuts and bruises, and no makeup.”

“I stand by my answer.” He took her hand. “Come on.”

By the time they reached the beach, there were already many groups of people gathered, staring at the horizon. Juliet tightened her hold on Billy’s hand. She’d read about sunsets, seen pictures in magazines. From her bedroom window, she could see parts of the brightly colored sky, but nothing could have prepared her for this awe-inspiring view of the sunlight reflecting off the Pacific Ocean.

The setting sun dipped lower, sending a line of orange light across the surf toward her, welcoming her to the world. Her eyes brimmed with tears as the sunset painted the horizon in reds and purples. The rhythm of the waves crashing on the sand calmed her fears, coaxing her to allow hope into her heart.

Billy leaned in close to her ear, his voice soft and low. “Makes our problems seem small, right?”

Until he mentioned it, she hadn’t been able to put her finger on the peace washing through her. “Yeah. I never realized the ocean was so…huge.”

“It’s hard to really understand until you see it with your own eyes.” He tugged her hand, moving them closer to the waves. “Let’s take our shoes off. You should definitely get your feet wet.”

He led her to a bench, and they popped off their

tennis shoes and stuffed their socks inside. Billy rolled the bottom of his jeans up, exposing well-muscles calves covered in fine brown hair. Her momma used to buy Nair and watch Juliet while she applied it. Momma would mutter about ladies having smooth skin and how dangerous razors were.

He cleared his throat, and her chin shot up, heat creeping into her cheeks. Billy raised a brow. "Everything okay?"

"Yeah." She bent over to roll up her pants. "You have hair on your legs." He chuckled, and she peeked up at him with a grin. "You can add this to my new-experiences list."

"I was in boxer shorts the first night you stayed at my house."

She nodded. "I remember, but I was so distracted by your chest…" She straightened up. "I didn't notice anything below your shorts."

He wiggled his toes. "Hope they live up to your expectations."

She nudged him, laughing. "I don't have any expectations."

"Ouch." He stood up and pulled her with him.

"Ouch?"

He raised a brow with a crooked smile. "You could have just told me you think I'm good-looking."

She rose on her tiptoes and kissed his cheek, then whispered, "I always have."

Before he could respond, she dropped his hand and

sprinted across the beach. The heat warmed the bottom of her feet, but the sinking sand made it tough to keep her balance. She glanced over her shoulder. He was catching up fast. Focusing on the water's edge, she pushed her legs harder until she splashed into the waves. Running outside with the sun in her eyes was so much better than she'd ever imagined.

"Oh my god!" she squealed.

Billy raced to her side. "Are you all right?"

She nodded and started to grin. "I wasn't expecting it to be so cold."

"The Pacific is really big and deep. It never heats up much even in the summer." He chuckled. "I'm always shocked when I first get in."

Another one crashed and rolled up the sand, swirling around her calves as the sun dipped below the horizon. "Thank you for making me get out of the hotel room. This is… I never dreamed it could be this amazing."

He laced his fingers with hers. "Night's not over yet."

"No?" She smiled up at him.

"You wanted to play a sport, too, right?"

"That was on my list."

"We can head back to the hotel and get the rental car. The bowling alley is only a few miles away."

The dimming light sparkled in his bright-green eyes. She bit her lower lip.

He squeezed her hand. "What's wrong?"

“I still don’t really know what bowling is.”

The warm tone of his laughter coaxed her to join in.

“Can’t believe none of the books and magazines in your house ever mentioned bowling.” He shook his head, biting back a smile. “I’m offended.”

She started to apologize, but he grinned. “I’m also kidding.”

“So you’ll teach me?”

“You bet.” He turned away from the ocean.

Juliet stole one more look at the colorful sky, memorizing it. She was struggling to keep the truth from stealing the beauty of the moment.

There was no guarantee she’d ever see it again.

CHAPTER 20

Julie-Eight giggled as her character pummeled Todd's on the TV screen. Video games were much more fun than the puzzles they did back home. She still had lots of catching up to do to have a chance against Vanessa in this *Super Smash Brothers* game, but Todd was struggling to keep up with her.

"Geez, girl!" He nudged her with his shoulder, mashing all the buttons on his controller.

"I'm getting good at this!" A few more combo moves and it was over. Julie-Eight sprang to her feet. "I did it!"

Todd set his controller on the table. "You won fair and square."

He raised his hand, and she smacked it. Todd told her it was called a "high five." Since Juliet had gotten them out of their house, Todd had become Julie's only real friend. Cindy was nice, but she didn't play with her like Todd did.

"Are you going to stay for dinner?"

He glanced over his shoulder at Cindy. "Sick of me yet?"

Cindy rolled her eyes and came out of the kitchen. Leaning over the back of the sofa, she draped her arms around his shoulders and pressed her lips to his temple. "I'll never be sick of you."

He tipped his head back and kissed her. Julie-Eight tried not to stare. Until she'd gotten outside, the only physical affection she'd ever seen was in magazines. Her parents never touched like this.

Cindy straightened up. "How about grilled cheese sandwiches and tater tots?"

"Should we wait on Vanessa?" Todd asked.

"No, I'm sure they'll grab dinner after the symphony." Cindy's gaze shifted to Julie-Eight. "Would you like to help me make it?"

Her eyes widened. "Can I?"

Cindy nodded. "'Course you can. Come on."

Julie-Eight raced around the couch and wrapped her arms around Cindy's middle, smiling when she got hugged back. Cindy stepped back and led the way into the kitchen area. It was about half the size of the one back home with a tiny oven and a refrigerator small enough to fit inside her Momma's.

Cindy opened the top door and pulled out a plastic bag. "You can be in charge of the tater tots."

Julie-Eight had no idea what a tater tot was, but she was eager for a chance to cook something. "Should I wear gloves?"

Cindy raised a brow. "Gloves? No. I think washing your hands is good enough."

After Julie-Eight washed and dried her hands, Cindy showed her how to preheat the oven and placed a cookie sheet and a can of something that said *PAM* on it on the counter.

"Let me know if you have any trouble reading the directions."

"I'm a good reader." Julie-Eight turned the bag over.

"Well, I'm here if you need me." Cindy put the first sandwich into the frying pan.

Julie-Eight sprayed the pan and carefully spread the frozen potatoes evenly. The oven beeped, and Cindy helped her slide the tray inside.

"Smells good." Todd came over and leaned against the counter. A knock at the door interrupted them. Todd straightened, tense. "Are you expecting anyone?"

Cindy shook her head, then looked at Julie-Eight. "I'm sure it's nothing but go hide in the bedroom just in case."

She sprinted for the hallway as the lock turned and the door opened. She looked back over her shoulder as three men dressed in black came in the room.

BILL WALKED BACK to their lane and handed Juliet a ten-pound bowling ball off the rack. "See if your fingers and thumb fit in the holes."

"This is heavy." She smiled up at him, and time

slowed.

He lived on campus at UCLA, surrounded by women with perfect white smiles, slender legs tanned to perfection, and sun-kissed blond hair, but none of them made his heart race like seeing Juliet smile.

Her dark hair, soft skin, and big brown eyes made her seem almost ethereal. She was beautiful, for sure, but there was so much more to her. She'd survived in a house where her life had depended on perfection. And after she'd broken free, instead of being shocked and overwhelmed, she seemed to welcome every new experience, hungry to see, learn, touch, and taste everything.

Seeing the world through her eyes intoxicated him.

Bill cleared his throat. "It's only ten pounds. Any lighter and you'll be pitching it down the lane overhand."

A wrinkle formed between her eyebrows, and he realized she had no clue what pitching overhand was. He held the ball for her while she slid her slender fingers into the holes.

"Got it?" She nodded, and he let go of the ball, allowing her to hold the weight on her own. "Now try a gentle swing."

Her arm moved forward and back slowly a couple of times before she set the ball on the rack at their lane. "Zack told me you're really good at bowling."

"I'm all right." He chuckled and grabbed his sixteen-pound ball out of his bag. This ball was drilled to fit his hand perfectly and unlike the plastic house balls on the racks, this one was made of urethane and gripped the oiled wood of the lanes.

He stepped up on the boards, found his mark, and focused. As he exhaled, his body moved with a fluid motion he'd honed through years of practice and repetition. His smooth steps toward the foul line were timed with the back swing of his arm until he released the ball and his toe slid, stopping just before the foul line.

His ball spun as it rolled down the lane, and at the last second, it hooked into the pocket. The pins cleared completely off the lane. Damn, that felt good. He grinned and turned around to find Juliet on her feet clapping. She came to him as he walked off the lane toward the ball return. He caught her around the waist, laughing as his lips brushed hers.

He set her down, marveling at how easy it was to be with her. No drama, no concerns about what she might *really* be thinking. Just being himself was enough for her. Wild.

"Your turn."

She slid her fingers into the house ball, and he helped her up to the foul line.

"At first, it's easier to forget the approach. Just stand here at the line and focus on keeping your arm straight, let the ball swing back and forward, then release."

He showed her the foot position, and she mimicked

his stance. Then he moved behind her, helping her with her swing. She didn't wear perfume, but she smelled better than any of his college dates. He shoved the thoughts away. The last thing he needed was to get aroused at the bowling alley.

"There you go." He mumbled close to her ear. "Count three swings, and on the third, let it roll down the alley."

She followed his directions, and the ball rolled straight from her fingertips. It veered to the right, clipping the two pins in the corner. He readied himself to give her a pep talk, but when she spun around, her grin lit up the building.

"That was amazing!" She bit her lower lip, her eyes sparkling.

Warmth spread through his chest. It would be so easy to love her. He could almost hear his psych professor talking about bonding through shared trauma. Genesis had touched both their lives now.

But this felt like…more. He arched a brow. "Not bad for your first time."

She came back to the ball return and grabbed the bright-red ten-pounder. "Well, I *do* have a good teacher."

He crossed his arms, watching her place her feet and swing the ball, but his mind wandered far from the bowling alley to the big Victorian house on his street. She'd been a prisoner all those years, and it hadn't broken her spirit. She was missing her little sister, but she still chose joy over sorrow.

This time she released the ball and it slowly rolled across the lane, hitting the two pins on the other corner. She turned around, laughing. "I may have overcorrected."

He shrugged. "Four pins in a frame is better than three, right?"

She came back, and he held out his fist.

Her smile faded to a puzzled frown. "What's wrong?"

"You tap your fist to mine. It's called a fist bump."

"Why?"

"For encouragement." He smiled. "Like saying good job, without words."

Her lips curved at the corners, and she touched her knuckles to his. "Fist bump. I like it."

JULIE-EIGHT FROZE, UNABLE to move her feet.

The man in front grunted. "Get the girl."

"Who the hell are you?" Todd shoved the one coming for her, knocking him to the ground.

A second man grabbed Cindy from behind, pinning her arms. She squirmed. "Todd! Look out!"

The third man, and the biggest of them, rushed toward Todd with something sparking in his hand. Todd spun around and dodged under the weapon, tackling the guy around his knees. The weapon crashed to the ground right before they did.

Todd and the man traded punches while Julie-Eight's pulse pounded in her ears, her hands trembling. They needed help. But what could she do?

The first man crawled toward the weapon, and finally, she broke free of her panic. Julie-Eight rushed forward, kicking the black, sparking gun away from his groping fingers.

One last punch from Todd and the other man lay still. Todd stood up and turned to face the man holding Cindy. "Leave her alone," Todd growled. "She's got nothing to do with this."

The man in black shook his head. "We came for the girl, and no collegiate jock and his girlfriend are going to stop us."

Blood trickled from Todd's nose and the corner of his mouth. "Your friend over there has already been stopped. Leave now and no one needs to know you were ever here."

The man holding Cindy chuckled. "You are in no position to make deals."

The other man shot up from the floor so fast, Julie-Eight didn't have time to scream. He covered her mouth with a big-gloved hand and wrapped his arm around her waist from behind.

"Got her," he growled. She wriggled like a fish, kicking his legs repeatedly, but his grip didn't loosen. He yanked her to the door, nudging the unconscious one with his boot. "Get up."

The other man jabbed a needle into Cindy's arm, and her eyes closed. Her body went limp in his arms. Julie-Eight struggled again. Was Cindy dead?

Todd bolted forward, but the guy he'd knocked out earlier was awake again. He grabbed Todd's foot and he crashed toward the floor, hitting his forehead on the edge of the table as he went down. Julie-Eight's eyes widened, but no one could hear her shout.

Todd landed facedown and didn't move.

The man holding her dragged her toward the door, calling to the others. "Get them on the sofa."

A slender woman with white hair stepped into the apartment, shaking her head. "Fools. How difficult is it to snatch a young girl?"

Cindy's grandmother turned around and stroked Julie-Eight's hair. "I'm sorry. I truly am, but family comes first, and if anyone discovers you're a clone, I'll lose my family *and* my fortune. You understand."

Julie-Eight slammed her head back into the man's chest, but his grip didn't loosen. She didn't understand any of this. She wrenched a hand free and lashed out, smacking Claudette Sutter's cheek before the man caught her hand again.

The older woman jerked back, and a big earring fell to the floor.

Her lips pursed into a thin line as she straightened. "Take her out to the van. Don't be seen."

"Yes, ma'am."

The other two men followed them out. Once they

had Julie-Eight in the back of the van, one stuffed a sock around her mouth while the other shoved her inside a large plastic container with bars on the openings.

"Good puppy," one of them grumbled.

Hot tears ran down her cheeks. She didn't know if Todd and Cindy were alive or dead, and she had no way to find Juliet. But Mrs. Sutter's words kept echoing in her head. *You're a clone.* Julie-Eight didn't know what the word meant, but it seemed bad.

She closed her eyes and prayed Juliet would find her. Somehow.

THEY FINISHED BOWLING, and Billy drove her back to the hotel. Her head spun with wonderful new memories from the amazing day. She wanted to freeze every single moment. She'd missed out on so much, but she tried to keep the bitterness away. It would be way too easy to give in to anger.

Her cell buzzed right before the chime on Billy's phone did. He looked over at her. "It's probably Zack. Maybe he's got something on Genesis."

She clicked the text message button. Her smile faded. "He can't find Todd."

"He could be watching a movie with Cindy and Julie." He glanced at the clock on the dashboard. "Maybe they went to bed early."

Juliet wanted that to be true.

Billy didn't seem to believe it, either, though. He drove quickly, and after he parked, he tugged his phone out of his pocket, sent Zack a text, and then took her hand. "Come on, let's get inside."

Once they were locked in their hotel room, Billy opened his laptop and checked his email. "Shit."

Juliet came up behind him, goose bumps crawling up her arms. The email had a picture of Julie-Eight with…their mother. Adrenaline pumped through Juliet's bloodstream as she scanned the email.

> *We know you have Juliet. Bring her home and we'll let Julie-Eight go. She's scraped up and useless to us now anyway. If Juliet's not home tomorrow by 11:00 a.m., then Julie-Eight will never leave this house again. Juliet knows what happens to imperfect children.*

Tears made the last line blurry. "I have to go back."

Billy got up, shaking his head. "Tomorrow's your birthday. They'll kill you both. Even if you give them what they want, they won't let Julie walk away. She's too big of an exposure risk for them to let her go. You know that."

"I can't leave her there to die." Juliet choked on a sob, her hands trembling at her sides. "They were going to kill me anyway. At least I got to be free, even if it was only for a few days." She forced her gaze from her sister's picture to Billy's face. "You'll take me back tomorrow morning, and then you have to run. You can still expose them with my father's journal."

He gripped her arms. "I'm not doing this without you."

"You have to." She searched his eyes. "Please."

He let her go and went to the window. She waited for him to say something, anything, but he stayed silent. An eerie calm settled over her as she digested her decision. There was no other choice. They'd created her for this moment. She didn't *want* to die, but if her death gave Julie-Eight the chance to live, then Juliet's life meant something beyond being perfect. Her end would be painless. They wouldn't risk harming her perfect form.

She reached up and pressed the sore lump on the back of her head as a sad, defiant smile curved her lips. Deep down her parents would know she'd ruined their perfect specimen. Her only regret would be leaving Billy behind.

Juliet crossed to stand beside him. "I wish I could stay with you."

He caught her hand in his, his grip tight. "There's got to be another way." He lifted her hand to his lips. "We have to try."

His resolve to change her fate warmed her heart and made her wish it were possible, but what could they do? Between her parents using her sister as leverage and the Genesis Foundation and the police searching for her, it seemed impossible to beat them.

But hope and determination gleamed in his eyes

anyway.

She squeezed his hand. “I’m so glad you came to my door all those years ago, Billy Manning. Thank you. For everything.”

“This isn’t over yet.” He bent to kiss her lips, tender and slow, until her pulse raced. He rested his forehead on hers and whispered, “Please, Juliet. Don’t you dare tell me goodbye.”

CHAPTER 21

JULIE-EIGHT HURT ALL over by the time they let her out of the giant crate. Momma waited outside the van. She peered up at her mother, but she didn't look happy to see her.

"Look what Juliet did." She tsked as she looked Julie-Eight over. "No one would believe you were ever perfect. Not anymore. You're ruined. Like a piece of garbage."

Angry tears welled in Julie-Eight's eyes as she clenched her fists. "Other kids don't have to be perfect, Momma."

She snatched Julie-Eight's arm in a tight grip and yanked her in close to her face, her bitter breath puffing on Julie-Eight's cheek. "That's because they're sick and weak. Now you're nothing. A waste of time, that's what you are."

Julie-Eight tugged, trying to break free from her mother's tight grip. "They aren't garbage. They're happy!"

"Is that so?" Her mother shoved her backward as she let go. "You've only been gone a few days and you've already ruined yourself. You're too selfish to understand. You could have changed the world."

An unwanted tear rolled down Julie-Eight's cheek. "I never wanted to change the world. I just wanted to be a kid, like everyone else."

The sting of the smack to her cheek shocked her. Her mother grabbed her arm again and dragged her through the back door into the kitchen. Julie-Eight's face burned, and she touched the corner of her mouth. She stared at her fingertips. Blood.

"You've needed that for years." Her mother tucked a lock of hair behind her ear.

Julie-Eight started to reply but thought better of it. Nothing she said was going to get her out of this house. It would only make her mother angrier. Instead, she spun around and ran up the stairs to her bedroom. She slammed the door and threw herself onto the bed, screaming into her pillow.

Heavy footsteps creaked on the staircase. Two sets. Out of habit, she sat up and wiped her face, wincing as her salty tears stung the new cut on her lip. The bedroom door opened with so much force the knob dented the drywall.

Her mother stormed into the center of the room, nostrils flaring. "How dare you walk away from me!"

Fear swelled, overpowering Julie-Eight's anger. She pulled her knees up to her chest, hoping to hide her newly blemished mouth. "Sorry, Momma."

Her father hovered behind, face stern and eyes narrowed. "All this work for nothing. Look at your damned knees. Scrapes. You're worthless."

A tear rolled down Julie-Eight's cheek.

Her mother struck like a cobra, snatching Julie-Eight's upper arm and yanking her off the bed so fast that she gasped for air. Momma slammed Julie-Eight against the wall. "If anyone should be shedding tears, it's me and your father. You have no idea how much we've sacrificed, you ungrateful piece of shit."

Julie-Eight blinked hard, struggling to keep from crying. Her heart raced. Usually when Momma got really mad, her father would step in and remind her not to leave a mark.

Not this time. He shook his head and turned away. "Not too rough, Martha. We need her alive. She's our leverage to get Juliet back."

His footsteps creaked on the stairs, and Julie-Eight's heart sank. Survival instinct kicked in. She struggled to pry her mother's fingers off her shoulders. "Let me go. Please, Momma. You're hurting me."

"Just like you hurt *me*." She jerked Julie-Eight away from the wall and dragged her down the stairs to the closet outside the kitchen.

The closet without a light inside.

"No!" Julie-Eight screeched, yanking backward, but her mother was too strong. "Please! I promise I'll be good!"

Momma threw her in. Julie-Eight hit the back wall and fell to her knees.

"You were so beautiful and perfect." She shook her head, speaking as she closed the door. "They polluted you. I could have kept you safe."

The lock clicked, and Julie-Eight screamed, banging her fists on the door as the darkness suffocated her.

BILL OPENED SKYPE while Juliet pulled a chair over to sit beside him. One more click and Zack's and Todd's faces filled the screen.

"Holy shit, Todd. What happened?" His friend's right eye was swollen shut, and the corner of his mouth was cut as if he'd just gone a couple rounds with a prizefighter.

Juliet sat by Bill and gasped. "They attacked you? Was it someone from Genesis?"

Todd shrugged. "I'm not sure who they were, but you should've seen the other guys." He sobered. "They got Julie. I'm sorry. Cindy and I tried to stop them."

Bill rested his hand on Juliet's leg, grateful when she laid hers on top. He needed her to stay strong and believe in him. Somehow, he was going to find a way out of this mess. He had to. He couldn't just hand her back to them like a lamb to slaughter. No way.

"I got an email from them. They want to trade Juliet for her sister. We need to be there by eleven o'clock tomorrow morning."

Zack leaned in closer. "It's a trap."

"Yeah." Bill nodded. "And there's not much time to come up with a better plan."

"Before you start planning, things are more complicated than we realized." Todd held up a sparkly earring with a quarter-sized pearl inlay.

Bill frowned. "What's that?"

Todd twisted it in the light. "When Cindy and I came to, we tore through her place looking for any clues to figure out who those guys were, and we found this."

"An earring?"

"It's a clip-on." Todd met his eyes. "Cindy said her grandmother is the only person she knows who wears them."

Bill glanced at Juliet and back to the screen. "I'm not following."

Todd held the earring closer to the webcam. "Her grandmother was there at the abduction."

Bill sat back in his chair, his mind spinning. "Her grandmother knows about Genesis? How is that possible?"

The color drained from Juliet's face. "My sister said Cindy's grandmother was asking her lots of questions. I thought her imagination was running away with her, but...what if she was right? Maybe she said the wrong thing and Cindy's grandmother called my parents."

The web kept widening. He'd thought Genesis was the Huffs, but then his parents were mixed up with it, and now Cindy's grandmother, too? How many people in Moonlight Cove were connected to the Genesis Foundation?

Juliet straightened, leaning closer to the computer screen. "Julie also told me she saw pictures of Cindy and her sister, and they were like us. Identical." She shook her head, a tear slipping free. "She was so angry that Vanessa didn't need to stay perfect like us. I told her she was wrong. But…what if she was right?"

"Whoa." Zack moved in front of the camera. "So Cindy's grandmother might be working with Genesis?"

"She's rich." Bill's mouth went dry. "She could be funding them."

Zack rolled his chair to the side, his fingers flying on the other keyboard while he spoke. "Let me check my reports for her name."

Todd looked over at him. "She has a nonprofit that gives away grants. I think it's called the Sutter Syndicate or something like that."

Juliet rubbed her forehead. "Where's Cindy? Is she okay?"

"Not really." Todd sighed. "Physically, she's fine. They injected her with a sedative, so she didn't get roughed up like I did. But when she found her grandmother's earring on the carpet…" He shook his head. "She's shaken up."

"Where is she now?" Bill asked.

Juliet reached for the hotel notepad and a pen and started writing.

"Cindy's at her place." Todd cracked his neck. "Her

grandmother is supposed to bring Vanessa home tonight, and if her grandmother really is involved somehow, Cindy doesn't want her to know we suspect her."

"Good plan." Bill leaned in closer. "What are we going to do?"

Zack looked up from his screen. "Right now, the options seem to be that Juliet either goes home or she doesn't."

Bill pulled his hair back from his forehead. "Both those scenarios end with someone dead. We need another option."

"What about the journal?" Todd asked.

Bill glanced at Juliet. "That research and the money trail are the only hopes of getting Genesis to leave you alone."

Juliet stopped writing and looked up. "What if I go back and tell them Billy won't turn over the journal until they deliver my sister to him. That could buy Zack some time to see if he can find evidence of a connection between the Sutter nonprofit and Genesis."

Oh, he hated this plan already. Choking back the dread, he forced his voice to stay even. "You're saying we do exactly what your parents asked and trade you for your sister? I'm not leaving you there, Juliet. We'll find another way."

She squeezed his hand. "Once you have Julie, you can demand a ransom for the journal or you'll give it to the media. I can tell them you want me to deliver the money. They won't want me to be the one to meet you for the exchange, but they won't have much choice..."

Bill turned the idea over in his head. "How do we know they won't have a sharpshooter nearby to kill us both? I'm a threat now, too. I know too much."

The memory of his mother's dead eyes taunted him, the tiny hole in her forehead. One minute she'd been talking, the next, gone.

"Wait a second." Todd leaned back in his chair. "If Claudette Sutter is really funding these scientists, maybe Cindy can help."

Bill's shoulders ached. When he used to wish he was grown up, he never dreamed the stakes would be so high. He stared at Todd. "How?"

"Cindy comes with us to pick up the ransom. If we grab Juliet and run, that sharpshooter wouldn't risk a shot if Claudette's granddaughter could become a casualty—not if she's funding them."

Juliet frowned. "Haven't we put Cindy in enough danger already?"

"She feels horrible that they took Julie, and if her grandmother is involved, too, it'd be tough to keep her away from all this."

Bill crossed his arms. "Be sure she knows what these people did to my mom. I don't want her to agree without understanding what she's getting into."

"You seriously think I *want* to put her in this position?" Todd raised the brow over his good eye. "Fuck you, Bill."

"Sorry." Bill shook his head. "I just don't want anyone else getting hurt."

Zack filled the screen again. "I'll keep looking for a connection with the Sutter Syndicate. There were definitely some large donations from nonprofits."

Todd rubbed the top of his head. "How did Cindy's grandmother get mixed up with scientists bent on cloning human beings in the first place?"

"I'm not sure." Bill shrugged. "My parents got involved after David died. My mom said the research was a way to make sure families in the future didn't go through the pain of losing a child. Maybe Mrs. Sutter lost someone, too."

Todd froze for a second, then straightened up. "Juliet, your sister told you that Cindy and Vanessa were like you?"

Juliet nodded, and Todd cursed under his breath. "Cindy had cancer when she was twelve. She needed a bone marrow donor, but her parents and grandmother weren't a match. Cindy's mom couldn't have any more kids, but Cindy's grandma found a surrogate. Vanessa was born via surrogate, paid for by Cindy's grandmother. She turned out to be a perfect match."

Bill's heart raced. "Oh shit. Claudette had Genesis clone Cindy's DNA."

"It's definitely a possibility." Todd looked over at Zack and back to the screen. "Maybe she's funding them out of gratitude or to keep them quiet about Vanessa. Either way, she's got to be mixed up in all this."

Bill blew out a pent-up breath. "Okay, since she's involved, and her love for Cindy was what got her tangled up in this mess, having Cindy with us at the exchange might work."

Zack stopped typing. "If I can get proof that the Sutter Syndicate is tied to Genesis, we'll have the upper hand."

Juliet set her pen down. "But if you don't have it by eleven o'clock tomorrow morning, I'm going back. When my parents release Julie, I'll tell them Billy has my father's journal and if they want it back, they'll have need to pay fifty thousand dollars, and I have to deliver the money or he'll give the journal to the media and the government."

Bill was not a fan of this plan, but at the moment, he couldn't come up with anything better.

Zack turned back to his keyboard, calling over his shoulder. "If the money trail exists, I'll find it."

"I'll talk to Cindy and be sure she's ready, too," Todd said.

Maybe this *would* work. Or it could all be wishful thinking. He shook his head. "Thanks, guys. I owe you big-time. We'll check in with you early in the morning."

Bill ended the Skype call and closed the laptop. He looked at to Juliet. "Talk to me. Do you really think this will work?"

She shrugged, wiping a tear from the corner of her eye. "I have no idea."

He took her hand. "I wish I could call the police, but they'll take you back even sooner."

"I know." She slid her hand free to dry her other eye.

Silence settled between them. He grabbed the remote and turned on the television, eager for a distraction. He watched the clock. It was almost midnight, almost Juliet's birthday, and he'd be damned if it passed without notice.

"I'll be right back. Don't answer the door for anyone." He held up the plastic card. "I have my key right here."

"Okay." She paused and added, "Where are you going?"

"It's a surprise."

He slipped out and went to the lobby. He couldn't risk leaving Juliet at the hotel alone so he'd have to improvise. Luckily, the guy at the desk was willing to help. With two warm chocolate cookies in hand, Bill stopped at the soda machine. He opted for two Sprites and headed back up to the room.

He opened the door and stepped inside. "Happy birthday, Juliet."

She got up and came over with a soft smile on her lips. "It's after midnight. I guess I'm officially eighteen."

He handed her a cookie and set the sodas down. "They didn't have any cake. I figured a cookie was better than nothing."

She took a bite and hummed. "Thank you. This is good."

He popped the cans of soda open and held his up. "We should toast."

She looked confused for a second. "Like champagne at New Year's?"

"Or Sprite on your birthday." He glanced at her can and back up. "So?"

She lifted her can, and he tapped his to hers. "Here's to many more birthdays."

Her smile faltered a little, but she sipped the soda.

He turned off the television and she got up, walking to the window as she finished her cookie. "I'm afraid to go back."

He crossed to her, sliding his arms around her waist from behind. "I wish there were another way."

"Maybe Zack will find the evidence we need." She rested her head back against his chest. "Once she's free, don't let Julie stay at Cindy's house again. If her grandmother is involved with Genesis, I don't want her to be captured again."

"I won't." Christ, he didn't want to talk about any of this. It just meant Juliet would be locked up in that house again. "I'll keep her with me until we get you back. I'll get another hotel. She'll be safe."

Turning around, she stared up at him. "Thank you."

She rose on her toes and kissed him. Her tongue brushed his lips tentatively, and he opened to her, moaning as he tightened his embrace. All his fear, anger, and hope poured into this one moment. He walked her back to the bed, laying her down without breaking the kiss.

Her hands slid under his shirt, exploring his back. Gradually, she pulled back. Breathless, her gaze locked on his. "Make love to me."

Blood was already pumping below his belt, and under normal circumstances, he'd think the universe was smiling on him. But he hesitated to reach for the condom in his wallet. He brought his hand up to cup her cheek. He started to speak, and she pressed her fingertip over his lips to silence him.

"Please don't try to talk me out of this," she whispered. "I've read about it in books. This may be my only chance…"

Her words hung between them. She didn't need to finish the thought. They both understood.

"We're going to get out of there." He brushed his lips to her forehead. "You're going to have plenty of chances." He couldn't believe the words falling from his lips. He wanted to shake himself. His erection pulsed between them, aching for release, but he still didn't make a move for the condom. "We don't have to rush anything."

The corner of her mouth twitched, hiding a smile. "From what I've read, guys like to rush in this particular area."

He didn't know what she'd been reading, but he

loved that she never stopped surprising him. He chuckled, whispering against her lips, "I've done my fair share of rushing at college, but I'd like to take my time with you."

Her teeth teased his lower lip. "I'd like to forget about tomorrow and live for tonight while I can."

His heart pounded in his ears. He stared down at Juliet, his voice hoarse. "You're sure about this?"

"Yes." She nodded, a sparkle in her eyes. "I'd like to be completely imperfect."

Imperfect. No way. He shook his head, eager to forget about tomorrow, too. "Juliet, nothing we do together could make you imperfect, or broken, or whatever those assholes told you. You're beautiful and intelligent and brave. No one can take that from you unless you let them."

She smiled, running her fingers through his hair. "Before we leave this room, I want you to know something."

Was she going to say what he thought she was?

He'd never told Cassie that he loved her. In fact, he'd never said those words to anyone he wasn't related to, but he was ready to put his life on the line to save Juliet. Spending time with her made the rest of the world fade away. He wasn't ready to give that up yet. Maybe he'd never be ready. Was that love?

He blinked. The words were on the tip of his tongue, but telling her he loved her now terrified him, like they were giving up on having a future together.

No way.

He kissed her before she could say anything more. When he drew back, he whispered, “Tell me when we get you out of that house. Right now, there is no tomorrow. Only tonight.”

She nodded and fused her lips to his as he reached for the condom in his wallet.

CHAPTER 22

FOR HOURS THEY touched, tasted, and explored each other's bodies. It was exciting and overwhelming, introducing her to a whole new kind of hunger. They'd had sex. Twice.

She'd imagined the act would instantly make her feel like a woman, some nebulous line would be crossed and she'd be an adult, mature. Mostly it just made leaving him behind even harder.

Now she knew what she'd be missing locked up in that house.

Billy drifted to sleep on his stomach, his arm draped across her waist. His back rose and fell, peaceful. She smiled in the dim light of the hotel room. He'd managed to keep her mind off the coming morning and showed her another thing worth living for.

But there was a good chance she didn't have much more time left to live. And sleep was the last thing she wanted to waste it on. The clock on the nightstand ticked away, counting down the seconds until she was back in that suffocating house.

She flicked her gaze to the ceiling. Her parents had

told her religion was myths and superstition. Maybe they were right, but just in case they were wrong, she sent up a silent prayer for Julie-Eight, for herself, and for Billy and his friends. It couldn't hurt.

In the darkness, bitterness swelled. None of this was fair. She was eighteen years old. She should be able to fall in love just like other girls.

But she and Julie-Eight weren't like other girls.

"Dammit." She slipped out of the bed and into a hotel robe.

Somehow her first curse word wasn't as fulfilling as she'd imagined it would be.

Billy stirred, lifting his head. "Are you okay?"

"Just need to use the bathroom."

He drifted off again, and she carefully closed the door. After turning the sink on high, she put the lid down on the toilet and sat down. Tears gave way to quiet sobs.

A gentle knock on the door interrupted her pity party.

"Juliet? Can I come in?"

She sniffled and wiped her eyes. "Yeah."

He opened the door, and although they'd just spent a very intimate night together, it still surprised her to see him standing naked in the doorway. Not a bad surprise, though. Not by a long shot.

He came in and knelt in front of her. "What's wrong?" He chuckled despite the worry in his eyes. "Besides everything."

She sniffed, rolling her eyes. "I don't want to go back there." She lifted her gaze to his face. "I'm angry. Really angry. I want more time."

He laced his fingers with hers, squeezing tightly. "You have every right to be mad. None of this is your fault. It's not fair."

She smirked. "You're not helping to dampen the rage here."

"Good." His bright-green eyes sparked with intensity. He was no longer the college kid who took her in a few days ago; she could see the man he was becoming. "Anger can make you strong. We're not going to leave you in that house." He swallowed, his voice a little lower. "I'm not going to lose you."

She wrapped her arms around him, clinging tight as he held her. She closed her eyes remembering her little sister telling her she wanted to grow up to be brave like Juliet. Right now, she didn't feel brave. More scared than anything. But she'd read somewhere that true bravery was being afraid but showing up anyway.

The thought struck a chord in her soul. Her parents and Genesis all thought she was just a thing they created in a lab.

She whispered against his ear. "I'm stronger than they know."

He stepped back to look into her eyes. "And that's exactly how we'll beat them."

JULIE-EIGHT SAT IN the dark with her knees pulled up to her chest. She'd run out of tears hours ago. The terror had given way to exhaustion, and sleep had given her an escape from the darkness. She had no idea how long she'd slept when her bladder woke her.

She banged on the door until her hand ached.

No one was coming for her.

She finally relieved herself in the back corner of the closet. And now she waited in the timeless inky blackness of her prison. Her stomach growled, protesting the lack of food, and her throat was dry from thirst.

How long had it been since her mother had locked her in here? Papa had said they needed her alive to get Juliet back. Did that mean her sister was going to give herself back to them?

Suddenly dishes clinked on the other side of the door. Her heart raced, and she fought the urge to bang on the door again. If Momma was still angry at her, interrupting her cooking would only lengthen the punishment.

The scent of eggs and bacon slid under the door like a serpent. She scooted closer, and lay down, pressing her face to the bottom seam, inhaling deeply. Her belly knotted up, eager for food.

Her mother's voice was muffled. "Ready to do what your told now?"

"Yes," Julie-Eight answered. Her throat was scratchy and hoarse.

The door opened, and she shielded her eyes from the bright light. Momma grabbed her arm and yanked her onto her feet. She pushed Julie-Eight forward to the kitchen. "Go sit at your place."

When she got to her chair, she stared at the plate full of bread crusts, scraps of bacon, and leftover yellow goo from the yolks of fried eggs. She glanced at her mother, puzzled.

Momma crossed her arms. "You're as useless as a dog now so you might as well eat like one."

"But someone already ate this food."

Momma nodded. "I was going to toss these scraps in the garbage, but then I remembered we had a *dog*."

Hot tears stung her eyes, but hunger won over her pride. There was no silverware so she used her hands, promising herself this wasn't going to be forever. Juliet was coming, and Julie-Eight would be outside again, just like before.

Somehow.

BILL GLANCED AT his friends. "For the record, I hate this plan."

They'd been in Zack's garage discussing all the details since six o'clock in the morning. Bill was beginning to think they might be talking themselves in circles. Todd's face was still healing, but Cindy looked uninjured standing beside him.

Cindy cleared her throat, looking over at Juliet. "I had no idea my grandmother was involved with Genesis. I never would have taken in Julie if I had known. I'm so sorry."

Bill ran his hand up Juliet's back, hoping to give her some support.

Juliet shook her head. "We'll get her back, but once she's out, she needs a new place to hide."

"I'm taking her to a new hotel in Los Angeles." Bill met her eyes. "I'll watch her myself until we get you out. Then we go right to the media."

Todd peered over Zack's shoulder, staring at the computer screen. "Any evidence yet, Z-Man?"

Zack groaned. "You know, hacking through a firewall isn't as simple as typing 'the Sutter Syndicate' into the search engine. I'm working as fast as I can." He looked up at Bill. "I did find one connection though." He pulled up another window on his screen and pointed to a news article. "This is from ten years ago. The Sutter Syndicate bought controlling stock in Eden Incorporated."

Bill gripped Zack's shoulder. "We've got them."

Zack shook his head. "Not quite. I still need the link between Eden and Genesis, but we do have proof the Sutter Syndicate is one of their biggest backers. We're close though."

Bill scanned the group. "What if we tell them Juliet

needs to deliver the money in twenty-four hours? They won't be able to put her in a glass case on her birthday like they planned because she needs to deliver the ransom for the journal, and hopefully that'll be enough time for Zack to find the money connection between Eden and Genesis so we can give it to the media and the police. It's our only insurance against Genesis."

"Not quite." Zack leaned back in his chair. "I'm also working on a backup plan. If I can't connect the Sutter Syndicate to Genesis, I did manage to hack into the 'vitamin' formula they claim to be manufacturing. It's definitely a cover for the cloning. According to the file I downloaded, the pills are basically a run-of-the-mill one-a-day multivitamin. It won't be as strong as the money trail, but that's still fraud."

Bill clapped his shoulder. "You rock." He glanced at the clock. His bagel from breakfast sat like a stone in his gut. "I guess we'd better get going."

Todd and Cindy went out to her car. Zack wasn't going with them. He'd stay here and keep looking for the evidence they needed.

Bill took Juliet's hand. "Let's talk really quick."

He led her out of the garage but didn't go to the car just yet. He stared into her eyes, his chest tight. "Promise me you'll be careful in there."

"I will."

He sighed. "I don't like giving you back to them on your birthday. They were going to have some creepy board meeting celebrating your body in a glass case."

"They need that journal, and they need me to get it."

"If all the board still shows up, there's a chance my dad might be there too." He cupped her cheek, wishing like hell they could just go back to the hotel. "Our family has a safe word. It's *iridescence.* If you say that to him, he'll know I trust you. Maybe he can help."

"He didn't before." Her gaze drifted lower. "Why would he help me now?"

Bill caught his finger under her chin, lifting it until she met his eyes. "Because you're going to tell him that I love you."

The words fell from his lips so naturally, he hadn't realized he was going to say them until they were out of his mouth.

A puzzled crease formed on her forehead for a second, then gave way to a smile. "I..."

He kissed her before she could finish her response. This wasn't going to be goodbye if he could help it, and he wanted some things left unsaid. It meant they'd need to be together again. They'd have unfinished business.

Or so he hoped.

Maybe he'd written too much fiction.

Resting his forehead against hers, he whispered, "Come back safe, and we'll finish this conversation." Her eyes shone with understanding. He'd never met another person who got him like she did. "You remember the word?"

"Iridescence."

"Good." He took her hand. "Let's do this."

WHEN CINDY PARKED on the street in front of the towering Victorian house, nausea bubbled in the back of Juliet's throat and panic churned in her belly.

This house was her prison.

Cindy got out first. If everything went according to plan, Billy would grab Julie-Eight and stay close to Cindy. They were betting their lives that no one would risk hurting Cindy, but Zack found the connection between the Sutter Syndicate and Eden Incorporated. Cindy's grandmother was definitely backing them.

She opened the passenger door and looked down at Juliet. "Ready?"

"No." Juliet's voice was hoarse.

Bill got out of the back seat and helped her up. "You're not going anywhere until we have Julie."

Juliet nodded and stood up. The front door of the house opened, and Julie-Eight stepped onto the porch. Momma was right behind her, gripping her shoulders so tightly she'd probably leave marks.

"Juliet!" Her mother shouted. "Come up here."

Her heart raced like a rabbit at the sound of her mother's command.

Maybe Billy sensed it because he yelled back. "Send Julie down to us, and Juliet will come up."

She narrowed her eyes. "You don't get to make the rules."

"Meet us halfway, or we'll get right back in the car."

"Fine." She shoved Julie forward and down the stairs.

Juliet walked toward her sister, with Cindy and Billy on either side of her. She glanced up at the windows, at her bedroom. So much had changed since she was last locked inside this place. When they were only a few feet apart from her sister, Julie-Eight broke free from their mother's grip and raced to Juliet.

Juliet hugged her tight.

Julie-Eight whispered, "Don't go in there. Momma is so angry."

Juliet pulled back to look at her sister and frowned. Julie-Eight's face was bruised and swollen. The fear faded as anger swelled. She glared at her mother. "You hurt her."

"No." He mother shook her head slowly. "*You* hurt her. You're so selfish. You took that perfect girl from this house, and then you let her get cuts and bruises. Years of work down the toilet." She held out her hand. "Let's go."

Julie-Eight wailed, clinging to Juliet's waist. "Don't. Don't go in there."

"I'll be okay." Tears welled up. "You have to go with Billy now."

"They'll hurt you." Julie-Eight sniffled. "Come with us."

Juliet peeled her sister free from her waist. "I'll see you soon."

Billy picked up her sister and carried her to the car with Cindy covering them. Julie-Eight's sobbing stabbed at Juliet's heart. "They hate us, Juliet. No…"

Momma grabbed Juliet's wrist so hard her breath caught. "Time to go."

Juliet craned her neck, looking back as her mother dragged her up the steps. Billy carried Julie-Eight to the car, and Cindy stayed too close for anyone to risk shooting Billy or Julie-Eight the way they did Billy's mom. Just like they planned.

Cindy drove away with Julie-Eight's tear-stained face pressed against the back window.

Juliet blinked hard. She wouldn't cry. She wouldn't give her mother the satisfaction.

The door opened, and something broke inside her. Her fight-or-flight instinct kicked in. She yanked her wrist out of her mother's grasp and turned to run.

"Juliet." Her name became a command when her father said it.

She hesitated.

"Wait in the kitchen, Martha." His voice was grim as he put his hand on Juliet's shoulder. "You know there's nowhere you can run."

Slowly she faced her father. "I'm not going to be your prisoner again."

"You'll be free sooner than you think."

Adrenaline teased her blood stream. "You never

cared about me or any of the Julies. We were just funding to you. Clones."

"I cared about each and every one of you. I did my best to keep all of you perfect." A muscle jumped in his cheek. "And I succeeded. The first perfect specimen. Because of you, children won't have to face sickness or infant death. Your DNA is going to change the world. Because of my work, you'll be remembered forever. You're going to be immortal, Juliet."

"My DNA?" The shrill tone of her voice surprised her as the rage sparked again. "I'm a human being. I want my *life* to change the world, not my DNA. I'm eighteen years old, and I've never seen a movie or driven a car. This is far from 'perfect.'"

He shook his head. "I know it might not seem fair right now, but you are proof my research works. We can genetically engineer more Julies based on your DNA. Children that we can guarantee will reach adulthood."

Research. That was all she'd ever be to him. Bitterness simmered in her belly. "I was only perfect because you kept me inside, constantly watched and protected. That's not perfection, it's torture." She shook her head. It doesn't matter. You won't be able to recreate your work anyway." She swallowed the lump in her throat. "My friends have your research journal. The one with my name embossed on the front."

Shock wiped the heretical spark from his eyes. He must've been too busy searching for her to notice it was gone. His jaw slackened for a second before he pressed his lips together, color rising from his neck up into his cheeks. "You stupid girl." He ground his teeth. "You have no idea what you've done."

She shook her head. "Actually, I do. My friends are willing to return the research journal for fifty thousand dollars." Juliet crossed her arms. "And I need to deliver the payment in person. You have twenty-four hours."

"No. Absolutely not."

"Then they'll hand it over to the police and the media." She balled her hands into fists and walked through the front door. "I'm either delivering the money to them or you'll have to tell Genesis all their research is about to be exposed. I guess it's up to you now."

His eyes widened, and his lips pressed so tight they became a white line. "You've killed us all."

CHAPTER 23

CINDY DROVE THEM back to Zack's while Bill watched for tails. No cars followed them. When she pulled into Zack's driveway, Bill ran a hand his hand down his face. They'd made it.

Hopefully Juliet was all right.

Zack came out to greet them with a tentative smile. "How'd it go?" Apparently, Julie's bruised face and Bill's bleak expression gave him his answer. He sobered. "Shit. What happened?"

Bill pushed his hair back from his forehead. "We left Juliet there with her cruel parents."

Julie sniffled, and he instantly regretted his words. Dammit.

He knelt beside her. "I'm sorry. I shouldn't have—"

She clamped her arms around his neck, sobbing against his chest. Bill held her tight and lifted her up. He glanced at Todd. "She should probably see a doctor to make sure she's okay."

Todd shook his head. "Too risky."

"I know, but..." All of this was too risky. What the hell were they doing? Did he honestly believe they could handle this on their own? If anything happened to Juliet…

He didn't even want to think about it so he changed the subject. "Did you find anything else?"

"Claudette Sutter paid Eden in three payments, and according to Cindy, one of the dates is Vanessa's birthday. I'm still trying to get the money trail between Eden and Genesis." Zack sighed. "I know it's there. I just haven't found it yet."

"You will." Bill carried Julie to the rental car and opened the door. After setting her on the passenger seat, her hold on him loosened. "I'm going to take you to Los Angeles. They won't find you there. I promise."

Cindy bent over close to Julie. "I'm so sorry." She frowned as she looked over the girl's banged-up face. "Did they do this to you?"

Julie nodded. "They're going to kill Juliet. She shouldn't have come for me."

Bill did his best to comfort her. "We have your dad's notes. They're going to have to let Juliet go if they want them back."

"Why do his notes matter?" She wiped her nose.

"Because they can't make more girls like you and Juliet without them."

She sniffled. "They're real mad."

Seeing the bruises on her face and arm tormented him. Were they beating Juliet right now, too? He prayed they still needed her "perfect."

For once, that obsession with perfection could actually save her.

JULIET SAT IN the kitchen, baffled by the panic in her father's voice.

"We can't let the board come here tonight, Martha. Not now."

Momma put dishes away like this was any other day. "It's too late. Some of them are already in the air flying here."

He paced the linoleum like a caged prisoner. "Then we need to run."

"Run?" She tossed the towel off her shoulder and onto the countertop. "This is your moment, Ed. You did it." She pointed at Juliet. "She's perfect. Just like you promised she would be. Birth to eighteen years old without a single cold or disease. Tonight, they'll enshrine Juliet as the first, and then you'll have all the financial backing you need. You're changing the world. We can't miss that."

Her mother grabbed the dishtowel and tucked it into the handle on the oven door as if they weren't discussing sacrificing Juliet in order to procure more funding.

Her father glared at Juliet. "The Manning boy has my research journal. They won't return it unless Juliet delivers the cash. She can't be preserved tonight."

Her momma's eyes widened as she turned to face

her. "You ungrateful waste of skin. You could've been the next Eve, bringing humanity back to the Garden of Eden. And you threw it all away, for what? The poison garbage outside and a worthless, stupid boy."

"Enough!" Juliet shot out of the chair. "Keeping me locked up in this house for eighteen years doesn't make me perfect, and it doesn't prove anything. Of course I never got sick. When did I ever meet anyone with a cold? All you've done is clone my DNA and killed innocent babies and children you deemed less than your ideal for perfection. How twisted is that? They were human beings, not test subjects. You didn't terminate *subjects*; you killed *children*."

"Shut up," her mother growled.

"No." Juliet shook her head. "I won't. In the time I was out there in the world, I learned something. No one is perfect, and that's what makes them unique and special."

Her mother pulled her hand back to slap her. Juliet winced, but her father caught her mother's wrist.

"No." He growled. "No bruises."

She yanked her arm away. "What does it matter now? They're all going to be here for the ceremony, and if we can't enshrine her, we'll have to tell them your journal is missing. They won't give us the money without it. They paid for data and research, but the database is useless without your notes."

"You think I don't know that?" He went back to pacing. "We have to buy some time." Stopping, he turned to his wife. "Do you know what they did to Anita Manning? They sent an assassin to silence her. We'll be next. No loose ends."

Martha's face paled. "Call Frank. We need an exit plan."

JULIET STARED DOWN at the street from her seat by the window. Locked in her bedroom, gloves back in place and puffy socks on her feet instead of the tennis shoes she'd borrowed from Billy's mom's closet. It was hard to believe she'd ever left this house.

But her time with Billy hadn't been a dream.

He loved her.

In the tempest of anger and fear, his simple, honest words were a tether to hope. She'd get out of this. Somehow.

They took the cell phone Zack had given her. She had no way to warn him that her parents were going to take her and run. And there was no telling where she'd end up. But nothing would keep her from finding Billy again. Nothing.

The door opened behind her. She turned around, surprised to find a familiar face in a lab coat.

Billy's dad. She knew that now.

She stood up. "Are you Frank?"

He took a tentative step inside, glancing over his shoulder. He kept his voice hushed. "Yes. Frank

Manning."

She didn't move any closer. "Why are you here?"

"You have to understand, this research has the capacity to change the world. Your sacrifice will save millions of lives."

Juliet stoked embers of her rage until it flared to life inside her again. What had Billy said? Stay angry. It made her strong.

She crossed her arms. "But *my* life is worthless? Are you saying the data is more important than my soul?"

"Soul?" He blanched but didn't apologize. "You're the world's most miraculous science experiment. Your DNA was the result of hours and hours of work and trial and error. We had others before you, but they couldn't maintain perfection. You were the first of the in vitro efforts to pay off."

Her brows pinched together. "The Huffs…aren't my biological parents?"

"You were genetically engineered, created in our lab. We implanted your embryo into Martha. Once you passed the first-year milestone, we replicated your DNA. The first several Julies didn't meet the standards, but we reached perfection again when Julie-Eight was born. Don't you see? You're…" He fumbled for words. "You're the property of the Genesis Foundation lab."

Baffled, she dropped her arms, her hands balling into fists at her side. "I'm not anyone's *property*. I'm eighteen years old, and I should have my whole life ahead of me."

"You don't understand."

"How you could raise Billy to be such a good person, and meanwhile you're working for people who kill children for being imperfect?"

He cocked his head. "Billy is exactly why I'm doing this work. I don't want him to have a child who might die of cancer, or have a birth defect, or countless other maladies."

"Billy loves me." She waited for her words to sink in. "He will *never* forgive you if anything happens to me."

He frowned, then raised his eyebrows. "I'm impressed with your high level of manipulation. I'll make a note on our critical-thinking data."

He didn't believe her. She was *still* just a "thing," a lab rat. "I'm not lying. We met years ago, before I escaped."

He shook his head. "Impossible."

"He came to my door on my ninth birthday. I kissed his cheek. Ask him."

"Enough." He frowned. "Come with me. We're leaving for a safe house."

She didn't move. "Iridescence."

Billy's father froze. "What did you say?"

"He told me it's your safe word so you'd know it came from him."

Mr. Manning stepped farther into her room, leaning on the vanity table. "Why would he tell you that?"

She searched his eyes. "Because I'm not a science experiment. I'm human, just like you, and I love your son."

He studied her for a moment, like he was really seeing her for the first time. He shook his head, his expression pained. "We have to go."

She went to the top drawer of her dresser and retrieved the graphic novels he'd given her over the years and fanned them out in front of him. "I learned to draw from these books you brought me. Billy and I want to publish his comic. He's writing it, and I'm illustrating."

She lifted her eyes to meet his. "I have a heart and soul. I want a future"—her voice wobbled—"with your son."

He cleared his throat. "I can't do this." He turned and closed the door. "Bill is all I have left in this world. If I help you, you have to promise me you'll persuade him to hide. I know he wants to finish college, but they'll find him there."

Juliet nodded, choosing not to mention their plans to expose Genesis. Her trust was with Billy and his friends, not the man that thought of her as property of a lab until a few moments ago.

"There was a fire at one of the other Genesis pods once. It killed the science team and destroyed the basement lab."

"Pods?" She frowned.

"Another house, like this one. We have to stay small, hidden in the suburbs." He checked the door again. "When word got out it was arson, the rumor was that Genesis had ordered its destruction. Dr. Huff deleted all his real research from the database. They were furious, but it was his insurance policy. We were no longer expendable. They'd need us alive. Tonight, they're all coming here for your ceremony and to wire transfer money in exchange for the data in your father's journal."

"That's why he's running. He doesn't have the journal."

He nodded. "Whatever you and Bill have planned, it won't work. All that matters is the research. Your lives are worthless to them."

"You're wrong." She swallowed. "We know one of the donors funding Genesis and her granddaughter is helping us."

His jaw dropped. "That's impossible. We don't even know the donors."

"We also know this donor paid for her granddaughter to be cloned. They live in town here."

Confusion shone in his eyes as he shook his head. "No, it's too risky."

"I'm not lying. I've met them both."

"Frank!" her father yelled up the stairs. "Bring her down. We need to go."

Frank glanced at the door and back to her. "Promise me you'll force Bill to hide."

Juliet nodded. "I will."

"All right." He reached for the doorknob. His hand trembled. "Be ready to run when I give you the signal. And don't look back." He grabbed some clothes from her dresser and tossed them in a tote. "Let's go."

ZACK DROPPED HIS piece of pizza back on the plate and stared into the webcam. "Bill, I think I found something."

Bill looked over at Julie passed out on top of the comforter of the hotel bed. She looked tiny all curled up on the California king. "Keep your voice down. She finally fell asleep."

"Okay." Zack nodded and leaned in close like that might help. Bill turned down the speakers.

"Eden Incorporated makes a monthly stipend under research and development to the Genesis Foundation. The payments reference the phony vitamin formulation. We've got 'em."

"Holy shit. You did it." Bill grinned, relief washing over him. "You're the best, Z-Man."

He buffed his knuckles on his chest. "Yeah, I know."

Bill tapped the pen on the desk. "I wish we'd made the drop in twelve hours. I hate leaving Juliet with them."

He'd be counting down the hours until the exchange at the mall. If everything went according to plan, when Juliet came in with the money, they'd grab her, run through mall to the emergency exit by the bathroom. Pulling the door would set off the alarm, emptying the mall. Zack and Todd would be waiting in Zack's van. Cindy would be with him and Juliet again. Hopefully it would keep any snipers from shooting.

It seemed to work when they dropped her off this morning.

"We'll have her out of there soon." Zack leaned back in his chair. "I'll poke around and see what else I can compile. I'm putting it all in an email with an attached PDF of the research journal and the funding connection. I'll set the email to send on a delay, just in case something goes wrong and we need to hold it back. And if things go south and they come after us, the *LA Times* will have the story tomorrow night, regardless of what happens.

Bill took a slow breath, trying to relax a little. "Thanks for everything, man. I'm sorry you got pulled into this mess."

He shrugged off the praise. "We've been friends for way too long for me to leave you hanging." His lips curved slightly. "Plus, I like this girl. She's special."

Bill nodded. "Definitely."

"Get some rest." Zack moved closer to the screen again. "We'll get her back in the morning. Just stick to the plan."

JULIET'S FATHER HELD up a black velvet bag. "This will be over your head. Behave, and we won't have to bind your hands."

"You can't tie me up anyway." Juliet ground her teeth. "It might leave a mark."

Her mother groaned. "We don't have time for this." She snatched the sack out of his hands, and Juliet was plunged into darkness. Disoriented, she stumbled behind her mother. They stepped out the door, and her mother froze.

"Going someplace?"

It was a female voice.

Her father replied. "Yes. We wanted to let her walk outside before the ceremony."

"Oh please." The voice laughed. "Everyone in the county knows she's already been out. You broadcast her picture all over the news for days."

A hand rested on her shoulder. She tensed.

"You're a little early." Her mother's voice broke the silence. "Go on inside. We'll be right back."

"I don't think so."

Metallic clicking. Juliet had never heard anything like it.

"Who are they?" Momma asked.

The woman's voice grew louder, as if she was closer now. "This is my cleanup crew. Thanks to *them*, you have the little girl back. We can't afford any more mistakes. Now let's go inside. All of us."

Juliet's heart pounded. This had to be Cindy's grandmother. She was there the night they took Julie, but she didn't seem to know her parents had traded her for Juliet.

"Where is the younger girl?"

"Locked upstairs." Her father's voice was tight.

"Good. The rest of the board will be here soon."

Juliet gasped as her mother shoved her back into the kitchen. If Bill's father was right, once they discovered there was no research journal, they'd kill them all.

Her pulse thrummed. She'd broken free of this prison once. She could do it again. But she needed to keep her head. Her life depended on it.

CHAPTER 24

BILL GOT UP from the chair in the hotel room and stretched. His muscles were tight. They had the evidence they needed—at least enough to expose her parents and one of their big donors—and Zack had the email to the *LA Times* cued up and ready. But that email wasn't going to help Bill get Juliet out of that house. Dread curdled in his stomach.

He walked over to the bed. Julie's face was still swollen, the bruises starting to turn purple. What if they were hurting Juliet right now? How could he sleep not knowing if she was safe?

Yeah. He couldn't. No way.

He flipped on the television hoping for a distraction when his cell phone chimed. He pulled it out of his pocket, and his breath hitched. He had a new email. With "Iridescence" in the subject line.

The board is here. We can't delay the ceremony.

I'm sorry.

Dad

"No." Bill stood up, backing away from the computer screen. "No, no, no!"

Julie stirred. "What's wrong?"

There wasn't time enough to explain it all. "We need to go get your sister. Now."

She immediately got off the bed and put her shoes on. He grabbed the car keys, and they hurried out to the rental car.

Bill pressed Zack's name on his phone and waited for him to answer. "Hey, Zack. They're doing it tonight."

"What?" Papers rustled on the other end of the line. "But we have the journal."

"I know, but apparently that doesn't matter." Bill unlocked the car. "I got an email from my dad." He glanced at little Julie, tempering his words. "The *ceremony* is happening tonight unless we can stop it."

"Shit. So what are we going to do?"

"Grab the journal and meet me at the Huffs' place. Call Todd, too. We're going to need Cindy. And a lighter. Bring a lighter."

He hung up the phone and checked Julie's seat belt in the passenger seat. "When we get there, I need you to stay in the car with the doors locked. And you have to stay hidden so they don't try to take you while we're helping Juliet."

She nodded, and tears welled in her eyes.

He patted her knee. "I'm not going to let them hurt her."

She didn't answer.

He pulled out of the hotel lot, scraping the bottom of the Prius on the way out. He had no idea what time the "ceremony" would take place, but the clock was ticking loud and clear in his head. Juliet needed a hero tonight.

But all she had was him.

The ride back to Moonlight Cove was silent other than the damned click of each second passing by inside his head. At least the traffic had lightened up a little. He was nearing eighty miles per hour in the carpool lane.

He found Zack and Todd already parked at the end of his street when he arrived. Bill pulled up behind them and opened the door. He started to get out and paused. He looked over at Julie. "Wait for me, okay?"

She nodded, and he clicked the power locks. Cindy got out of Todd's pickup as he approached.

Zack held up the journal. "What's the plan?"

"You already scanned all of it into the computer, right?" Bill asked in a hushed voice.

"It took all day, but yeah." Zack glanced at Todd and back to Bill. "We're unarmed. Are you sure this is a good idea?"

"I'm not sure of anything except that Juliet will die if we do nothing." Saying the words out loud had Bill's armpits sweating. This was real.

Todd kicked at the pavement. "After my go-around with their trained thugs, if we go in without any weapons, they'll have us in glass cases right next to Juliet."

"Actually..." Bill wiped the nervous sweat from his brow. "I was thinking you and Z-Man should wait it out here. In case things don't go well, I don't want them to come after you. Between Cindy, me, the journal, and the lighter, they won't attack us. It's too dangerous. If they hurt the granddaughter of their biggest donor or lose eighteen years of research in this journal, they'll have to start over."

Cindy raised her chin, but fear was plain in her eyes. "I'm ready."

Zack handed Bill the journal, then a fireplace lighter. "This is epic, man. Like David and Goliath to the extreme." He shook his head. "Shouldn't we should call the police or something?"

Todd crossed his arms. "He's right. You don't even know how many people are on this board. There may be even more dudes in black with guns and Tasers. You're going in blind without a gun or even a baseball bat. What are you going to do if they tell you to stick it?"

"Then I burn all this damned research." Bill's mouth was dry while he struggled to dig up some heroic bravado. One of his characters in the Triad would have a much better speech prepared to fire up the team before they headed into battle. "It'll cost those bastards a fortune. Plus, it'll take them years to recreate if they have to start over. They need this book. And once your email hits the *LA Times*, they're finished."

"We hope." Zack jammed a hand in his pocket. "They won't print it instantly. They'll want to fact-check my reports. The Sutter Syndicate has power around here. They fund a lot more than Genesis. The paper won't smear them until they're sure it's true."

"Shit, Zack. Reality isn't what I need right now." Bill rubbed his hands on his jeans. "Give me an epic speech like Aragorn in *The Lord of the Rings* before the final battle." He looked between his two best friends. "At least tell me I'm doing the right thing."

Todd sighed, dropping his arms to his sides. "You always do the right thing. And I hope this works." He lowered his voice. "Look, I know you care about this girl, but this isn't fiction, dude. These bruises on my face are real. They could've killed me."

Bill stared at his friend's swollen, discolored eye. Todd was right, but there wasn't time for backup, and if he called the police, the Huffs could say *he* kidnapped Juliet. Then they'd find little Julie in his car…

Shit. He couldn't protect Juliet if he was locked up in a jail cell.

"If anyone gets how real this is, it's me." His voice cracked at the thought of what these pricks had taken from him. "They murdered my mom while she was sitting right across the table from me. Juliet will be next if I don't get my ass in there."

Todd embraced Cindy. "You sure about this,

babe?"

She nodded. "My grandmother won't let them hurt me."

He chucked her chin. "Who's the hero now?"

"Did you think you were the only one in this relationship?" Cindy cracked a small smile.

"Not a chance." Todd sobered. "Be careful."

Bill tossed the Prius keys to Zack. "Julie is in the Prius. If things go south, get her as far from here as you can."

"TIME TO GO upstairs and change into your birthday dress."

Juliet didn't move from the kitchen chair. "I'm not putting on a dress for you to parade me around like a science experiment."

"That's *all* you are. Martha treated you like a child to make it easier for you, but you were the product of my lab." Her father stalked across the kitchen until his nose was almost touching hers. "So either go back up there and get changed or I can strip you naked right here and dress you myself. Your choice."

Repulsed, she rocked back. "You're sick. All of you."

Juliet got up and ran up the stairs. By the time she reached her bedroom, tears welled in her eyes. None of this was going according to plan. The ceremony was still happening. These people didn't see her as a daughter or a young woman with a life ahead of her. She was a trophy to be displayed on their shelf—nothing more.

And she wasn't going to be able to escape it. She had no way to get a message to Billy. She'd be long gone while he waited at the meeting place in the mall to exchange the journal. A tear rolled down her cheek as she approached her bed. A white formal gown was laid out on the mattress. It had a beaded bodice with a full skirt that billowed like clouds.

A wedding dress for her eternal marriage to death.

No one would miss her. They would clone her over and over again. They'd taken so many samples from her during her lifetime, they probably had enough DNA for an army of little Julies.

Julie-Eight's face popped into Juliet's mind, adding to the suffocating pain in her chest. She'd never see her sister again. She hadn't gotten the chance to tell her she loved her and that she could be anything she wanted to be now.

At least Juliet wouldn't be sacrificing her life in vain. Julie-Eight was out of this house. She was safe.

Juliet changed clothes, imagining she was Anne Boleyn bravely facing the king's executioner. But there wouldn't be any pain for Juliet. God forbid they left a mark on her perfect skin. She stopped in front of the mirror and dried her cheeks.

But she wasn't perfect anymore. Not by their

standards.

She ran her finger along her lower lip. It seemed like ages ago that she'd kissed Billy and explored his body with these lips. She tried to cling to those memories.

When she was just a girl in love with a boy and being perfect wasn't a requirement.

Whispering outside of her bedroom door caught her attention. She moved closer, holding her breath so she could hear them.

"Ed, we have to tell them," Billy's dad whispered.

"I'm trying to get out of this alive. You saw what they did to your wife. That journal is the only leverage we have, and now it's gone."

"As long as Juliet is breathing, we can get it back." Mr. Manning paused. "Just explain we need a little more time."

A body thudded against the door. "I already told you the plan. We go through with the ceremony, and while the board is sipping champagne in celebration, we slip out the back door."

Mr. Manning's voice was choked. "You're willing to lose everything?"

"We'll still have our lives. I made perfection once. I can do it again. We don't need Genesis to change the world. We're the ones with the science to make it a reality."

More rustling and finally her father spoke again. "I'm going downstairs to welcome the board. Bring

Juliet down before they have time to start asking questions about the data. The sooner it's done, the sooner we can escape."

Footsteps creaked on the stairs, and Juliet backed away from the door. She went to the window and sat on her bench for the last time. Her stomach knotted with regret. She should've made Billy listen. She should've told him she loved him, too. If she could just see him one more time…

She froze, narrowing her eyes.

Billy was walking toward the porch. But there were armed guards inside. Juliet had to warn him. She tried to open the window, even though it was screwed shut. She waved her arms, willing him to look up at her.

He stopped at the base of the porch stairs and tipped his head back, staring up at her window. Their eyes locked for a moment, and her heart lurched. What was he doing here? This wasn't the plan.

And Cindy was right beside him. He broke eye contact with Juliet and vanished onto the porch. Her door opened, and Juliet gasped. Mr. Manning stood in the doorway, his voice soft, defeated. "It's time."

Juliet came closer and whispered, "I saw Billy. He's outside."

"No." Concern lined his eyes. "I told him the ceremony was happening anyway. He knows the board is here. He shouldn't have come." His gaze met hers. "If you get the chance, run, and take my son far from here. I'll try to give you a head start."

She nodded solemnly, her heart racing. This would either be the end or the beginning of her life.

He took her arm. "We can't keep them waiting."

Together, they walked down the staircase. Billy's dad held on to her as if she might plummet at any moment and ruin the perfection they were about to kill.

All conversation stopped as they entered the room where the board and donors were gathered, and everyone stared up at them.

Juliet tried to memorize the faces. Cindy's grandmother and her three armed guards stood near Juliet's parents. But the others were new. The men were all dressed in tuxedos, and the other two women wore formal gowns as through this were some kind of celebration instead of a murder.

Mr. Manning's words echoed in her mind: *You're the property of the Genesis Foundation.* She was only a doll to these rich people, and they were putting her in a box to keep her in mint condition.

She froze three steps from the bottom. Mr. Manning tugged her arm gently, but she didn't budge. Scanning the crowd, Juliet found her voice. "Thank you for coming to my eighteenth birthday. My parents imprisoned me in this house since birth so I don't have any friends to share this day with."

A few of the board members shifted their weight uncomfortably, glancing at the Huffs. Maybe they hadn't realized she could speak.

Her father stepped forward. "Unfortunately, Juliet has discovered the purpose of our meeting tonight. I had hoped she would peacefully drift away, but she's made that impossible now."

"Peacefully?" Angry tears filled her eyes. "Were you going to give me a birthday cake laced with sedatives?" She tore her gaze from her father to the rest of the crowd. "I'm not your property. I have hopes and dreams just like all of you." She scanned the crowd for anyone who might help her. "I fell in love. Experiments don't do that, right? I have a heart and a soul. Please…I want a life, too."

The elderly woman pressed her red lips into a stern line. "Silence her, or I will." She turned and pointed her perfectly manicured crimson fingernail at Juliet's father. "This is all because of your incompetence. Your experiment only exists because of our money, and we didn't fund this research to be made to feel like murderers." She glanced at Juliet and forced a pitiful attempt at a smile. "You must understand—even if we wanted to let you go, it would be impossible. You know far too much, and this project is too important to the human race to be stalled by bureaucrats and sentimentality." She lifted her chin a notch. "Regardless of what you may think, you *are* an experiment. Without Genesis, you wouldn't even exist."

The other board members seemed to relax.

Mr. Manning whispered, "We have to keep going."

Juliet didn't move.

Suddenly the three bodyguards pushed through the crowd and shoved Mr. Manning aside. Juliet screamed as they carried her to the center of the room and placed her on a stool. The board closed in around her, some touching her hair, fingers stroking her back and down her arms as awed whispers surrounded her.

"Perfect."

"We've done it."

"Perfection."

"The eighth prototype is perfect, too."

Julie-Eight? Her parents still must not have told them her sister was gone.

A knock on the door gave her a reprieve from the nightmare unfolding around her. Cindy's grandmother glared at the Huffs. "Expecting company?"

Her father shook his head.

Juliet's heart pounded in her ears as she made eye contact with Mr. Manning. It had to be Billy.

Her father went to the door and cracked it open. "We don't want any."

Instead of Billy, it was Cindy who pushed her way inside, Billy right behind her.

She scanned the room and sighed, staring at the older woman. "I hoped I was wrong."

"Cindy?" The woman frowned. "What are you doing here?"

"I found your earring." Cindy's voice cracked. "After I woke up from being *drugged.* You were there when they kidnapped a little girl."

Her grandmother rolled her eyes. "It's so easy for you to judge. You're too young and idealistic to understand. This project is bigger than any of us. We can end childhood diseases."

"By cloning kids like me without their knowledge?"

Her grandmother's jaw went slack.

Billy came forward, his gaze locked on Juliet.

Her grandmother's posture stiffened. "I saved your life. Vanessa is a perfect match in every way."

"You told Vanessa, didn't you? That's why she's so angry. You told her she's a copy of me, a clone."

Billy slid through the crowd and reached for Juliet. She stretched out her hand, but one of the bodyguards shoved him back. He stumbled and scrambled to stay upright.

Holding the journal over his head, Billy clicked the lighter, igniting a long flame below the pages. "I'm here for Juliet. Just let her go, and I'll leave the research notes. Otherwise, you can all watch them burn."

CHAPTER 25

Bill held his breath. This was the moment of truth. They'd either kill him like they did his mom or they'd negotiate. But it was his only chance to get Juliet out, so whatever happened, he had no regrets.

One of the guards pulled a gun from his holster and cocked it. "Give us that stolen property and we won't shoot you dead where you stand."

Bill's pulse skyrocketed as adrenaline coursed through his veins, but as he opened his mouth to respond, Cindy moved in front of him.

"You'll have to kill me first. But maybe that wouldn't matter." She looked at her grandmother. "You could just pay to make a replacement, right?"

"No!" Her grandmother came closer. "Don't shoot."

Bill shouted. "I've got all the research and data you need in this book. Let Juliet go."

"No!" Ed Huff pushed his way forward. "She's proof our project works. I have the data, but without Juliet there's no way to prove it works. We would have to start over and gestate another subject. Too much money's been spent. We need her."

Bill clicked the lighter again and held it to the cover. Fire licked at the edge, and an audible gasp went through the crowd. He started to lift it when his father launched himself forward from the stairs, tackling him. He grappled with his father for the journal, snuffing out the flame in the process.

Against his ear, his father said, "I'll distract them. Get her out of here. I love you, Bill."

Bill stopped struggling but didn't let go of the journal, unsure for a second if his own father could be trusted.

"They'll kill you," Bill whispered.

"Just get away. Hide. Live. That's all we ever wanted." He broke free of Bill's grasp with the journal and got to his feet. "I've got the notes."

His father walked farther into the group of investors, holding the notebook high. As he passed Juliet, the guards followed, everyone's attention on the object they'd spent untold amounts of money on.

Bill scrambled to his feet and grabbed Juliet's hand. She didn't hesitate. They ran for the door with Cindy right behind. As they sprinted across the front lawn, shots started flying. Cindy screamed, but she kept stumbling forward, running for the street.

Zack's van rolled up, and Todd opened the side door. He helped them jump in and yelled to Zack, "Go, go!"

Zack punched the gas, and the tires squealed while

Todd slammed the door closed. Little Julie scooted toward them, hugging Juliet. Two bullets hit the back of the van, startling them all, but Zack kept driving. The Victorian house shrunk in the distance.

"I can't believe it worked." Bill started to laugh. "We did it."

But Juliet stiffened, moving away from her sister. "Cindy?"

Zack called from the driver's seat. "Everything okay?"

Cindy's face was pale, sweat beaded on her forehead. She lifted the hand she had pressed to her side. Blood. She lowered it again, and blood seeped between her fingers.

"Cindy's hit!" Todd shouted. "We need to get her to a hospital."

"Shit." Zack gave the van more gas. "Is she conscious?"

"Yeah." Juliet crawled over to help her. "Someone tell me what to do."

The blood suddenly made the nightmare real. Bill cleared his throat, searching for his voice. "See if there's an exit wound on the other side."

He'd watched plenty of medical dramas on TV. If the bullet didn't go all the way through, she'd need surgery to find it. Todd and Juliet carefully moved her forward so they could see her back.

Cindy winced and gasped. "She let them shoot at us—at me."

"You don't know that." Juliet shook her head. "They might've just panicked when we ran or…"

"No. They worked for *her*." Cindy grimaced as the van rolled over a bump. "Genesis is more important to her than I am."

Juliet looked at Bill. "No wounds on her back."

Todd kissed her forehead. "Five minutes, baby. Hang in there."

Cindy's eyelids starting drifting closed.

Bill ground his teeth. "She's losing too much blood."

Todd pulled his shirt over his head and pressed it against the wound. Cindy's eyes popped open as she groaned. He took her bloody hand in his. "Sorry. I know it hurts. We're almost to the hospital. You need to stay awake, okay?"

She nodded. "I'm trying."

Zack stopped the van at Mercy Hospital, and bright light flooded them as nurses rushed forward. A gurney followed. Bill kept Juliet and Julie close while Todd stayed with Cindy, telling the doctors all they knew.

Bill nudged Zack as they sat in the waiting area. "You should take the van back to your place and be sure that email sent."

"I'm on it." Keys in hand, he started for the van, but Bill caught his arm.

"And bring all the evidence back with you." Bill lowered his voice, trying not to worry Juliet. "Just in case the police show up. I doubt the Huffs would call them, but neighbors would've heard those gunshots."

JULIET'S WHITE DRESS had a new red stain in the center. Cindy's blood. People came and went, but their stares were impossible to miss. Wedding day accident?

No one would believe the truth.

She was learning quickly that time runs slower in the emergency room. It felt like they'd been there all night, but according to the clock only two hours had passed. Still no word on Cindy.

Two men entered the waiting room and flashed badges to the front desk. The hospital employee pointed at her.

The men walked straight toward her. "Juliet Huff?"

"Yes?"

Julie-Eight squeezed her hand, and Juliet tightened her arm around her sister's shoulder, keeping her close.

The first man had very short black hair like Todd's. "I'm Detective Miller, and this is my partner Detective Jones. Can you come with us? We have some questions about the shooting victims."

"Victims?" She glanced at Bill, then back to the officer.

Detective Miller nodded slowly. "We'll fill you in, but we need a more private place to discuss it."

She started to move, but Bill laid a heavy hand on her knee. "I think she needs a lawyer."

The other officer raised a brow. "And who are you?"

"I'm her boyfriend."

She was covered in a friend's blood, barely escaping a group of mad scientists who wanted to kill her. Hearing Billy refer to himself out loud as her boyfriend should *not* have made her pulse jump. But it did.

The officers made eye contact and shared a silent nod. "We can call a public defender. Let's move to a more private place to talk. Why don't you all come with us?"

Billy got up, and Juliet followed suit, holding her sister's hand. The officers led them into a break room and sat at the table. "We received a call about shots fired at 1400 Lilac Drive. We've got one man dead and a young lady in surgery. The witnesses on the scene gave us a description of the shooter. She was about your height, with long dark hair and dressed in a floor-length white ball gown. Big coincidence, huh?"

Someone was dead? Juliet's hands trembled. She should've seen this coming. When would the Genesis Foundation stop surprising her?

Billy held her hand and stared at the detectives. "Her parents are trying to set her up. She needs a lawyer."

Detective Jones rested his forearms on the table. "We just want to understand what happened. We can help."

Billy rolled his eyes. "Juliet didn't shoot anyone."

"I was running *from* them." Juliet turned her palms up as if she could show them her lack of a gun. She didn't know what else to do. "I wouldn't know how to shoot a gun if you put one in my hands."

Detective Miller scribbled on a notepad. "You've been missing for a few days." He looked at Julie-Eight, obviously cataloging the injuries he could see. He shifted his attention back to Juliet, his expression going stoic. "You kidnapped your little sister." To Julie-Eight, he asked, "Did she hurt you?"

Her sister shook her head, her brow furrowed. "Juliet saved me. My momma did this to my face. They hate us. They were going to kill my sister today on her birthday. Juliet would never hurt anyone."

The officer remained focused on Julie-Eight. "We should have a doctor look you over. They can make you feel better." He offered his hand, but her sister leaned away, hiding her face against Juliet's side.

"I'm not leaving Juliet!"

The detectives shared a silent look, and Miller sighed. "All right. Wait right here." The officers stood up. "We've got a social worker on the way, and an officer posted outside this door. Don't go anywhere."

After they left, Juliet turned to Billy. "What am I going to do?" Panic and exhaustion weighed on her until she wished she could just curl up in a ball and sleep. "They told the police *I* shot everyone."

"We don't know if anything the officers said was

true. They're trying to scare you into confessing to something." He took her hand. "They can do a test on your hands for gun powder residue, and you won't have any. I'm sure Genesis is just hoping to slow the police down enough to give them time to cover their tracks and empty your father's underground lab."

Julie-Eight poked her leg. "Juliet, what's a social worker?"

She glanced at Billy. She'd never met one in person, but in books they protected children. Usually by taking them away. She tried to keep her expression calm, but inside, she wept. Without any schooling or a job, she couldn't take care of her sister. They'd put Julie-Eight in foster care, and most of the stories she'd read about them weren't good.

"They protect children when their parents treat them badly."

"So they'll help us?"

Billy met her eyes. He knew, too. Juliet swallowed hard. "I hope so."

Eventually Detective Miller returned with a woman in a gray pantsuit with thin, white pinstripes. Her auburn hair was short, and her eyes were kind. She took a seat across from them.

"Hi, I'm Hannah. You're Juliet and Julie, right?"

Her sister shook her head. "My name is Julie-Eight."

Hannah frowned, making a note on her pad. "Like the number eight?"

Julie-Eight nodded. "I'm sick of people changing it. It's Julie-Eight."

"Okay, Julie-Eight, did your sister take you away from your parents without their permission?"

A crease formed in Julie-Eight's brow. "Well, they never would have given their permission."

"So she abducted you."

Juliet frowned. "No. That's not how it happened."

Hannah sobered, meeting her eyes. "It might be best for me to chat with Julie-Eight alone."

Before Juliet could reply, Bill's cell rang. "It's Zack."

Juliet stared at the social worker. "His friend has documents and a digital copy of my father's research journal. They prove our parents kept us locked in that house as prisoners. Research projects." Juliet wrapped an arm around Julie-Eight's shoulder. "I didn't kidnap my sister. I set her free."

AFTER TWO HOURS of questions from the police and the social worker, Todd finally joined them. "Cindy's parents are in the waiting room with Vanessa. They have a lot of questions."

"I can imagine." Bill nodded. "How's Cindy doing?"

"The surgeon found the bullet. They had to remove her spleen, but it looks like she'll make a full recovery."

"That's good news." Bill pulled him into a tight

hug. "Thanks for everything tonight."

Todd stepped back. "Just glad we're all going to make it." He frowned, lowering his voice. "Sorry. I meant…us." He shook his head. "I'm screwing this up. Sorry about your dad, man."

"What?" A vise tightened on Bill's chest. "Oh. I…" He couldn't string his words together. He'd known they might kill his father, but somehow, he had convinced himself his dad had made it out. His dad had given them the journal. Why would they hurt him?

Bill's eyes burned, his vision blurring as he dropped back into his chair resting his forearms on his legs.

"Oh shit. They didn't tell you, did they?" Todd sat beside him. "I'm an asshole."

Bill's voice was shaky. "I'd rather hear it from a friend." He pinched the bridge of his nose, struggling to hold back the tears. He could cry later. For now, he needed to keep a clear head. "Did they tell you what happened?"

"Not exactly." Todd sighed. "They claim witnesses saw Juliet shoot him and Cindy, but I told them it must've been a trick shot since she was running away from the house right next to Cindy."

"I'll never know what really happened." A tear slipped from the corner of Bill's eye.

Juliet took his hand, her touch like a lifeline. "He loved you. He saved us both."

"Yeah, he did." He laced his fingers with hers.

Todd stood and rested a hand on Juliet's shoulder.

"Stay with him."

She nodded. "I'm not going anywhere."

Bill wasn't so sure about that, but he kept his mouth shut. Even after the police figured out Juliet wasn't a suspect, that social worker wasn't going to let her stay with her sister. Juliet had just turned eighteen years old. She wasn't eligible to go into foster care with Julie.

Julie-Eight.

Todd knelt in front of Julie-Eight's chair. "Hey, kid. How're you holding up?"

"I'm okay." She lowered her voice. "The social worker said I don't have to go back to Momma's house."

Todd nodded. "Good thing. I'd have to break you out again."

They both had crooked, swollen smiles right now. She scooted forward in her chair and hugged his neck.

Bill swallowed the lump in his throat. In the past couple of weeks, he'd discovered his parents weren't the people he'd thought they were, and before he could reconcile it, they had been taken from him by the Genesis bastards.

The social worker came in and frowned at Todd. "Who is this?"

Todd straightened up. "I'm Bill's friend."

"He's my friend, too." Julie-Eight crossed her arms. "This is Todd."

Hannah's expression brightened. "Friends are

good." She looked over at us. "Maybe I can take Julie-Eight and Todd to the snack machine. I'm sure she's hungry."

Julie-Eight grinned. "Can I?"

Juliet looked at Todd, but he answered before she could say a word. "I won't let her out of my sight."

She smiled at her sister. "All right."

Julie-Eight took Todd's hand, and they followed Hannah out of the room. Bill stared at his hands, his mood darkening with revenge fantasies, when Juliet's voice cut through the darkness.

"Billy? I need to say something."

He blinked, lifting his head to meet her eyes. "Okay."

She glanced at the door and back to him. "This probably isn't the right time. I'm so sorry about your dad."

He swallowed hard. "If tonight has taught me anything, it's that there might never be a right time."

Her dark lashes brushed her cheeks as she stared down at their joined hands. With his free hand, he lifted her chin. "I need to tell you something, too."

"All right," she whispered.

"My parents had a trust set up for me. I don't know all the details, but you can stay with me until we figure things out, okay?" His pulse thrummed, reminding him he was still alive.

"Thank you." A single tear tracked down her face. "When I thought they were going to put me in that glass box tonight, I had one regret." She caressed his cheek. "Through all this hell, I fell in love with you. You gave me hope, and for the first time, I have dreams about a future outside that house."

A bittersweet smile curved on his lips as he leaned in to kiss her forehead. "Does this mean I'm not in trouble for telling the police I was your boyfriend?"

She chuckled, but it didn't reach her eyes. "Actually, I liked the sound of that."

His smile faded. "Why do I get the feeling you're saying goodbye?"

She blinked back tears. "I love you, Billy Manning."

Shit, he couldn't lose her, too. He took her hands in his. "You're not going to stay with me, are you?"

She broke eye contact, focusing on their joined hands. "I'd like to, but I have to figure out how to please that social worker. I've read horror stories about foster care in magazines and books." She lifted her gaze, tears shining in her dark eyes. "They're going to give Julie-Eight to strangers. I have no way to support her. I took her out of that house and brought her into a world without any skills to care for her. How do we live in it?" Her voice cracked. "I'm all she has left."

He tightened his grip on her hands. "You're not alone, Juliet. We'll figure this out, just like we did with Genesis." His heart raced like a thoroughbred while he struggled for words. "Finding you has been the only good thing to come out of all this. I can't lose you, too."

CHAPTER 26

JULIET WIPED HER eyes as the door opened again. Detective Miller came in with his hands clasped in fists. He had a new partner with him. "Ms. Huff, this is Agent Hank Kitterman. He'll be taking lead on this case from here out."

Agent Kitterman was dressed in a black suit with a crisp white shirt and black tie. He was tall with short, copper-colored hair and light-green eyes. He offered Juliet his hand, and she gave it a tentative shake. "Are you working with Hannah?"

He frowned and glanced at Detective Miller. The detective filled in the blank. "She's the social worker assigned to the case."

With an almost imperceptible nod, Agent Kitterman's attention shifted back to Juliet. "Where is she now?"

"She took my sister to get a snack. They should be back soon."

"I'll wait." He turned to Detective Miller. "I can take it from here."

A muscle tensed in the detective's cheek, but he

complied and left the room. Agent Kitterman took a seat, his attention settling on Billy. "You're the boyfriend?"

"Yeah." Billy squeezed her hand. "I'm Bill Manning."

The agent opened a folder. "Good to meet you, Bill. Your parents worked for Genesis, am I correct?"

Juliet glanced at Billy. How did this man know about Genesis already? The police detectives hadn't mentioned it.

Billy nodded slowly. "They did."

Before he could go on, Juliet's little sister burst through the door and ran to her side. "Who is this?"

Agent Kitterman's eyes narrowed, his head tilting slightly as he studied Julie-Eight.

Juliet's throat tightened up. He definitely knew her sister was really her clone. But there was no way the newspaper report had come out yet. Had he already read the information Zack had turned over to the police? Or was this man part of the Genesis Foundation?

She didn't know who to trust.

Her heart raced, but she forced herself to speak slowly, contemplating every word before she said it aloud. "This is Agent Kitterman. He's going to help us."

Hearing her voice seemed to snap the agent back into the moment. He flipped through papers in the folder and plucked one out for Hannah. "I have a court order remanding the Huff girls into my custody. Social services won't be needed on this case."

"*Your* custody?" Hannah frowned, skimming the document. "Which branch of the government do you work for exactly? She's a minor..." Her voice trailed off as she continued reading. She looked up at him and shook her head. "I don't know how you got this through, but I'll be having my superior look into this case."

"I would expect no less." He closed his folder. "But until then, you should go."

She opened her mouth to respond but thought better of it. Instead, she pulled a small card from her briefcase and handed it to Juliet. "Call me anytime."

"Thank you."

Once the door latch clicked, Agent Kitterman leaned closer to her sister. "You must be Julie-Eight."

She nodded slowly.

He mustered a hint of a smile. "I'm Agent Kitterman, but you can call me Hank, okay?"

"All right." Julie-Eight stayed close, pressed against Juliet.

His voice remained soft, nonthreatening. "Do you know how special you and Juliet are?"

Juliet stood, wrapping her arm around her sister's shoulders. "You still haven't told us who you work for."

He sat back in his chair. "The less you know, the better."

She didn't relax her posture.

He rubbed his brow. "You've been through a lot." Agent Kitterman plucked out a leather case from his belt and opened it to show a badge and his photo. Before Juliet could inspect it any closer, it was clipped to his waist again. "I'm with a top-secret branch of the federal government, Department 51. We handle threats to the American people that most people would believe to be...extraterrestrial."

"Like the X-Files?" Billy arched a brow. "Juliet and her sister aren't aliens, and they're not a threat to anyone."

"True." He nodded. "But my department has been tracking the Genesis Foundation for decades with very few leads." He looked at Juliet. "You're the first person to escape from one of their pods."

"How did you know our names?" Juliet asked, still unsure if anything he was saying could be true.

"We knew Genesis had a pod in Moonlight Cove, but we'd never been able to find the location until one of the agents on my team saw the Huff's on television. When they showed your pictures, we placed some surveillance equipment at the residence."

"Then you had to know what they were doing to Juliet and her sister when they got them back, but you didn't do anything to stop them." Bill clenched his jaw and glanced at Juliet before facing the agent again. "Why should we trust you?"

"That's a good question." Agent Kitterman settled

back into his chair. "My department only had jurisdiction over technology that could be considered extraterrestrial in nature. If we busted into an American citizen's home, it would expose our entire department."

Juliet frowned. "Then why did you just tell the social worker you were handling our case?"

"Because now we believe your knowledge could help us stop them." He paused his gaze drifting to Billy and back to her. "The Genesis Foundation is well funded, not only with money but with rare…technology. That's what initially drew the attention of our department. They want to believe it's all their science, but they have something…not of this world that sparked their progress. There's a reason their scientists are miles ahead of the government-funded cloning projects. It's also why Genesis falls under my jurisdiction." He paused. "I assume it's safe to discuss this with your…sister in the room?"

Juliet sat down again, and Julie-Eight settled on Juliet's lap. Julie-Eight crossed her arms. "We're like twins but born far apart."

"That's a great way to think about it." He focused on Juliet and Billy again. "We've taken custody of the Huffs, as well as Claudette Sutter, and I've already intercepted the documents your friend emailed to the *LA Times*."

"Wait. Why?" Billy's eyebrows pinched together. "Are you kidding? We can expose them. It's the only way to stop them. The world needs to know what they're doing."

"It's not that simple."

Bill shook his head. "How did you stop an email?"

The agent sighed. "We've been surveilling your friend's house as well. When you left tonight, I instructed my agents to delete the email."

"I don't understand." Juliet shook her head. "You said you wanted to stop them."

He opened his file again and handed Juliet a picture.

She showed it to Billy, then looked at the agent again. "This is our friend, Cindy."

Did this man know about Cindy and Vanessa, too? She gave the photo back.

"What's she got to do with this?" Billy asked.

Agent Kitterman steepled his hands together. "Look, all of you have had a rough couple of weeks, I get it. But we're on the same side here." He scratched his head. "Bottom line is, my job is to protect the American people from otherworldly threats. We can't expose Genesis publicly. If word got out that a human had been cloned successfully, society would break down."

Billy cocked a brow. "How so?"

"Parents who lose a child might sell every possession, maybe even their own organs, for a chance to see their child alive again." He held up the picture. "Your friend Cindy was dying from leukemia, and because her family had the money, they created a perfect-match donor. And what if record labels decided to clone Elvis and Michael Jackson? Would they own their creations, then? They paid for them. Do clones have the same rights?" His voice trailed off as he shook his head.

A chill crept down Juliet's spine. He was right. None of the people in that room tonight had defended her. They believed they'd bought and paid for her. She was theirs to store in a glass case—less than human.

As if he could read her mind, he went on. "It wouldn't stop there. People could start selling their own genetic material. What if an Olympian was down on his luck or injured in an accident? He could sell his DNA to the highest bidder. This science leads us down a dark path. We have no way to regulate cloning, and the moral implications could be debated for years. I'm here to keep that from happening." His gaze flicked between them. "For now, the government will bury this story. I can offer you, and your friends who are aware of the connection between Juliet and Julie-Eight, federal pensions in exchange for your silence, similar to the citizens involved in the Roswell, New Mexico incident."

Billy looked at Juliet and back to the agent. "Your department buried the whole thing? Are you from Area 51?"

Agent Kitterman smiled. "How do you think it got its name?" He shook his head, sobering. "Department 51 will help Juliet pass her GED and receive job training, and Julie-Eight will be given a birth certificate and the opportunity to stay with her sister and go to school instead of being placed into foster care. Everyone wins here."

Juliet cleared her throat. "And what happens to Genesis?"

"I'm hopeful we can gain some information from Ms. Sutter and the Huffs. My department will find the rest of the Genesis Foundation and shut them down without the entire world discovering humans have been successfully cloned."

He made it sound simple.

She squeezed Billy's hand and tightened her other arm around her sister. "If we can stay together, we won't tell anyone."

Agent Kitterman stood with a smile. "I'll send my assistant in with the documents. Excuse me while I have a chat with—" he checked his file "—Zack and Todd. I'll loop them into this conversation as well."

TODD WAS STANDING right outside the door. He stepped back for Agent Kitterman to pass. "Sorry. Am I interrupting?"

The government agent straightened. "Actually, I wanted to speak with you and your friend Zack. Can you find him and bring him in?"

"Yeah. Sure." Todd glanced at Bill. He nodded, and

his friend closed the door.

Bill focused on Agent Kitterman again. "Genesis killed my parents and kept Juliet a prisoner inside her house for eighteen years. I want to be sure the Huffs and the Sutter Syndicate don't get to trade information for their freedom. My parents, Juliet, her sister, and our friend Cindy deserve justice."

"We won't offer them any plea deals." He shook his head. "And we've got top agents digging into the Genesis Foundation investigation. We won't stop until we're certain we've shut them down. Permanently. You have my word on that."

The door opened again, and Todd and Zack both entered the room. Agent Kitterman filled them in on the federal pension, and Zack's eyes lit up. "Just like the people in Area 51. This is how you muzzled them while you fed the story about a weather balloon instead of an alien spacecraft, right?"

Todd nudged his friend. "When he's not computer hacking, Z-Man is a conspiracy theorist, too."

Zack groaned. "Dude, don't talk about hacking in front of a federal agent."

Agent Kitterman almost smiled. "Zack, your work on this incident with Genesis is really impressive. After you finish your degree, my agency would be interested in interviewing you to be a part of our team." He chuckled. "And your interest in conspiracies would be an asset in my department."

"Nice." One side of Zack's mouth quirked up.

"You're giving me a job offer for hacking, instead of fines and charges?"

"You could say that." Agent Kitterman turned to the rest of them. "Are you all in agreement? If so, I can have the pension documents drawn up and in your hands in a few hours."

Bill nodded begrudgingly. It wasn't like they had much choice. He crossed his arms. "And you're going to keep searching for the rest of the people involved in Genesis?"

Agent Kitterman rolled back his shoulders. "They're a top priority."

Sounded like government bullshit to Bill. His parents, Juliet, and her sister were real people hurt by Genesis. Real casualties. And he wanted to see Genesis punished.

"There were ten people at that ceremony tonight. Zack only found a money trail to Claudette Sutter." Bill clenched his teeth and forced his voice to say even. "That means nine more rich people are still out there funding those scientists."

"I assure you we will find them. Now that we have some suspects in custody, we have a starting point to locate the rest of the pods. My department exists for cases like this." Agent Kitterman glanced at the others. After everyone agreed to the deal, he sent a message on his phone.

A few minutes later, a woman came into the room. She had on a similar suit to Agent Kitterman's, but she wore a black skirt instead of slacks. She nodded to all of them and handed Agent Kitterman a sack of stapled packets.

He nodded to her. "Thanks, Tish." He passed the packets to each of them. "Let's go through the details of this affidavit. Once I have everyone's signatures, I can get to work on the pension packages."

Zack skimmed the first page and looked over at agent Kitterman. "I assume we can't run this by a lawyer first?"

"Correct. The first item on the affidavit is confidentiality. You will never be able to discuss the details about Genesis or any of the persons involved with anyone outside of this room. Breech of that clause will terminate your pension package and possibly open you up to prosecution." The Agent scanned the group. "Any other questions?"

Bill flipped pages, barely noticing the words. This wasn't justice; this was paid silence. He'd be stepping aside and trusting this "department" to stop them. He wanted Genesis's name smeared across the papers and television, but if he spoke up, the Feds would muzzle him anyway. One way or the other.

His father's final words to him echoed in his head: *Live. That's all we ever wanted.*

His folks had been sucked into Genesis because they quit living the day his brother died. And now they were gone, too.

This agreement could be an escape hatch to let go

of his appetite for revenge against Genesis and move on with his life.

Bill picked up the pen and initialed and signed.

Zack raised a brow. "You didn't even finish reading it."

Bill set the pen down with a shrug. "They're paying me to back off and let them hunt Genesis. I can take their money and live my life. They'd shut me up one way or another anyway. Why not take their compensation?" He pushed the contract to Agent Kitterman. "I'm a fiction writer. Hypothetically, if I used the word *Genesis* in any of my books, would you be at my door?"

The corner of the agent's mouth twitched as if he wanted to smile, but he didn't let it break through. "It's a common word. The first chapter in one of the oldest books on earth. This pension is an agreement that you won't talk about it in the context of a corporation that's cloning humans."

"Works for me."

Beside him, Juliet finished signing, and Agent Kitterman took her paperwork. He looked over at her little sister. "Julie-Eight, since you're under eighteen years old, I have different form for you." He slid another document toward Juliet. "This one makes Juliet your legal guardian." Then he laid one more paper in front of Julie-Eight. "And this one is for you."

She read the top and frowned. "I have to change my name?"

He nodded slowly. "Only the people in this room

know that you're the eighth replication of your sister. To the rest of the world, you can be whoever you'd like to be, and I'm guessing you are much more than a number, right?" He winked, drawing a smile from Juliet's sister.

"I can pick *any* name?" she asked.

"Yep." He tapped the blank on the page. "Fill this in, and my office will produce a birth certificate and social security number with whatever name you choose."

JULIET'S HEART RACED. This could be the fresh start she'd been dreaming of. A new beginning without perfection weighing on them.

Julie-Eight stared at the paper and finally smiled up at Juliet. "I want to be Mary from *The Secret Garden*."

Her favorite book.

Juliet laughed hugged her sister tightly. "Mary. I love it."

Once all the documents were signed, another man in a plain dark suit opened the door. "Kitterman, Cindy Sutter is awake."

"Good. I'll be right there."

He gathered all the paperwork. "I need to go have this conversation with Cindy and her sister—" he checked the file "—Vanessa." He looked over at them again. "Because we're still looking for the other investors, we're assigning officers to monitor your houses for the next couple of weeks just to be safe." His gaze settled on Juliet. "We'll be taking custody of the Huff property and clearing all evidence of Genesis. While we do that, I'll be escorting you and Mary to Washington, DC, for debriefing. We'll get identification paperwork together for both of you, and then you can choose where you'd like to settle and live."

He scanned the room. "Any last questions about the documents you signed?"

Zack raised his hand. "You'll protect my parents, too? They don't know anything."

"Yes." Agent Kitterman nodded. "If you notice any strange activity, you can reach out to me anytime. My number is on the card."

He left the room, and Billy glanced over at his friends. "Can you guys take Jul—*Mary* out to get a soda?"

"But I'm not thirsty," Juliet's sister whined.

Juliet kissed her sister's hair. "I'd like to talk to Billy alone for a minute."

She grinned. "Are you gonna kiss him?"

Juliet rolled her eyes. "None of your business."

The young girl giggled and got up. She took Todd's hand, and they left the room. Once the door clicked shut, Billy angled his chair to face her. "I don't like that they're bringing you two to Washington, DC, alone."

"It won't be forever." She studied his face. Concern

lined his eyes. Was she trusting the wrong person? "He said I can choose where I want to live."

"That's what he says right now." He took her hand, and her pulse skipped. "I know I signed that paper saying I wouldn't talk, but if anything happens to you, I'm telling every news agency out there what happened, and I'll let them broadcast this agent's card. Everything."

She leaned in to kiss his cheek. "No one has ever worried about me before."

A crooked smile tugged at his lips. "I'm being serious."

"I know, and I am probably a little naive, but Agent Kitterman is my only chance to keep my sister with me and to get a shot at a normal life." She wasn't sure if she was trying to convince him or herself. "I can't do this on my own."

He nodded, breaking eye contact. "You're right." He shook his head slowly. "I've never met anyone like you, Juliet. When we stayed up all night brainstorming the Triad graphic novels…I still want that. I don't want you to leave me behind to mourn my folks and go back to UCLA like none of this ever happened."

Her heart pounded in her ears. "I don't know how long we'll be gone."

"You could take the cell phone Zack gave you. Just buy more minutes with the pension money."

She stared into his bright-green eyes, hoping she wasn't dreaming. "What are you saying?"

"I'm saying I want to keep being your boyfriend. And when it's safe, I want to take you on real dates." He chuckled. "Okay, screw safe. I just want to be with you, dangerous or not."

Juliet laughed as she leaned in to kiss him. She wrapped her arms around his neck until there was a tap on the door.

"Just a second." Billy rested his forehead against hers. "I'll be right here waiting for you."

She smiled and whispered, "And I'll be back to continue this kiss."

CHAPTER 27

BILL'S FINGERS FLEW over his keyboard while he fought the urge to check the clock. In the three months that Juliet had been gone, just about everything had changed.

Except his feelings for her.

After letting UCLA know he was taking a semester off, he put his parents' place up for sale and moved into an apartment. The house was too full of memories, and just driving up the street in the shadow of the big Huff house made his stomach churn.

The fresh start agreed with him so far. The monthly pension payments also gave him the chance to chase the dream he'd always coveted: writing. His first novel was cooking along. He wanted to have it finished before Juliet and Mary got back, but he was going to be a couple chapters shy of that goal.

Still, not too shabby.

It was winter break, and Todd and Z-Man were home visiting. They were on their way over to his apartment right now with Cindy. They were going to set up a surprise party for Juliet and Mary while Bill went to the airport to pick them up. He finally checked the clock and grinned. It was almost time.

After a quick shower, he let his friends in and jogged out to his car. He'd traded in the truck. It was probably ridiculous for him to worry about, but Julie was going to be eleven soon and she wouldn't be able to fit in the middle of the bench seat much longer. Plus, he'd convinced himself a starving novelist shouldn't have a gas guzzler.

He had gotten his Prius in red, though. He was about to turn twenty, not fifty.

FLOWERS IN HAND, he waited by the baggage claim. In the months they'd been apart, he and Juliet had Skyped almost every day. Now he knew her favorite color was green and her favorite flowers were violets.

He was also crazy in love with her. If his parents had still been around, he had no doubt his mom would caution him that they were too young. And maybe that would've been true if he were a normal twenty-year-old.

Instead, he'd witnessed his mother's murder, helped the woman he loved escape from a secret foundation that kept her and her sister locked up like lab rats, and now he regularly watched over his shoulder for any sign of Genesis raising its "perfect" head again.

He'd already lived at least an extra twenty years in the past six months.

And he'd learned that life was way too short.

The second he spotted Juliet on the escalator, the ambient noise in the airport faded away. She scanned the crowd below, and when her eyes locked on his, a bright smile lit up her face. He started making his way through the crowd as she and Mary neared the bottom.

As soon as she stepped off the escalator, Juliet rushed into his arms. He caught her, fusing his lips to hers. Damn, he'd missed her.

Someone poked his side. "Hi, Billy."

He broke the kiss, his eyes lingering on Juliet for one more moment before he turned and grinned at her sister. She was already an inch or two taller. "Hey, Mary. How was your trip?"

She babbled all the way to the baggage carousel and out to the car, but he hardly noticed.

Juliet was back, and if he had his way, they'd never be apart again.

"I don't try to describe the future. I try to prevent it."

—Ray Bradbury

2017

EPILOGUE

JULIET SAT ON the edge of her stool at the drawing table, her legs spread wide to allow for her sizeable belly. She was two days past her due date and starting to wonder if this baby was ever going to come out and meet them.

Billy rubbed her shoulders and leaned down to brush a kiss to her ear. "You should put your feet up and rest."

She chuckled and kept working on the new panel for the latest Triad graphic novel. "Time passes too slowly if I lie down. I'd rather work."

Their first baby. It still seemed surreal. She'd basically raised her sister, Mary, but actually giving birth and caring for a new baby scared her a little. Billy's parents were dead, and her parents were in a secret Federal lockup somewhere.

She drew faster, feverishly. Even though the nursery was all set up and the hospital bag was packed, she felt like she was forgetting something. They were going to be parents.

What if they weren't ready?

Mary was away at college in Washington, DC. Agent Kitterman had helped with the admission. His office continued to monitor Mary's health closely, too. Juliet tried not to think about it, but the shadow of Mary's cloned DNA was inescapable.

From her father's journal, Juliet learned that her DNA had been created in the Genesis lab, possibly using the technology Department 51 was so interested in, but all the Julies that came after had been clones of Juliet. Cloned animals lived half the lifespan of the original. Would humans be different? No one knew. Her sister was an anomaly, and no one could predict what the future held for her.

Billy was quick to share his father's advice, to take each day as it came. We could worry about tomorrow when it got here. But some days that was easier said than done.

She shaded in the scimitar and worked on the angle of the villain's nose. Their Triad comic series had been picked up by a major comic book publisher recently, and now there were whispers of a movie deal. On the side, Billy had been publishing a sci-fi novel series about a nefarious corporation that used children for its research and development. He'd been pushing the envelope with the government, and although she cautioned him, he wove his stories with boldness and fury. Agent Kitterman wasn't authorized to give them updates about their progress against Genesis, and every month that the pension hit their account, Billy's rage would fester.

But everything had changed the day the stick turned blue.

When they'd found out she was expecting, Billy had contacted Todd. He was a police sergeant now, and within a couple days, Todd was teaching both of them to shoot handguns. They hadn't seen any trace of Genesis since Juliet's eighteenth birthday, but having a Glock locked in a gun case seemed to give Billy a little peace of mind.

A sharp pain shot down her abdomen, followed by a trickling sound. She frowned, unable to see her feet on the floor. "Billy!"

Hurried footsteps and then he filled the doorway. "Everything okay?"

She set her pen down and pointed at the floor. "Did my water just break?"

He glanced down and rushed toward her. "Oh my god. The baby's coming!"

"We've trained for this day." She hoped she sounded more like a superhero than a giant pregnant woman trying to waddle toward the door. "I need to change."

Billy zoomed past with the hospital bag. "They'll put you in a gown when we get there anyway."

She raised a brow. "We have hours until this baby comes. I'm not arriving in wet pants."

"Okay." He didn't look thrilled with her decision, but he knew better than to argue with a pregnant woman. "Do you need help?"

“I can make it.” In her bedroom, she winced as another contraction seized her belly. She slowed her breathing, waiting for it to pass. Once the pain subsided, she changed into a new pair of sweats and sent a text to Mary to let her know she was about to become an aunt.

When she got to the door, Billy was already had his car keys dangling from his hand. “Let’s do this.”

Juliet laughed and kissed him. “This baby is so lucky to have you for a dad.”

THE WOMEN’S CENTER was hopping with activity. Women with large bellies walked the halls with nervous soon-to-be-dads in tow. Nurses came and went, and a pale woman with a tiny baby in her arms was being pushed down the hall in a wheelchair.

Billy kissed Juliet’s temple. “We’re going to have one of those soon.”

Juliet nodded, her gaze sliding farther down the corridor. She swore there had been a doctor there, watching her. Dread tightened in her chest even though she struggled to dismiss it. No one knew her past.

“Juliet Manning?”

She gasped, turning to find a nurse in Disney scrubs.

The nurse frowned. “Sorry. I didn’t mean to startle

you. I'm Jenny."

Billy ran his hand up Juliet's back. "Is everything okay?"

She nodded. "Yeah, I just…thought I saw something."

"We have your room ready." Jenny smiled. "Can you walk or do you need a wheelchair?"

Another contraction gripped her, stealing her voice.

The nurse took that as an answer. "I'll be right back." By the time she returned, the pain had subsided. "Your chariot."

Juliet took a seat. "Thank you."

"Your first baby?"

Juliet nodded.

Billy held her hand, walking beside the chair as he spoke. "Her water broke forty-five minutes ago, and the contractions are about three minutes apart."

All the pregnancy books he'd read were paying off, and Juliet almost chuckled before another contraction made her wince.

The nurse parked the chair in a private room, took Juliet's vitals, and entered everything in the computer. "You can change into the gown, and the doctor will be in soon."

THE NEXT TWO hours passed in a fog of pain and sweat

until the epidural kicked in. Billy stayed by her side as the sun set, rubbing her back and texting her very excited sister back East.

The obstetrician came by again to check her cervix. She held her breath, hoping it might be time to push.

Her doctor straightened and pulled off her gloves. "Everything is progressing nicely." She entered something in the computer and smiled. "My shift is ending in an hour, so if the baby hasn't crowned yet, the next obstetrician on duty will deliver you."

Juliet tightened her grip on the bed rails. "Another doctor?"

She nodded slowly, shaking her head with an empathetic smile. "This happens all the time in labor and delivery. I can assure you that you'll be in great hands."

She tried to convince herself there was no logical reason for this anxiety, but she couldn't shake it. "I really wanted *you* to be here."

Her gaze shifted up to Billy and back to Juliet. "And maybe things will progress faster now. I've seen stranger things." She patted the footrest on the hospital bed. "Everything looks great. You and the baby are doing just fine."

Billy moved into Juliet's line of sight as soon as the door closed. "Talk to me. What's wrong?"

She pulled her eyes from the door and stared up at her husband. "I'm sure it's nothing."

"If it's nothing, then you can unload it on me, right?"

She huffed out a breath. "I thought a doctor was watching us when we checked in. He had a mask on so I couldn't see his face, but when I looked down the hallway again, he was gone."

Billy squeezed her hand. "Doctors come and go all the time in this place."

She nodded. "I know. I don't know why it even caught my eye. It's probably just my mind playing tricks on me. We haven't seen or heard from Genesis in years. They can't possibly know I'm pregnant."

"I'm usually the paranoid one." He searched her eyes and let out a slow breath. "So if *you* think you saw something, then I believe you." He pulled out his cell phone. "I'm texting Agent Kitterman just in case."

"Thanks."

In the next half hour, a new nurse came by to take her vitals. She went to the computer and back to the machine monitoring the contractions. "Let me find the doctor. I think you might be ready to push. Just breathe for me, okay?"

Juliet nodded, smiling up at Billy. "Dr. Garner might still be here."

Right on cue, she came in, gloved up and ready. "I hear there's a little Manning waiting to make a grand entrance."

Juliet looked up at Billy. "I hope so."

After positioning her feet in the stirrups, Dr. Garner finally said the words Juliet had been longing to hear. "Okay, on the next contraction, bear down."

Billy coached her through it, counting the seconds for each push. Juliet closed her eyes, trying to focus. Was anything happening? The epidural made it impossible to tell.

The doctor called to the nurse. "Have the forceps ready."

Juliet turned her head and frowned. It wasn't Jenny. Had her shift ended? The nurse fumbled with the surgical tools.

Dr. Garner looked up at Juliet. "Give me one big push."

She groaned, closing her eyes again.

"That's it. Great job. The head is out."

Juliet gasped for air, opening her eyes. The nurse was still by the medical instruments, the forceps still on the stainless steel tray.

Dr. Garner called for another tool. "Shoulders are next. We need your biggest push, okay? I know you're tired, but you can do this. Ready?"

Billy kissed her forehead. "Almost there…"

Juliet closed her eyes and grunted with effort. A baby's cry echoed back. Her eyes snapped open as Dr. Garner stood up to show her the wriggling infant. "She's a beautiful baby girl."

She handed the newborn to the nurse, who wrapped her in a towel. As she turned to place the baby on the scale, the florescent light reflected off something, catching Juliet's attention. She narrowed her eyes, struggling to make out the shiny spot on the nurse's scrubs. A pin.

A round green… No. It couldn't be.

Juliet's pulse raced. "I need to hold my baby."

Dr. Garner cleared her throat. "We're just getting her weight and Apgar score."

The nurse glanced her way, her lips curved in a barely-there smile. She picked up the baby from the scale with a dark glint in her eyes.

With each step closer, the pin became clearer. A round green center with the infinity symbol.

Juliet's heart raced. *Genesis.* She tried to move, but her body wouldn't respond, the epidural deadening her nerves from the chest down.

Billy leaned in close, his eyes full of happy tears. "She's beautiful just like her mother."

"No." The nurse handed the blanket-wrapped baby to Billy. "She's absolutely *perfect.*"

Acknowledgments

Thank you so much for reading the first installment of the Genesis Trilogy. If you enjoyed the book, I hope you'll leave a review. Even short ones help readers discover the book.

Big thank you to my daughter, Panda and my husband Ken for encouraging me to put this book out. This idea has been with me for years, but it wasn't my usual genre, so I was hesitant to send it out into the world. But diving back into this world was so much fun for me and I'm excited to finish the trilogy.

Thanks to my amazing editor Danielle Poiesz-Luby from Double Vision Editorial for all your amazing insights to make Perfect even better. I love working with you!

Thank you to my amazing patrons on Patreon! I couldn't put out these indie books without your support! And to my incredible Night Angel reader group on Facebook thanks again for reading and posting your reviews. You all make publishing so much fun!

All my gratitude to the Wordmakers and the Write Owls for all the writing sprints. I love writing with all of you!

And finally extra thanks go to my husband, Ken! I

had so much fun making the Perfect Podcast with you! Your steadfast, unwavering support for me and my books makes me the luckiest writer around. I love you!

Also by L.A. Kessler

The Genesis Trilogy

PERFECT

FLAWED

TAINTED

As Lisa Kessler

The Muse Chronicles

LURE OF OBSESSION

LEGEND OF LOVE

BREATH OF PASSION

LIGHT OF THE SPIRIT

DEVOTED TO DESTINY

DANCE OF THE HEART

SONG OF THE SOUL

The Night Series

NIGHT WALKER

NIGHT THIEF

NIGHT DEMON

NIGHT ANGEL

NIGHT CHILD

The Moon Series

MOONLIGHT

HUNTER'S MOON

BLOOD MOON

HARVEST MOON

ICE MOON

BLUE MOON

WOLF MOON

NEW MOON

The Sedona Pack

THE LONE WOLF'S WISH

SEDONA SIN

SEDONA SEDUCTION

SEDONA SCANDAL

SEDONA SURRENDER

SEDONA SERENITY

SEDONA SACRIFICE

SEDONA SUSPECT

SEDONA SANCTUARY

SEDONA SALVATION

The Salem Pack

WOLF'S WITCH

The Sentinels of Savannah

MAGNOLIA MYSTIC

PIRATE'S PASSION

PIRATE'S PLEASURE

PIRATE'S PERSUASION

PIRATE'S PROMISE

PIRATE'S PARADOX

Summerland Stories

ACROSS THE VEIL

FORBIDDEN HEARTS

A WINTER'S WISH

Standalone Works

BEG ME TO SLAY

FORGOTTEN TREASURES

Stay up-to-date on new releases and giveaways by subscribing to Lisa's newsletter here: https://goo.gl/56lDla

L.A. Kessler is the pseudonym of award-winning horror and paranormal romance author Lisa Kessler. She's a two-time San Diego Book Award winner for Best Published Fantasy-Sci-fi-Horror and Best Published Romance. Her books have also won the PRISM award, the Award of Excellence, the National Excellence in Romantic Fiction Award, the Award of Merit from the Holt Medallion, and an International Digital Award for Best Paranormal.

Her horror short stories have been published in print anthologies and magazines, and her vampire story, Immortal Beloved, was a finalist for a Bram Stoker award.

When she's not writing, Lisa is a professional tarot reader and vocalist.

You can learn more at Lisa-Kessler.com

Made in the USA
Columbia, SC
19 February 2024

31821045R00219